LINDA LAEL MILLER

Country PROUD

ISBN-13: 978-1-335-92482-7

Country Proud

Copyright © 2021 by Hometown Girl Makes Good, Inc.

This edition published by arrangement with Harlequin Books S.A.

For questions and comments about the quality of this book, please contact us
at CustomerService@Harlequin.com.

HQN
22 Adelaide St. West, 40th Floor
Toronto, Ontario M5H 4E3, Canada
www.Harlequin.com

Printed in U.S.A.

For Laura Wiley and Alan "Chipmunk" Robertson,
two of the finest, bravest people I know.
Guys, you are Country Strong and Country Proud
partly because you're both Country Born.
It's an honor and a joy to be considered kin to you.

My very dear readers,

In my considerable experience writing fiction—easily half a century—I've met with success in unexpected hours. I've also struggled through the "slough of despond," but why dwell on that? We all have our shadow valleys and dark nights of the soul, and since I'm writing this and you're reading it, it seems safe to assume that either we've come out on the other side or we're bearing up under our particular problems and pressing on toward a brighter day.

Writing *Country Proud* was a special joy to me, especially in this time of wild challenges and uncommon adversities. (I will remember this year as, among other things, the year I lived in my pajamas.)

The story people—Brynne and Eli, Cord, J.P., Melba and Dan—kept me focused on what really matters in this life. As I worked with them, I saw in these imaginary friends the qualities I most admire in others and work hard to cultivate in myself: honesty and integrity, courage in the face of adversity, compassion for all living things, respect for other people's right to speak their mind (whether I agree or not), the ability to take the ultimate risk and love another person.

Times are tough, and they might get tougher.

It's up to us to get tougher still.

That said, I don't get paid to preach, but to tell a story—hopefully a good one. If you enjoy reading *Country Proud* half as much as I enjoyed writing it, I will have succeeded.

Stay strong,

Linda Lael Miller

CHAPTER ONE

Sheriff Eli Garrett gazed out his office window at the gently falling snow and sighed.

Christmas was over—although it seemed to him that the holiday would roll around again in approximately fifteen minutes—and another New Year was just around the bend.

Eli cupped his hands behind his head and leaned back in his chair, still watching the snow and hoping this little skiff wouldn't work itself up into a mega blizzard, burying some or all of Wild Horse County in plain misery.

According to the weather app on his phone, it could happen. The meteorological jury was still out.

If the storm materialized, he and his four deputies would be on round-the-clock duty, prowling the roads and highways for accidents and stranded motorists, checking up on shut-ins and crotchety recluses, hauling drunks out of snowbanks, hopefully before hypothermia set in.

Like bar brawls, incidents of domestic violence rose over the holidays, given the preponderance of alcohol, but a few feet of the white stuff imprisoning people in their unhappy homes for an indefinite period would obviously exacerbate the problem.

Same as most cops, Eli dreaded domestic violence calls above all others.

His county was a relatively peaceful one, but he'd served in law enforcement since he'd graduated from the academy in Phoenix, first as a deputy and finally as sheriff, and he'd seen some crazy-assed shit.

Once, he'd spent upwards of forty-five minutes standing in the weed-choked front yard of a run-down house, trying to talk a methed-up ex-con holding a gun barrel to the underside of his own chin into surrendering the weapon.

Eli had told the poor bastard everything would be okay, which was a lie, since he knew a woman and several children were trapped inside the house behind the man, and there was no telling what kind of shape they were in. The offender was a felon in possession of a firearm, which was five kinds of illegal, and there would be drug charges as well as assault and God knew what else.

Hell, the most liberal judge in the state, never mind the county, would have sent this waste of space straight back to the pen—this time, for good.

Three strikes, you're out.

Fact was, Eli would have said—or done—damn near anything to get the woman and those kids safely past that pistol-wielding maniac and into the ambulance waiting just out of shooting range.

"You don't have to do this," he'd said, for the umpteenth time.

Eli hadn't drawn his own weapon; a mistake, he supposed, since even a stoner could probably take him down before he pulled his revolver out of the holster, but he hadn't wanted to ratchet up the tension, which already vibrated like a wire tightened to the breaking point. The two deputies backing him up were almost surely ready to shoot if the need arose.

He'd taken a single step toward the man, hands dangling loosely at his sides, palms out. He was no grandstander, no hero—just a committed cop who wanted everybody involved to survive the episode.

"Think about your wife," he'd reasoned calmly, though he could feel sweat pooling between his shoulder blades. "Think about your kids. You want them to see you blow your brains out?"

The man bellowed, maybe with rage, maybe with the pain of all he'd done to eff-up his own life.

Sensing a stir behind him, figuring one or both of the deputies were about to make a move, Eli had growled, "Stand down. *Do not fire your weapons.*"

He hadn't taken his eyes off the suspect, and he saw a terrible rictus of a grin cross the other man's face, followed by a gruff laugh.

What happened next was surreal. It seemed to take place in slow motion; the air turned to a thick, pulsating fog and the ground felt spongy beneath Eli's feet, causing him to sway slightly.

The shot echoed in all directions and the dead man folded to the ground.

Inside the house, the woman and the kids shrieked in horror.

"Oh, shit," Eli had murmured. "*Shit.*"

The two deputies rushed past him, toward the house. The ambulance, parked up on the road until the shot was fired, sped down the driveway.

Eli walked toward a nearby maple tree, stepped behind it and lost his lunch.

Some hero.

As it turned out, the woman had a pair of black eyes and a broken arm. The kids were thoroughly traumatized, but physically unharmed, as far as he knew.

After the state police arrived, with their CSI team and the county coroner, Eli had returned to the sheriff's department—the very office he was sitting in now—to write up the required reports. Then sheriff at the time, Dutch McKutchen, had been out of town that day, taking his wife, Clara, for her first round of chemotherapy, so he'd missed the action.

Upon his return, Dutch made up for lost time by reaming out his "brain-dead idiot of a deputy" for the better part of half an hour. "When you approach an armed suspect," he'd raged, "you have your weapon drawn and ready. You *do not* go into a *situation* like some fricking hotshot TV cowboy—you could have been killed!"

After the lecture, Dutch had bought Eli a drink over at Sully's Bar and Grill, told him not to come near the department until he'd been (1) debriefed by the appropriate state officials, and (2) cleared by an officially sanctioned shrink.

Eli smiled sadly, remembering Dutch. The old man had died of a heart attack ten years ago, a month into his retirement, while fishing up at Flathead Lake.

Deciding his thoughts had taken an unnecessarily grim turn, Eli lowered his hands, sat forward with a creak of the springs under his chair and stood.

Given some of the problems he'd faced, he reckoned a potential blizzard wasn't the worst thing that could happen in his county. Not by a long shot.

Most likely, the storm would fizzle out before it did any

real damage. Those weather people, in his opinion, were given to drama.

Just the same, Eli felt a little uneasy.

His sister, Sara, would say he was borrowing trouble.

Dutch McKutchen would have told him to pull his head out of his backside and be grateful for all the good things in his life. Like his two best friends, Cord Hollister and J.P. McCall. And his job, which he loved, about 85 percent of the time. He had a fair amount of money put away, savings and an inheritance from his and Sara's paternal grandparents, and he owned his house and a few acres of land outright.

Had a good truck, too. Paid for, and still under warranty.

And then there was Brynne Bailey, back home to stay.

Brynne, his high school sweetheart. The girl he'd essentially betrayed

Eli was thankful that she'd returned to the Creek, for sure. Never mind that she barely gave him the proverbial time of day, probably still carried a torch for the man she'd left behind in Boston. But she was *here* now, in Painted Pony Creek, Montana, running her parents' popular restaurant and bar, Bailey's.

And speaking of Bailey's...

He'd agreed—a little reluctantly—to meet his friends there for coffee and a few rounds of good old-fashioned bullshit.

Eli checked his watch. It was one of those jazzy Dick Tracy gizmos, a Christmas gift from Sara and her kids, Eric and Hayley.

A text bounced off some satellite and came in for a landing with a *ping*, startling him a little. He wasn't all that big on modern technology; sometimes wished he'd been born in the days of swinging saloon doors, dance-hall girls, dusty streets and buckboards.

He shook his head, amused.

He was a seasoned officer—he'd stood toe to toe with armed criminals, not just that once, but half a dozen times over the course of his career, but this damn watch made him jumpy. God only knew what it was up to, behind that chunky square face...communicating with aliens, maybe. Or tracking his every move and reporting to—whom? Men in black? The Illuminati? Walmart?

Amos Edwards, one of his deputies, was big on conspiracy theories, and he'd taken a dim view of the device, claiming that "they"—whoever "they" might be—were using all forms of technology to spy on law-abiding citizens as they went about their daily lives. Intimate moments included.

Eli chuckled ruefully. Videos of *his* moments, intimate or otherwise, would be boring as hell.

He swiped the tiny screen to bring up the text.

It was from Cord. J.P. and I are here. Are you on your way, or out somewhere making Wild Horse County safe for Democracy?

He grinned. Managed to access the tiny virtual keyboard and bumble-fingered out, Be there in five minutes. At least, that was what he'd intended to say. The actual message read as if it had been punched in by a chimpanzee.

Cord and J.P. would just have to decode it for themselves.

Brynne Bailey liked snow. Didn't mind driving in the stuff, or shoveling the sidewalk in front of the café. In fact, it was romantic, especially around this time of year.

By February, of course, she'd probably be whistling a different tune. Longing for spring and mooning over seed catalogs and websites pitching tropical vacations.

At a signal from Cord Hollister sitting at a corner table,

across from J.P. McCall, Brynne grabbed the coffeepot and headed over. Filled their cups.

The place was quiet, since the midafternoon lull was on. Things would pick up around four, when the early diners would rally for the supper special—tonight, it was meatloaf, spiked with Brynne's own famous onion jam.

Curled beneath the table, J.P.'s retired service dog, Trooper, lifted his head and acknowledged Brynne with a doggy smile.

She smiled back.

"Thanks," Cord said, and J.P. nodded in agreement.

Cord was married, but J.P. was available, and a real catch by anybody's standards—like Cord, he was successful, smart and sexy as hell.

Oh, yes. J.P. McCall was a prize—a war hero, no less, with a sense of humor and a legendary investment portfolio. Women fell all over him, much to his delight, but so far, he'd remained single.

Brynne *liked* J.P., just as she liked Cord, but there was no spark between them. No chemistry whatsoever.

Which was a bummer, since she might have had a shot, otherwise.

Brynne was a pragmatic woman, and she was aware that, with her dark blue eyes, naturally silver-blond hair and decent figure, she turned heads.

Her appearance had been an asset in some ways, but she'd learned early that pretty girls had problems of their own; boys—and, later, men—hesitated to ask them out, lest they be rejected. She'd been popular in high school, a varsity cheerleader, proficient at both softball and soccer, a star player in the drama club, and she'd gotten good grades, too.

Senior year, she'd been prom queen.

Awkward, since she hadn't actually had a date. By then, Eli had dropped her for Reba Shannon.

Even after all these years, Brynne felt a pang at the memory.

She'd put on a good front that long-ago night, kept her chin up and her shoulders back, but once she was home, in the privacy of her bedroom, still clad in the lovely lacy dress her mother had made with such care, she'd flung herself down on her bed and ugly-cried until her mascara ran and her whole face was puffy.

Watching Eli and Reba dance together had crushed her.

Things were better when she went away to college, at least when it came to the dating scene. At Northwestern, she'd been a very small fish in a very *large* pond, sheltered and naive; gently raised in Painted Pony Creek, Montana, she'd been homesick and totally overwhelmed during her freshman year.

Guys asked her out, though. They took her to parties and football games, dances and concerts, movies and festivals.

And, with few exceptions, they expected sex in return. *Immediately.*

No getting to know each other. No taking the time to become friends, let alone build a relationship.

That kind of slam-bam-thank-you-ma'am approach had come as a shock to Brynne, though of course she'd known it was a thing. Sure, she'd grown up in a Podunk town, and she'd still been a virgin at the time, but plenty of the kids she'd gone to high school with had indulged. Two of her friends had been pregnant on graduation day.

But in college, sex wasn't an option, it seemed to Brynne. It was a *given.*

She hadn't been a prude, but she hadn't been a pushover, either.

In her mind, there was sex—and there was *lovemaking.*

Sex had its place, she knew, but it wasn't currency, to be exchanged for pizza and beer or an invitation to a party.

Soon enough, word had gotten around campus that Brynne Bailey didn't put out; if she went out with a guy, it was Dutch treat—no exceptions.

And no hanky-panky.

After college, Brynne had moved from Chicago to Boston and made a life for herself, working in various high-end galleries, first in sales and eventually in management. She'd squeezed her personal artwork—mainly abstract acrylics, with diversions into watercolor landscapes, animals and birds—in whenever she'd had that rare combination of time and inspiration.

And then there had been Clayton.

Clay.

She didn't want to think about him. Especially not in the middle of a workday.

So she shifted her attention back to Cord and J.P.

She'd gone to school with them, from kindergarten right on through high school and they were good friends, the kind of friends a person could depend upon, in the best of times—and the worst.

She refilled their coffee cups.

"You guys have a lot of leisure time," she teased. Since there were no other customers in the café at the moment, she decided to chat a little.

Cord trained horses, and he was world-renowned for his ability to establish a rapport with even the most troubled animal. J.P. had been injured in Afghanistan, years before, and had parlayed a modest government settlement into a fortune.

J.P. looked around, taking in the empty tables and unoccupied seats at the counter. "So do you," he said.

Brynne made a face, then laughed.

"Want to sit down?" Cord asked.

"No, thanks," she replied. She had a personal rule: she didn't sit with customers, even when the eatery was nearly empty and the invitation came from two of her oldest friends. "I'm on duty."

J.P. saluted, the smart-ass.

Just then, the number one vehicle from the sheriff's department whipped into the parking spot next to J.P.'s fancy rig. It was a massive SUV, dark green under sprays of mud, tricked out with top-of-the-line gear and emblazoned with insignia.

Brynne felt a lurch in the pit of her stomach.

Even after all this time, he still got to her, especially when the encounter was unexpected. And she figured she ought to be over it by now, since they weren't kids anymore.

Nevertheless, there it was.

She watched as Eli got out of the rig, shut the door behind him and headed for the entrance.

He was easy on the eyes, especially in that uniform, but Brynne had other rules, besides the one about not sitting down with customers—she didn't date cops.

Not anymore.

She was a law-abiding citizen and all that, but cops, like firefighters—she didn't date them, either—were in almost constant danger, even in places like Painted Pony Creek, Montana. Back in Boston she'd had friends in law enforcement, before and after she'd fallen in love with a policeman.

She'd seen too many marriages break under the stress the job naturally entailed, visited too many hospital rooms, and attended too many funerals.

To Brynne, loving a cop meant being afraid, 24/7.

And if there was one thing Brynne Bailey didn't need in her life, it was fear.

The little bell over the door jingled merrily as Eli came in from the cold.

Trooper crawled out from under the table and went, tail wagging, to greet the newcomer.

Eli smiled and bent to ruffle the dog's ears, murmuring a greeting. According to his sisters, Sara, who was Brynne's friend, he'd recently adopted a dog of his own, and named him "Festus," after a character on that old Western chestnut, *Gunsmoke*.

"Coffee?" Brynne asked automatically. She wasn't abrupt around Eli Garrett, just strangely *careful*.

"Sure," Eli said. "Thanks."

Brynne wondered if he ever thought about their history; if he regretted dumping her as gracelessly as he had.

Probably not, she decided.

To him, high school was a distant memory, water under the bridge.

Brynne didn't dwell on the old days herself, of course, but sometimes recollections of losing Eli to another girl—Reba Shannon in particular—ambushed her.

When that happened, she had to remind herself that that was then and this is now. She and Eli, once so close, were mere acquaintances now.

Resolved to keep her cool, she went back behind the counter for a clean cup and saucer, grateful to have something to do, even though the task took less than a minute.

Eli was seated and reading the menu when Brynne set the cup down in front of him and poured coffee.

"What can I get you?" Brynne inquired lightly. It was what she said to everyone. Nothing special.

"Is the grill off?" Eli asked, without looking up from the menu.

"I can fire it up," Brynne replied. "What'll it be?"

"Burger with everything and an order of curly fries," came the answer.

Brynne turned quickly and headed for the kitchen.

"Missed lunch," she heard Eli explaining to his friends. "I could eat the north end of a southbound skunk."

Brynne rolled her eyes, amused by the colorful, if hackneyed, description.

Men. Especially *Montana* men.

In the privacy of the kitchen, Brynne set to work. The fry cook was at the dentist and would be back in time for the evening rush. Brynne listened to the low rumble of male voices as she turned the dial on the grill to medium-high, washed her hands and gathered the makings of a deluxe burger—a thick meat pattie from the fridge, then a bowl of sliced onion, a plump tomato, a block of cheese, a slab of bacon.

One of the three hunks started up the jukebox.

Charlie Daniels fiddled his way into "The Devil Went Down to Georgia," and Brynne tapped one foot to the rhythm as the burger sizzled on the grill in front of her. The song was an oldie, but it was still a popular choice among the patrons of Bailey's, along with a lot of other golden relics.

She added a slice of cheese to the burger, dropped the fries into the basket and lowered them into the bubbling oil, and, against her better judgment, let her thoughts drift back to her time in Boston.

And Clayton.

Clayton "Clay" Nicholls, a detective with the robbery division of Boston PD.

Brynne had met Clay when the gallery she managed had

been robbed. Tall and muscular, with sandy-colored hair and a truly disarming smile, he'd caught her attention in that first moment they'd shared and held on to it long after the reports were filed and the investigation had been successfully closed.

Like museums, art galleries were usually targeted by very sophisticated thieves, familiar with state-of-the-art security systems and patient enough to plan their heists for months, if not years, before making a move.

In this case, the perps were young, inexperienced and impulsive.

The pair had been identified and tracked down within a few hours, balaclavas notwithstanding, caught on camera as they lugged armloads of paintings out the back way and piled them—Brynne still winced at the memory—into a rusted-out van with its doors open and its license plate clearly visible.

The plate would have led to an arrest all by itself, but these two, like most petty criminals, were a few trillion gray cells short of a brain. They'd yanked off their balaclavas, in plain sight of the security camera above the back door, high-fived each other in jubilant self-congratulation.

Clay and his team had had them in cuffs before the sun went down.

The stolen artworks had been recovered, expertly restored their former glory and returned to the gallery walls.

Of course Brynne had been relieved and grateful and, when Clay called three days after the incident to ask her out, she'd said yes without hesitation.

They'd gone for coffee on their first date and talked for hours.

Brynne had told Clay all about growing up in Painted Pony Creek, Montana, and Clay, a lifelong citizen of Boston, had told her about his career—he'd been born to be a cop, he'd said, following in the footsteps of his father, grandfather and great-grandfather. He was recently divorced, he said, with two children, a boy and a girl—the marriage had been solid for a long time, but the stresses and strains of his job had worn him and his wife down.

Finally, there had been nothing left besides their mutual love for the kids, and they'd sadly agreed to call it quits.

Brynne closed her eyes at the memory of that long-ago, sunlit afternoon on the patio of a café near the gallery.

She'd fallen for Clay somewhere between meeting him on the agreed street corner and the final café Americano long after the sun set.

More dates followed: dinner, movies, concerts—the usual things.

Unlike the college boys and entry-level executives she'd dated previously, Clay didn't expect sex from the get-go. He'd wooed her, actually *wooed* her, the old-fashioned way, with flowers, phone calls, handwritten notes and the like, and when she'd talked, he'd *listened,* instead of simply waiting for her to shut up so *he* could speak, the way the others had done.

A year later, Brynne moved in with Clay.

Gradually, she got to know his children, Davey and Maddie, and come to love them almost as deeply as if she'd given birth to them herself.

Clay's ex-wife, Heather, had been friendly enough, on the rare occasions when she and Brynne encountered each other—family birthday parties for the kids, brief vacations, picking them up for or dropping them off after their weekends with their father.

Back then, Brynne's mom and dad were still living in Painted Pony Creek and running the family business, and as soon as their daughter had given up her apartment to share

Clay's larger one, they'd started asking when she intended to bring her "boyfriend" out west for a visit.

Naturally, they wanted to meet him.

Size him up as a potential son-in-law.

Although they never said so outright, Brynne had known her parents were bothered by the fact that Clay was (1) divorced, and (2) a cop, with all the dangers and other drawbacks of the job.

Brynne and Clay hadn't really discussed marriage at that point.

Being together had been enough.

Brynne's days had been full, between her work at the gallery, which she loved, and her own art. Most evenings, Clay was home, and they talked, read, cooked together and made love. Sweet, vibrant love.

The folks at home had begun to ask pointed questions during their weekly phone calls. Brynne loved her mom and dad, and hadn't blamed them for wondering where her relationship with Clay was headed—she was an only child, after all—but she'd avoided direct answers.

As wonderful as Mike and Alice Bailey were, they'd been somewhat too eager to see Brynne married, settled, and producing grandchildren. Alice, not surprisingly, had been the one most invested in the dream.

Clippings had begun to arrive in the mail—Brynne's mom had never gotten the hang of email—images of bridal gowns, exquisite floral displays, glamorous venues ranging from mountaintops to European castles, towering cakes fit for a Windsor wedding.

Brynne had barely registered those pictures at first, but she'd stuffed them into a drawer instead of tossing them.

They'd accumulated, over the weeks and months, and they'd become harder to ignore.

Then Heather, Clay's ex, a trust fund baby, had suddenly married her personal trainer, temporarily transferred full custody of their children to Clay and dropped the kids off at the apartment to set out on a six-week world tour with her new husband.

Brynne had been thrilled to have Davey and Maddie around full-time; in those six weeks, she'd played mom and delighted in every aspect of the role. She'd taken them to school, picked them up afterward, brought them to the gallery, where they remained until quitting time.

Clay was pleased with the situation, too—he was an excellent father and sorely missed his children when they weren't around—but, although Brynne hadn't realized it then, something inside him had shifted when Heather remarried.

It was a subtle change, but it turned out to be momentous.

Upon her return from the whirlwind honeymoon, Heather greeted her son and daughter with tears and hugs, but, as she confided to Clay and Brynne, she and her bridegroom needed "us time." Time to get used to being married.

Would Clay mind keeping the children just a little while longer? She would see them regularly, of course, but she just wasn't ready to be *both* a wife and mother just yet.

Again.

Clay had agreed, though he insisted on a new custody agreement, and Heather had gone along with the plan.

The kids, who adored their father, had been delighted, and Brynne had been, too.

Clay, too, had been glad to keep the kids, but he'd seemed oddly embittered all of a sudden regarding Heather's new marriage. He'd scoffed when Davey and Maddie came home after a brief visit with their mother and showed him pictures of the places they'd visited and the things they'd done together, as a family.

He'd begun to refer to the new husband—"Geoffrey with a *G*"—as a gym monkey and a mope, the latter being cop slang for a loser.

And it wasn't like Clay to be so petty.

Slowly, so slowly that Brynne hardly noticed, things began to go wrong between her and Clay. He was often short with her, and he began to work longer and longer hours.

Brynne busied herself with her job, her art and the children, and told herself to be patient with Clay. His job was difficult, not to mention dangerous, and the police had recently been under fire in the media.

The first crack in the relationship occurred when Clay's partner was shot and nearly killed. Then she and Clay had stopped in at a convenience store to buy fountain drinks, and interrupted a holdup.

Clay had wrested the gun from the robber's hand, and a second bullet had missed him by inches.

He'd taken the incident in stride—*This is what it is to be a cop*, he'd said—but Brynne, despite previous exposure to the high costs the job too often involved, had been deeply shaken. Before Clay's partner's shooting, she'd been one step removed from the realities.

Afterwards, she'd started having nightmares, fretting when Clay came home late.

Impatient, he'd called her clingy, and that single word had wounded Brynne almost as badly as what happened next. Where, she'd wondered, was the line between "understandably concerned" and "clingy"?

And what, exactly, had happened next?

Geoffrey, aka the gym monkey, had showed up at the gallery in a state, demanding to see Brynne *now*.

She'd been busy with a client, and asked her assistant to take Geoffrey to her office, give him a glass of water, try to calm him down. She'd be with him as soon as possible.

Geoffrey wasn't having that.

He made a scene.

Brynne had been forced to move to plan B.

Her assistant took over the clients, and she half dragged, half cajoled Heather's blathering husband out of the main gallery, along the hallway and into her usually quiet office.

Geoffrey, clad in spandex shorts, a skimpy muscle shirt and a pair of very expensive trainers, sank into a chair and began to weep.

Loudly. With plenty of sniffles and snot.

Brynne handed him a box of tissues, took a bottle of water from her private minifridge, and gave it to him with a one-word command. *"Drink."*

He drank. Copiously.

The torrent subsided a little, though he was flushed.

"What is it?" Brynne asked, annoyed and oddly jittery. A part of her knew what was coming, though she couldn't bring herself to acknowledge it just yet.

Geoffrey took care of that little problem.

"They're cheating," he blurted. "Heather and Clay, I mean."

The core of Brynne's being shifted on its axis.

She collapsed into the chair behind her desk, and began grasping at the proverbial straws. "No," she said. "They can't be."

They can't be cheating, because I will die if they are.

Because I love Clay Nicholls too much to lose him.

They can't be cheating because that will be the end and I will probably never see the children again.

"They are," Geoffrey insisted gruffly, fiddling with his smartphone and then thrusting it at Brynne.

Her hands trembled as she took it.

The first image—Clay and Heather, half-dressed and kissing so deeply that they might have been trying to swallow each other—struck Brynne like the engine of a runaway freight train.

"Scroll," Geoffrey ordered.

She did.

The pictures were graphic, and undeniably recent. The small, bullet-shaped tattoo on the back of Clay's right shoulder, commemorating his near-death experience at the convenience store, was only a few weeks old.

"How did you get these?" Brynne asked bleakly, wondering, even as she spoke, why that mattered.

"Nanny cam," Geoffrey replied.

And that was it, the proverbial straw that broke the camel's back.

Brynne Bailey decided never to date another cop.

It was too damn risky.

CHAPTER TWO

Brynne set the cheeseburger down in front of Eli with a slight thunk, turned and walked away.

"Was it something I said?" Eli asked.

Cord studied him over the rim of his coffee cup, while J.P. quipped, "More likely, something you *haven't* said," he replied.

Eli cut the burger into four pieces and scowled. "Such as?"

"Such as, asking Brynne out," Cord said reasonably, finished with his coffee now. "You know you want to."

"Yeah," J.P. agreed, with a grin and a nod. "Grow a pair, man. Ask the lady out for dinner. Take her to a movie. Live on the edge."

"I 'live on the edge' practically every day of my life and you damn well know it," Eli snapped, before taking a defiant bite of the best cheeseburger deluxe in three states. Brynne might be citified, but she could sure as hell cook.

Cord examined the check Brynne had left him earlier and reached for his wallet. "Give us a break, cowboy. This is Painted Pony Creek, Montana, not old Dodge City."

Eli might have reminded his friend about some of the incidents he'd handled right there in the old hometown, but his mouth was full. Plus, he didn't want to talk blood-and-guts when he was eating.

"Time you got serious about finding a good woman and settling down," J.P. pontificated, still grinning.

Eli chewed, swallowed, took a gulp of water and shot back, "Says the man whose romantic life consists of swiping right on Tinder a little too often."

J.P. frowned. For once in his life, he seemed stuck for an answer.

Cord laughed. "He's got you there," he told J.P.

Easy for *him* to be cocky. He was happily married.

J.P. got to his feet, reached for his own check. He still looked annoyed.

Truth hurts, Eli thought uncharitably.

"You guys are just going to leave me here?" Eli demanded, in a loud whisper.

Trooper emerged from his post under the table, stretched and yawned big.

"Yeah," Cord replied. "We are."

"That's a crappy thing to do," Eli protested. "*Especially* when you invited me here in the first place!"

J.P. arched an eyebrow, braced his hands on the back of his chair and met Eli's gaze head-on. "You were late," he said.

Eli glared at his friends, first J.P., then Cord. Then he ate another hunk of his cheeseburger. He was pissed, but he was hungry, too. Hadn't eaten since breakfast.

And breakfast had been a leftover burrito nuked in his microwave.

"Fine," he bit out, after swallowing. "Go. Leave me hanging in the wind!"

Cord rolled his eyes. They were very blue, Cord's eyes; women tended to tumble into them, head over heels. "Spare us the drama, Eli. We're trying to *help* you, here."

"By leaving me alone?"

J.P. grinned again, that cocky tilted semblance of a smile that sometimes—like now—made Eli want to punch him out. "You're not alone, dude," he drawled. "Brynne's here."

Eli was well aware that Brynne was there. The air seemed to pulse with the energy of her presence. "Do *not* call me 'dude'!" he retorted.

J.P. laughed.

Then he and Cord ambled on over to the cash register, Trooper meandering along behind them.

Brynne came out of the kitchen immediately, smiling at that pair of polecats in a way that made Eli feel just a tad bit crazy.

They paid their checks, chatting with Brynne about the upcoming New Year's Eve celebration to be held right there at Bailey's. Practically everybody in the county was planning on attending.

Eli planned on working that night, since his already small crew would be stretched thin anyhow. The prospect gave him a lonely feeling, which was odd, because he was used to holiday duty.

Plus, he'd had Christmas Eve off this year—spent part of it with his sister, and his niece and nephew, and part of it out at the Hollister ranch, with Cord and his wife, Shallie, J.P. and his highly forgettable date, and a whole bunch of other friends. He couldn't expect to take New Year's Eve off, too; it would be unfair, and if he could help it, Eli was *always* fair.

Cord and J.P. left, and Eli watched them go, silently vowing to pay them back for ditching him like this.

Brynne, still behind the cash register, gazed after them, her beautiful face expressionless.

Maybe she was watching the falling snow—fat flakes now, spiraling as they descended, picking up speed.

Presently, she approached the table.

Eli admired her trim gray slacks and dark blue blouse, which exactly matched her incredible eyes.

"Something wrong with the burger?" she asked, apparently noticing that he'd only eaten half of it. "I'll be happy to make you another if there is."

Eli cleared his throat. "No," he said gruffly, embarrassed. "It's fine." An awkward pause followed. Then, "Brynne?"

Brynne waited, not frowning, but not smiling, either.

Eli pushed his chair back and stood. "Would you mind sitting down?"

She considered, looked around at the empty café, then peered through the front window to check the sidewalk.

No customers.

No excuse.

"Okay," she said, sounding bemused. She pulled back the chair Cord had occupied before and sat. "What is it?"

Eli was still ravenous, but he didn't touch his food. "Do you like it here? In Painted Pony Creek, I mean?"

Brynne looked puzzled. "It's home," she said. "Why do you ask?"

"Because—well—it can't be all that exciting, after Boston."

Her perfect brows drew together for a moment. "Eli," she asked quietly, "what on earth are you getting at?"

"I'm just trying to make conversation."

"Why?"

He felt a flush climb his neck. "Does there have to be a reason? We went to school together."

"We did," Brynne agreed, with a wisp of a smile and no trace of bitterness whatsoever. "We went steady, in fact. Then Reba Shannon came to town and you ghosted me."

It was true. "That was high school, Brynne," Eli reminded her, but he knew he was losing ground, if he'd ever held any in the first place. "I was a dumbass kid with a perennial har—" He stopped himself just in time. Or maybe not. "I was a dumbass kid," he repeated.

Reba hadn't been prettier than Brynne—practically no woman was—but she'd been willing, and to a horny seventeen-year-old boy, that made her irresistible.

She'd also been a tease, playing not only Eli himself, but J.P. and Cord, too, for fools.

A few months ago, Reba's daughter had shown up in the back room at Sully's, the living image of her late mother, and announced that one of them—Eli, Cord or J.P.—was her birth father.

A lot of drama ensued.

As it turned out, Cord was Carly's dad.

In his heart of hearts, Eli still felt a twinge of disappointment at the knowledge. It would have been a fine thing to have a daughter, even if she was practically grown before he'd even met her.

Now he and J.P. were the girl's honorary uncles, and they tended to spoil her accordingly.

Suddenly, Brynne unleashed that smile of hers—it was blinding, like headlights on a dark highway, set on high beam. "I'm over it, Eli," she said.

I'm over you, Eli.

When he didn't answer right away—he was still catching his breath—she went on. "What's this all about? We were *both* kids, we had a thing for each other, and it ended badly, at least for me. A lot of time has gone by, in case you haven't noticed."

"Did I ever apologize?" He hoped he had, because no matter how long ago it happened, he'd acted like an asshat.

Brynne pretended to consider the question, though her lips quirked a little at the corners. "I don't think so."

"Okay, then," Eli said, after clearing his throat again, "I'm really sorry. That I treated you the way I did, I mean."

Brynne studied him, gave a slight shake of her head. "Like I said, I'm over it. Have been for a very long time. But I still want to know—what brought all this on?"

Eli pushed away his plate. Hungry or not, he wasn't going to get another bite of food past the cinch-like tightening in his throat.

When he spoke, he was surprised by his own words.

"What are you doing New Year's Eve?"

What the hell? He was scheduled to work that night. And she would probably say she had a hot date. Thanks, but no thanks.

"I'll be here at Bailey's," Brynne said, confused. "The party—" She blinked. "Eli Garrett, are you trying to ask me out?"

He hesitated, then decided he was in too deep to back out now. "Kind of," he admitted.

"'Kind of'?" Brynne repeated. "Are you or aren't you asking me out, Eli?"

He sighed. Interlaced his fingers on the tabletop in front of him. "I am," he said,

"Then the answer is no," Brynne said, without rancor.

"No?" It was the reply he'd expected. So why did he feel as if he'd just been kicked in the stomach?

"Yes. I mean, no." Brynne was smiling now, as though they'd just settled some existential dilemma.

Eli wished the earth would open right up and swallow him whole, but he had his pride, too. "Why not?"

"Why won't I go out with you?"

He was exasperated now. "No," he countered. "Why don't you install a zip line and offer a discount for senior citizens? *Of course* why won't you go out with me!"

"A zip line might not be a bad idea," she said thoughtfully.

"Damn it, Brynne—"

"All right." She met his gaze calmly, and her tone was matter-of-fact. "I don't date cops," she said.

He'd run into that policy before, throughout his career— women who were scared to fall for a man who might get shot in the course of a day's work, women who disliked any kind of authority, women who only dated men with six-figure incomes. Even a few who had warrants out for their arrest.

"You don't date cops," he said, nonplussed.

"That's what I said."

"Why not?"

"I have my reasons," Brynne responded, looking and sounding a little miffed now.

"Would you mind sharing them?"

"Yes, actually," Brynne said, bristling by this point.

This was not going well.

Damn J.P. and Cord and their bright ideas.

"Fair enough," Eli said, pushing back his chair. "Can I have the check, please?"

"No," Brynne said. "This conversation isn't over."

"Well, you couldn't prove that by me," Eli answered.

"I don't date police officers," Brynne reiterated.

"So you said."

"But I don't mind having them for *friends*."

"Friends? I thought we were friends already." He paused, made a huffing sound. "I'm not sure where I got that idea, though, now that you mention it."

Brynne laughed then, and the sound reminded Eli of the merry little bell above the front door. "Will you just dial back your male ego a notch or two and listen to me, please?"

He glared at her. "I am all ears," he said.

She laughed again. "Your face! When was the last time you asked a woman out and got turned down, Sheriff?"

"About two minutes ago," he replied.

"And before that, about twenty years, I'm guessing," Brynne said.

Let her think that. He wasn't obligated to tell her about the times he'd struck out.

"It's my turn to ask. What the hell are you getting at?"

Brynne smiled again. "If you want to come to the New Year's Eve shindig as *my friend*, and not my date, I wouldn't mind."

"That's generous of you," Eli said, drawing out the words.

Just then, the little bell over the door jingled, and a flock of high school kids blew in, including Eli's sixteen-year-old nephew, Eric, and Carly, Cord's daughter.

They were laughing, teasing each other, pushing and shoving a little.

"Hey, Uncle Eli," Carly called brightly, unbuttoning the bright red pea jacket she'd gotten for Christmas.

"Hey," he echoed, his voice hoarse again.

The girl looked so much like Reba had at that age. Fortunately, Carly was a better person than her mother had been, and talented, too. She sang, wrote songs and had built an impressive following on YouTube, though these days she was busy with school and working with animals.

Brynne was out of her chair, smoothing the floral print apron she wore over her slacks and blue blouse, greeting the kids cheerfully and helping them to push several tables together, in order to accommodate the sizable group.

Apparently, more friends were about to join them.

Eli was standing when Carly came toward him, snowflakes nestling in her caramel-colored hair and just beginning to melt.

Facing him, she stood on tiptoe to kiss his cheek.

"We interrupted something, didn't we?" she whispered. A mischievous twinkle lit her amber eyes.

Embarrassed again, Eli deflected. "Of course you didn't," he said. "Brynne and I were just talking, that's all."

"Liar," Carly countered with a smile, keeping her voice low. "Did you *finally* ask her out?"

"Is the whole damn town playing matchmaker?" Eli demanded, but he couldn't help a twitch of a grin.

"Probably," Carly answered. "Did you?"

"Did I what?"

Carly rolled her eyes and, in that moment, she looked more like Cord than Reba. "Did you ask Brynne out?"

"Yes," he answered. "Are you satisfied?"

"No," Carly said. "What did she say?"

"She said she doesn't date cops."

More kids were coming through the door, and a few called out hellos to Eli as well as Carly.

Carly sighed dramatically. "She dated a police detective in Boston," the girl confided, sotto voce. "I heard her telling Shallie about it once. Evidently, it was a real shitshow, and Brynne got her heart broken."

"Language," Eli said, with mock sternness.

Carly laughed. "Right."

"Go join your friends," he told her.

She kissed his cheek again, then did as she was told.

Eli carried his check to the cash register and waited for Brynne to take his money.

When she did, he handed over a twenty.

She made change. He add it to the tip.

The kids were making a ruckus, but it was a happy sound, full of holiday merriment. They were hoping for a heavy snowfall so they could sled and go snowboarding in the nearby mountains.

"So," Brynne asked quietly, meeting Eli's gaze and holding it. "Are you going to be my guest at the New Year's Eve party or not?"

He imagined the scene. Practically everybody there would be a friend of Brynne's, so he wondered how she thought this thing was supposed to go.

"I might stop in," he allowed.

"I hope you do," Brynne replied.

And the conversation was over.

Eli waved to the kids, and Eric gave him a thumbs-up. He and his nephew hadn't always been on the best of terms—the kid had gone through a rough stage, gotten involved in some stuff he shouldn't have—so Eli reckoned the gesture was better than a middle finger.

His shift was almost over for the day, and he was glad.

He'd go home, let the dog out, crack open a beer, kick back and watch a little Netflix.

Damn, he needed a hobby.

Outside, he surveyed the darkening sky, gunmetal gray

and boding ill for snowplow operators, nervous drivers and the sheriff's department.

The noise from inside Bailey's was muffled, but it was poignantly joyous, too.

He thumbed the fob to unlock his SUV and headed toward it, head down, snowflakes chilling the nape of his neck.

Once her work-day was over—after 10 p.m.—Brynne climbed the stairs behind the kitchen to her apartment on the second floor.

Her cat, a rescued tabby named Waldo, met her at the door, winding himself around her ankles and meowing piteously for a snack.

Brynne smiled and bent to pet him. "Don't give me that poor-starving-cat routine," she said. "You had supper at six, like always."

Waldo subsided, but only slightly.

Brynne flipped on the lights and surveyed her spacious living room with a sense of lonely satisfaction. When she'd taken over the restaurant after her parents retired, she'd had the former storage/office space completely renovated, putting in a living room with bay windows overlooking Main Street, along with a streamlined kitchen, a master suite and a truly decadent private bath.

There were two small guest rooms as well, linked by a full bath and, of course, a powder room down the hallway.

Brynne sighed, kicking off her shoes and padding across the kitchen to fill the electric kettle and plug it in. A nice cup of herbal tea and a long, decadent soak in her garden tub would help her to decompress.

Running the café wasn't exactly stressful, but it was a thriving concern, as it had been when her mom and dad ran it, and it kept her busy for as many as twelve hours a day.

And that was good, because when Brynne wasn't rushing from one task to another, solving problems and putting out fires—sometimes literally—she started thinking about her life.

The mistakes she'd made.

The opportunities she'd missed.

The three years she'd wasted loving Clay Nicholls and believing that he loved her in return.

"Stop it," she said aloud.

Waldo meowed again, more insistently this time.

"Beggar," Brynne scolded fondly. While the water heated for her tea, she took an open can of tuna from the refrigerator and spooned a few flakes into Waldo's empty dish.

He devoured the treat, then sat primly, watching Brynne as she washed her hands at the sink, took a mug from the cupboard and dropped a tea bag into it.

Minutes later, teacup in hand, she shut off the kitchen and living room lights and headed down the hallway toward her suite.

There were photos on the hallway walls—her mom and dad with their recently purchased RV, living it up at the Grand Canyon, wearing mouse ears and huge grins at Disney World, standing in front of Mount Rushmore. Interspersed were small paintings Brynne had done herself, mostly watercolors, and pictures of Davey and Maddie, Clay's children.

Clay had taken some of them, Brynne had taken others.

They'd all been so happy back then—or, at least, Brynne had *thought* they were. She certainly had been, as had the children, but then there was Clay.

Had he ever been happy, or had he been pretending the whole time?

He'd told Brynne he loved her, and she'd believed him.

Until Geoffrey-the-Gym-Monkey had clued her in, that is.

She tore herself away from the photos—there she went, *thinking* again, and continued along the hallway.

She passed the closed doors of the two rooms she'd put in— *admit it, with visits from Davey and Maddie in mind*—resisting the temptation to open the doors and peek into those rooms, one decorated for a boy, one for a girl.

At times, like now, for instance, she wondered what she'd been thinking to set aside so much space for children who weren't her own and would *never* wind up in Painted Pony Creek. She ought to tear out a few walls, create a nice studio for herself, or at least convert one to an office.

Because hope died hard, even when it was completely unfounded, Brynne hadn't made the decision. She didn't have time to paint these days, and her dad's old office downstairs, a converted supply closet, filled the bill.

Besides, if she renovated again, there would be all the commotion that comes along with construction, not to mention the expense.

Brynne had earned a good living in Boston, and she'd saved a lot—sold a few of her own paintings, too, for sums that still surprised her—but, while Bailey's brought in a decent income, she wasn't going to get rich selling breakfast, lunch and dinner to the locals.

She was still young by modern standards—thirty-four— but she was also an unmarried woman, with zero prospects, and she had to think ahead. After all, she'd be old one day, probably sooner than she thought.

Entering her bedroom suite, Brynne chuckled at herself. She took a steadying sip of raspberry tea and admired the space around her.

It was as much her own design as any of her paintings—French country furniture, a few cherished artworks on the walls, a working white brick fireplace, visible from the bath as well as the bedroom.

Here, as in the living room, a set of mullioned bay windows overlooked the street out front. Brynne's small Christmas tree sat between them, dark and magical, tinsel swaying as if stirred by the snow falling beyond the glass.

In that moment, she figured she needed a little Christmas, so she went over and tapped the switch on the cord to set the bubble lights bubbling.

How she loved those old-fashioned lights. They brought back so many happy memories of her childhood.

Waldo, having toddled after her, took his place in the wing-backed chair next to the fireplace, where Brynne had expected to spend quiet nights reading, and nestled in for the night.

Brynne entered the bathroom, separated from the sleeping area only by a low tiled wall, started the water running in the tub and stripped to the skin. Then she added a generous sprinkling of the scented bath salts she'd received as a Christmas gift from Miranda, her favorite waitress, climbed into the water and sighed with relief as the day's tensions began to dissolve.

She sipped her tea and wished momentarily that she'd taken the time to start a fire in the hearth to complete the ambience, then decided it didn't matter. The little tree in front of the bay windows blazed with light and color, and Brynne found herself feeling almost festive, even though her feet still hurt and there was a twinge in her lower back.

She stayed in the tub for a long time, adding hot water when necessary, and finishing her tea.

She'd be glad when the holidays were over—Christmas had

been quiet, with friends and staff members gathering down-stairs to celebrate—and Brynne had enjoyed a long video call with her parents.

They were at their condo in Arizona this month, playing golf and attending flea markets, having the time of their lives, to hear them tell it. Brynne worried about them often, out there on the open road in their cumbersome RV, but they seemed happy, referring to themselves and their occasional traveling companions as the Geriatric Gypsies. They'd be swinging back through Painted Pony Creek come summer, to live in the house they still owned, over on Pine Street, the house Brynne had grown up in.

Her dad would tinker with the RV, keep the lawn trimmed with his ancient push mower and swap yarns with his cronies over at Sully's on hot afternoons, while her mom would gar-den and haunt the café during working hours, making sure things were shipshape.

It wasn't that Alice Bailey interfered, exactly. She'd run the place, along with her husband, for close to forty years, that was all, and she had a vested interest, emotional if not financial.

Brynne enjoyed having her mom around—mostly. Alice always introduced new recipes to the menu, and her many, many friends came from all over Wild Horse County to lunch and sip sweet tea and hear all about the Baileys' adventures on the road.

In the quiet times, though, when it was just Alice and Brynne, and sometimes Brynne's dad, Mike, Alice asked ques-tions.

Had Brynne been seeing anyone special?

She was over that man from Boston, right?

Was she sure she wanted to stay in Painted Pony Creek? Maybe she ought to sell the business—Alice *swore* she and

Mike wouldn't mind—and spend a year in Paris or possibly Florence, just painting.

Or what about New York? She'd probably love New York, all that color and motion and sensual stimulation…

Brynne sighed, finished her bath and let the tub drain as she wrapped herself in a fluffy towel and stepped out onto the mat.

She loved Paris—who didn't?—and Florence *and* New York, and she knew it would be good for her to work less and paint more—sometimes she actually *ached* to pick up a brush—but she wasn't an heiress or a trust fund baby. She had responsibilities, right here in Painted Pony Creek—she had friends, her art, a business, a cat. She couldn't just go haring off to another city or another country at a whim.

As she brushed and flossed and rinsed, she thought about Painted Pony Creek.

It certainly wasn't cosmopolitan, by any stretch of the imagination, but it was, as she'd told Eli earlier, *home.*

The scenery was breathtakingly beautiful, too—snow-capped mountains, stands of timber reaching as far as the eye could see, shimmering lakes brimming with fish, four distinct seasons, and canyons and valleys. When it came to landscapes fit to paint, Montana had everything and more.

The drawbacks? Painted Pony Creek was a small town—ironically, one of its charms—and that meant there wasn't a lot to do.

Oh, there were events—the big rodeo, the Fourth of July blowout and barbecue at the town park, classic car shows and the like—but, at least at the Creek, no museums or galleries, no film or art festivals.

Unless….

Unless someone, like Brynne, decided to *start* something—

not a museum or a gallery, and not a film festival, since folks in rural Montana probably wouldn't go for subtitles and intellectual angst, but a celebration of various arts and crafts, well, that just might fly.

There were lots of artists in the state—producing everything from chainsaw sculpture to exquisite landscapes in oils. There were wood-carvers and potters, quilters, doll makers—the list was practically endless.

Something quickened within Brynne as she thought of the possibilities.

The city park was huge, with plenty of room for booths, a stage featuring local bands, like The GateCrashers—the group Carly sang with—and concessions galore.

With adequate promotion, such a gathering would draw visitors from all over the region. Bailey's, Sully's Bar and Grill, and the various fast-food places around the Creek would be jumping, and the bed-and-breakfasts, the new hotel and even Russ Schafer's motel off the old highway would be booked to capacity.

Oh, yes. An art festival could give the whole community a boost, financially and otherwise.

Unless, of course, it fizzled.

Putting something like that together would be a job of gargantuan proportions; Brynne would need permits, some kind of liability insurance, and a virtual army of volunteers. They would have to attract and vet artists, musicians, food-service people.

And the publicity? Well, she didn't even want to think about that, not at eleven thirty at night, with a twelve-hour workday behind her.

The whole idea was probably a crazy tangent, and nothing more.

After a good night's sleep, Brynne decided as she turned off the tree lights with a tap of her bare foot, she'd be in her right mind again.

Probably.

CHAPTER THREE

The snow kept right on coming down.

After leaving Bailey's, Eli stopped by the office, checked in with Melba Summers, the deputy he'd hired in November, after Oliver Boone moved on to another job in another state.

All was quiet on the western front, for the moment anyway, so he clocked out for the day.

That conversation with Brynne, back at Bailey's, had left him with a lot to think about, and he wanted to do that thinking in a quiet place—*his* place.

A mile or so out of town, he met a snowplow heading back toward town.

The driver, Laura Wiley, waved as they passed each other, and Eli waved back.

That was one of the best things about living in a place like the Creek—knowing everybody. It gave a person a sense of security, and there were a hell of a lot fewer surprises.

Not that the town was composed of saints and angels; far from it.

★ ★ ★

The area was populated by human beings, some good, some bad, with the vast majority falling somewhere in between those two extremes.

There were plenty of creeps and lowlifes, that was for sure, but Eli knew who they were, and he kept an eye on them.

Strangers, of course, were another matter, and the Creek got its share of those, too, mostly just passing through. During the big rodeo, in mid-June, for instance, spectators came from all over Montana and well beyond its borders, too.

Most were decent folks, looking to have a good time and go peaceably back home again, but there were thieves, con artists and other no-goods, as well.

At rodeo time, Eli hired temporary deputies and put in eighteen-hour days himself. The town's Fourth of July celebration could get pretty rowdy, too, but so far, with his regular crew and a few extras, he'd managed to keep the lid on.

His mind tripped back to the kids at Bailey's—Eric, his nephew, and Carly, in particular. He hoped they'd put off the planned sledding and snowboarding until morning, but they were kids, after all. Invincible.

He'd text Eric later, remind him that he was still on probation; the boy seemed to have undergone a major change of heart, but it would be all too easy for him to fall into his old ways, start hanging out with thugs like Freddie Lansing and his buddies again.

Nothing good would come of that.

If Eric were caught drinking or taking drugs—or running with Freddie and the gang—he'd be headed back to court, and this time, he wouldn't get off with community service and a stern warning.

Although a few people around town thought Eli had used

his influence as sheriff to keep his errant nephew out of jail, the truth was, he hadn't.

Sara, the kind of mother every kid should be lucky enough to have, had gotten her son into therapy right away, and kept him there. He'd been grounded for months, banned from playing his beloved video games, lost the use of his tablet entirely, and allowed to use his phone only when absolutely necessary.

Now, his grades were up, he was talking about college again, and his therapist whom he was still seeing, said he was back on track.

While he wasn't about to bend the law for his nephew's sake—or anyone else's—Eli would do everything he could to keep the kid from turning to the dark side, for Sara more than for Eric.

Eli loved his sister; she and the kids were the only real relatives he had left, since his and Sara's parents had died in an accident nearly a decade back.

Sara and Eli had been typical siblings before the tragedy, young adults, busy with their own lives, going their own ways, but they'd grown close afterward. Sara, being a single mother on a tight budget, had started worrying about Eli then, fretting over his tendency to throw himself into his job—he'd been a deputy then, and a junior one at that—forgetting to eat right, get enough sleep, etc.

She'd driven him a little crazy, actually, but, in terms of family, she and the kids had been all he had.

He'd grown to love, appreciate, and admire his sister, and he hoped the feeling was mutual.

Sara was beautiful, with a fine mind, bookish and artistic, sensitive and shy.

Eli, on the other hand, was more outgoing, and while he'd

certainly missed his mom and dad, he hadn't taken the loss quite as hard as Sara had. She was two years older than he was, and something of a homebody, even as a child.

Growing up, Eli had spent practically every spare moment with Cord and J.P., fishing and hunting, bucking hay bales, digging post holes, riding horses, herding cattle. Thanks to the Hollisters, Cord's grandparents, and J.P.'s happily married folks and older sisters, he'd been almost as much a part of those families as he was of his own.

Being who she was, Sara had longed for a home and family of her own. After a year of college, she'd hitched herself to Zach Worth, a crap stain of a human being, and Eric and Hayley had come along quickly. *Too* quickly for Zach; he'd bailed when the kids were toddlers, gotten himself a Mexican divorce and has never been seen or heard from again.

Sara, though unhappy, had admitted, albeit reluctantly, that she hoped Zach stayed gone for good, and that was a sentiment Eli and most of their mutual friends had heartily agreed with.

Even now, more than a decade later, Sara was still gun-shy when it came to men. She said she didn't trust herself not to pick another loser, just like Zach, and if she woke up one morning married to a man like that, well, she'd go batshit crazy, that's all.

So she kept her head down, raising the kids, maintaining her modest little house across the street from the First Baptist Church and posing as a mild-mannered daycare worker by day and plugging away at her home computer in secret every night, after Eric and Hayley were in bed, spinning yarns.

She wrote thrillers set in the West, under the name Luke Cantrell. Probably no more than half a dozen people knew that, even now that she'd been able to give up her daycare job, and Sara was fine with that. Her first book had been a hit of sorts and she was nearly finished with her second.

While her publishers would have preferred that she drop the anonymity and actively publicize her work, Sara refused. She reasoned that the reception book one had received in the marketplace might have been a fluke, and if the next turned out to be a flop, well, she didn't want everybody in town feeling sorry for her.

If she failed, she'd fail privately.

Eli didn't think she had anything to worry about on that score.

On another, he wished she hadn't summarily written off the entire male gender, in terms of love and romance. She had a lot of living to do yet, and Eric and Hayley were growing up fast—one of these days they'd be off to college, landing jobs and getting married, and she'd be on her own. The fictional cowboy detective wasn't going to warm her bed, laugh with her or hold her when she cried.

Realizing what a hypocrite he was being, Eli laughed and thrust a hand through his snow-dampened hair. At least Sara had been married once—he'd never gotten past the hot-and-heavy stage with any of the many women he'd been out with.

His longest relationship, with a kindergarten teacher named Penny, had lasted six months. Penny had given him an ultimatum one fine day: *propose to me, damn it, or I'm leaving town for good.*

School was out the next day, and by then, Penny had accepted a job in Omaha. She left the Creek in her pickup truck, tooting her horn as she passed Eli's country mailbox and hauling everything she owned behind her in a rented trailer.

Like just about every other hometown woman he'd dated, Penny had accused Eli of being hung up on Reba Shannon, even though, by then, Reba had been long gone and good riddance to her.

Had he still cared for Reba back then?

No.

She'd screwed him over and nearly tanked his friendship with Cord and J.P. once and for all, and he hadn't missed her.

Who he *should* have been missing was Brynne Bailey, but he hadn't had the God-given sense to do that. Oh, he'd thought of her often, and wondered how she was doing, first in Chicago, where she'd gone to college, and then in Boston, doing whatever she'd done there.

Since she'd come back to the Creek and taken over Bailey's though, she'd been on his mind with some regularity.

He thought back to that afternoon, when he'd finally gotten up the nerve to make a move, however tentative.

She'd been polite enough. Even asked him to stop in at her New Year's Eve party, as a "friend."

For all that, the message had been clear enough.

Don't call me, Eli, I'll call you. Not.

He'd deserved to be shot down, no doubt about it.

He'd hurt her, way back in high school, and been too much of an idiot to realize it.

Even now, Brynne was clearly wary of him.

And she'd relegated him politely but firmly to the friend-zone.

What was the point?

He'd be just another fool, standing around and hoping the next year would be better than the last one—or, at least, no worse.

Barely able to make out the shape of his mailbox, just up the road a way, Eli flipped the turn signal switch, even though there wasn't another car in sight, coming or going.

It was habit.

Laura had passed this way with the plow, since the left-hand side of the road was relatively bare, but there was a two-foot berm blocking his dirt driveway, which was under about ten inches of snow as it was.

Eli didn't stop at the mailbox—he paid his bills online and nobody wrote letters anymore—he merely shifted into low gear and barreled down the driveway, depending on momentum to keep him from spinning out and getting stuck.

He could see his house up ahead, between the dizzying flakes flying like frenzied bugs now, a plain log structure, rectangular in shape, with a stone chimney at one end and a cyclone fence out front.

There was one of those at the back, too, to contain his dog, Festus, who couldn't be trusted not to chase a deer or a rabbit or some other critter into the next county, if he got loose.

Festus had a pet door leading out of the kitchen, so he wouldn't be waiting for a toilet break, but he'd sure as everything be ready for some company.

Most dogs were sociable. Festus was obsessed with human companionship—so much so that Eli let him ride in the county's SUV with him most days.

Today had been an exception only because Eli had had to be at the courthouse for most of the morning, testifying in a burglary case.

Smiling a little at the prospect of Festus's enthusiasm, Eli thumbed the button on his visor to open the door of his detached garage—made of logs, like the house—parked the truck inside and shut it again. He left by the side door and hurried toward the house, stomping the snow off his feet when he reached the back porch.

Festus, a lop-eared mutt of indeterminate ancestry, shot

outside to greet Eli, the rubber door flap swinging behind him. He barked jubilantly, and Eli paused to ruffle his brindle-colored ears, even though it was colder than a well digger's ass outside, and he wanted to build a fire, slam back a beer, take a hot shower to get the chill out of his bones, and pull on sweatpants and a T-shirt.

After that, he intended to rustle up some supper, sit himself down and think about Brynne Bailey in peace.

Weigh his options and decide, one way or the other, whether he ought to try to get back into her good graces or just leave well enough alone.

He managed the hot shower—after wrestling with a very playful Festus for nearly fifteen minutes—proceeded to the kitchen and then opened the refrigerator.

Since he hadn't gotten around to shopping for groceries— what with all the Christmas shindigs he'd gone to, he hadn't needed much in the way of grub—he settled for a boxed meal from the back of his ice-furred freezer, which tasted only slightly better than it looked when he slid it out of the carton and onto the counter.

While the food pirouetted inside the microwave, Eli filled Festus's bowl with kibble and topped off his water.

He'd pick up some supplies in the morning—beef and chicken, bacon, spuds, some decent vegetables and fruit. Maybe even a couple of those salads that came in a bag, complete with croutons and dressing.

Half the county might be snowed in by then, but Eli wasn't worried for himself. That truck of his would go damn near anywhere, especially with chains on the oversize tires.

The packaged dinner was everything he'd expected it to be, and less, but he choked it down anyway because he was hungry and he hadn't finished his burger and fries back there at Bailey's.

He'd been too distracted by the waitress.

He grinned, grabbing a beer from the fridge and heading for the living room. Brynne wouldn't like being called a waitress, he figured. No, sir.

She might have come back to the Creek to take over her parents' dining joint so they could retire, but she wasn't like other women who'd grown up in rural Montana and liked it there just fine.

Brynne dressed big-city and talked big-city.

Eli's grin faded. Sara, who was friendly with Brynne, said she'd wind up back in Boston one day soon, or maybe New York, because Painted Pony Creek was nothing but a backwater to her.

Oh, she hadn't said as much, according to Sara, but it was obvious to anyone who paid attention. Brynne had been hurt, and badly, by a man she truly loved, and she'd come back to the Creek to nurse her wounds.

Once she'd gotten over the worst of it, she'd be gone again, off to a world of symphonies and operas, five-star restaurants, museums and galleries.

Although he would have liked to believe otherwise, Sara's theory made a lot of sense. Even as a kid, Brynne hadn't been your typical Montana girl. She'd mostly spurned the standard blue jeans and tank tops or T-shirts for sophisticated outfits she'd designed and sewn herself, and, though she'd been popular, there had been a certain air of remoteness about her.

During the latter part of their junior year in high school, over that summer and a few months into their turn as seniors, Eli and Brynne had been an item. He'd been crazy about her, but she'd been reserved, though sweet and funny and so damn beautiful he sometimes couldn't catch his breath.

Then came Reba.

She was out of school, working with Shallie out at the run-down motel owned by Russ and Bethanne Schafer's folks. Reba was bold, full of life, vibrant and wild and very, very pretty.

Unlike Brynne, Reba was more than ready for sex: the more of it, the better.

Older, out of school, on her own.

And hot for him.

Like the dumbass kid he was, he'd believed her when she said she only wanted him and nobody else. The lie was flattering so he'd bought it.

After all, he was seventeen.

The trouble was, the whole time she was going out with Eli, she was playing the same game with Cord *and* J.P.

Things had come to a head at a party out in the woods, just days after graduation. J.P. and Cord had been away that weekend, competing in a rodeo, but they'd come back early, showed up at the secluded beer blast.

They'd found Eli and Reba practically wrapped around each other, and all hell had broken loose.

The three of them, Eli, J.P. and Cord, had gotten into a jealous brawl, and they might have done each other some genuine damage if several members of the football team hadn't hauled them apart.

Reba had quietly sneaked away, and none of them had ever seen her again.

They'd gotten their hearts broken good and proper, the unholy trio, and it had been months before they'd been forced into talking things out at a Christmas get-together. Cord's grandfather had shut them up in a storage closet and refused to let them out until they'd set things straight.

After that, their friendship had recovered, albeit slowly, and they'd forgotten about Reba and all the trouble she'd caused, over the coming years.

Forgotten, that is, until Carly showed up in the back room at Sully's that rainy night, when they'd gathered for their weekly poker game.

Carly's arrival had changed things for Eli, as well as for Cord and, he suspected, J.P., too. Even after learning that Cord was the girl's biological father, not him, Eli still felt oddly disoriented.

Before, he'd been complacent, comfortable in his own skin. He'd known who he was—or thought he did: Eli Garrett, sheriff of Wild Horse Country, best friend of Cord Hollister and J.P. McCall, brother of Sara Worth, uncle of Eric and Hayley Worth. And so on.

Finding out he might also be the father of a young woman, well, that had thrown him. And the discovery that he *wasn't* Carly's bio-dad, oddly enough, had rattled him even more.

He'd been deeply disappointed, in fact. Examining that disappointment as dispassionately as he could—not very—he'd come to the realization that he wanted a wife and family of his own, among other things.

That had highlighted his loneliness; he was still plumbing the depths of that, and that snowy night, alone in his house, except for the dog, it seemed bottomless.

He ached with it.

Felt as if he might actually *drown* in the simple sorrow, just go under and never resurface.

Festus made a whimpering sound and rested his furry head

against Eli's right leg. His eyes, one blue and one green, were raised to his master's face, full of sympathy.

"You're a good friend, old buddy," Eli said, his voice thick, the backs of his eyes smarting suspiciously. He patted the dog's head and chuckled, a husky sound, partly choked. "I think we'd better do something constructive right about now," he went on, scanning the room.

His gaze landed on the bedraggled Christmas tree in the corner of the living room. Sara and the kids had put it up, right after Thanksgiving, and decorated it, too.

There were still unwrapped gifts beneath it—a good woolen shirt, fur-lined leather gloves, a plaid bathrobe Eli wouldn't have been caught dead in.

By now, the tree was leaning markedly to the left and shedding needles onto the hardwood floor.

Out with the old, Eli thought.

He took the gifts from beneath the tree and tossed them onto the couch.

He found the storage boxes in the basement and began removing colorful glass balls, the dime-store angel topper, the strands of lights. He rewrapped the ornaments in their paper towels and tissue paper, not out of any inclination of his own, but because he knew Sara would lecture him when Christmas rolled around again and it was time to decorate another tree.

Closely observed by Festus, Eli dragged this year's tree through the house and out the back door, through the everdeepening snow to rest, dry limbs bouncing and still faintly fragrant, beside the burn barrel.

Back inside, shivering, he carried the boxes of decorations back to the basement, placed them on the appropriate shelf.

Upstairs again, he swept up the dry pine needles, dumped them into the bin, and put away the broom and dustpan.

Job completed, he was at a loss, like before.

So he opened another beer, switched on the TV and sat on the couch, Festus beside him.

Yeah, he'd planned to think about Brynne, work out how—and *if*—he wanted to pursue some kind of relationship with her. He was 99 percent sure he did.

And equally sure she wasn't interested.

Brynne awakened to a clear, crisply cold winter morning that was blanketed in snow. Roofs, roads, sidewalks, all covered.

Even after the plows came through to clear the way, most folks would stay at home today, nibbling at Christmas leftovers, taking down their trees, shoveling sidewalks, removing strings of outdoor lights from eaves and shrubs.

She would open for business at the usual time, but there would be few, if any, customers. Only the most intrepid would wade through knee-deep snow merely for coffee and pie, or anything else she served.

Brynne smiled, sipping her coffee. Suddenly, she was a kid again, excited and pleased by this deep and glistening gift of nature. Back then, a storm like this one meant no school. Going sledding with the other kids. Building snowmen and having snowball fights in the park.

"Snow day," she said, glancing down at Waldo curling around her slippered feet and purring persuasively.

He didn't care about snow days or happy memories.

He just wanted his breakfast.

Brynne turned from the window and headed for the kitchen, where she poured kibble into the fancy pottery bowl Miranda Clark had given him for Christmas.

In her spare time, Miranda dabbled in pottery, and she was

good at it. Her pieces were colorful and unique, reflecting her personality.

Miranda, of course, would be a prime candidate for the art festival Brynne had in mind. In fact, she'd bounce the idea off Miranda first, get her perspective on the pros and cons.

She'd call Shallie Hollister, too, for sure.

Like Brynne herself, Shallie was an artist, though her medium was photography. A woman of many talents, she also worked side by side with Cord training horses and, with her friend Emma Grant, she was planning to open a local center for riding therapy. Disabled children especially benefited from this kind of treatment.

With these thoughts in her mind, Brynne left Waldo to his breakfast and went off to shower and dress for a new day. Afterward, she donned black cords and a long-sleeved pink T-shirt, brushed her teeth, blew her chin-length blond hair dry and applied a little lip gloss.

That done, she gathered up her laptop and cell phone and went downstairs to warm up the grill, brew the obligatory pots of regular and decaf, and unlock the front door.

No one was out and about, as far as Brynne could see, and it was no wonder. The ancient thermometer, just visible through the frosted front window, read a shivery ten degrees.

Too cold to snow, her dad would have said, had he been there.

Brynne returned to the kitchen, whipped up her customary mixture of yogurt, fruit and granola, and took a seat at the end of the counter, where she'd set her laptop and phone.

She ate while the laptop booted up. The phone rang, not surprisingly, as soon as she'd put a spoonful of the breakfast concoction into her mouth.

She swallowed, thumbed the appropriate button and answered, "Hello, Miranda. Calling to tell me you're snowed in and can't come to work?"

Miranda laughed her throaty, infectious laugh. "You're psychic," she teased.

"Something like that," Brynne replied.

"I don't imagine you'll get a whole lot of folks coming in to eat," Miranda said.

"Most likely not."

"I hate not getting to work. Especially when we have so much to do to get ready for the New Year's Eve thing."

"We'll get everything done," Brynne assured her, looking around at the Christmas decorations—sagging tinsel swags, vintage Santa and snowman faces that lit up, the wonderfully tacky aluminum Christmas tree in a far corner. She'd take it all down herself. Make good use of the day.

"We always do," Miranda agreed, with a sigh of pleasant resignation. Then she added, "Well, I'll be in as soon as the roads are passable."

"Not before then, though," Brynne warned. She didn't want her employees—all friends—risking their necks to get to work.

Five more calls followed, in quick sequence. Everybody was snowed in—two fry cooks and three waitresses—and Brynne ordered them all to stay home.

Once the call-ins were over, she scanned her email and was pleased to find a message from Davey, Clay's son. He'd attached about a dozen photographs of the loot he and Maddie had scored over Christmas—most of it from Heather's wealthy parents.

Brynne smiled as she surveyed the bikes and board games, electronics and clothes, all carefully staged for best effect.

Davey, she suspected, was a budding photographer—he took pictures of *everything*, sometimes things he shouldn't.

After admiring the kids' treasures—remarkably, the siblings weren't spoiled—Brynne turned to Davey's email. She'd been saving that for last.

From: Daveynicholls@bughunter.net
To: BrynneBailey@BrynneBailey.com

Hi Brynne. Hope you had a good Christmas. We really liked the books you sent, and Dad says we have to write you an actual thank-you note, 'cause an email isn't enough.

There isn't much news to share. Mom is still with Geoffrey, that douchebag, and Dad is dating some woman he met at a nightclub. Mom says she's a floozy.

Maddie and I are spending New Year's Day with Dad, at his place. He says the floozy won't be there, 'cause she's nobody we need to know.

Trust me, that's a relief.

Anyway, Dad said if it's okay with you, we could Skype or FaceTime with you while we're with him.

Would that be okay with you?

If it is, which day and what time?

That's about all there is to say for right now. Maddie and I both miss you a whole lot.

Love,

Davey

Brynne swallowed, waited for her vision to clear and replied, Text me the times that work for you. When it comes to you and Maddie, I'm available anytime.

About five seconds after she'd clicked Send, a response arrived from Davey, with no subject line. The body of the message was a row of thumbs-up emojis.

She smiled and replied with two hearts and four kisses.

Then she cried for a while.

Not over Clay. No, she had no tears left for him—she'd cried them all in the months after the breakup.

She cried because she loved Davey and Maddie, and missed them terribly, and because the way things were shaping up, she might never have children of her own.

She could go the single-mom route, of course—lots of people did, these days—but Brynne was too damn old-fashioned for that. She wanted the whole enchilada—loving husband and all.

She closed her laptop, sniffled and plucked a napkin from one of the holders on the counter, dabbing at her eyes and then blowing her nose noisily.

That done, she tossed the napkin, washed her hands and got to work.

She took down the aluminum Christmas tree and the plastic Santa heads and other decorations left over from her mom and dad's day, then fetched a stepladder and climbed onto it to begin taking down the lights strung around the front window.

The roar of an engine startled her so that she nearly tumbled off the ladder.

Annoyed, Brynne palmed away some of the fog from the window and peered out, only to find Eli Garrett in front of her café, mounted on the biggest snowmobile she'd ever seen and grinning like a kid.

He was wearing a heavy coat and gloves, but no hat, the damn fool. His ears were red with cold.

Now that he knew she'd seen him, he gunned the engine a couple of times.

Brynne hurried to the door, jerked it open and was immediately struck by a blast of bone-chilling cold. "Eli Garrett," she sputtered, "are you crazy? Get in here before you freeze to death!"

Mercifully, he shut the engine down. Lord, that thing was loud enough to qualify as a menace.

Eli dismounted, dropped the keys to his gas-powered chariot into the pocket of his coat and came toward her, that insufferable grin still in place.

"What are you doing here?" Brynne demanded, as soon as they were both inside and the door was closed.

Dripping melting snow, Eli tugged off his gloves, shoved them into another pocket, then removed his coat. Hung it from one of a dozen pegs alongside the door.

"I was under the impression a man could get a cup of coffee here," he answered, in his own good time. "Was I wrong?"

"Oh, for heaven's sake," Brynne said, more flustered than angry. She was flashing back to her youth again, only this time not to school closures and sledding parties. No, this time, she went back to high school, when she'd worn Eli's senior class ring on a cord around her neck. When she'd believed, with all her naive young heart, that someday she would marry Eli Garrett and have his children.

Instead, he'd chosen Reba Shannon.

She was still furious with him. Still hurt.

"Aren't you supposed to be out patrolling the roads or something?" she asked, going to the coffeepot and pouring a cup of regular.

Eli took his coffee black.

He came in often enough, always with J.P. and Cord, for her to remember.

"I can be reached if I'm needed," he said, holding up his

phone before setting it on the counter, beside the mug she'd practically slapped down in front of him.

"Good," Brynne said, snappishly, because nothing else came to her.

"How is it that you're already pissed off at me? I just came through the door about five seconds ago, and I haven't had time to put my foot in my mouth."

Brynne sighed. "I'm sorry," she said. "I didn't mean to be abrupt."

"Okay," Eli said mildly. "Thanks for that, anyway."

"Eli, what are you doing here?"

"Drinking coffee?"

"You never come in for coffee. Not without Cord or J.P." She paused. Maybe she'd jumped the gun, pointing out their absence. They might be on their way to Bailey's right now, riding snowmobiles of their own.

Eli took a pensive sip from his cup. Then he grinned at her and said, "Cut me a break here, Brynne. I'm trying to be—sociable."

Brynne didn't know what to say to that.

So she poured herself a cup of coffee and stayed where she was to sip it, keeping the counter between them. In that moment, she sorely wished some of her regulars would show up: the sweet old codgers who always ordered the Rancher's Breakfast; the members of the Silver Streaks book club; or even Roy, from over at the post office, who could nurse a single cup of coffee and a slice of pie for the better part of an hour and always tipped one bright, shiny quarter.

No one came.

"Do you want breakfast?"

"Nope," Eli replied.

Brynne was flummoxed again, at a complete loss, which made her feel foolish, which, in turn, made her about half-mad.

"Well," she said.

Eli looked her over, though not in a rude way. He might have been assessing the state of a fence post, deciding whether to shore it up or cut it into chunks for firewood.

"Put on something warm. Snow boots, good gloves if you have them."

"Why would I do that?" Brynne countered, all too aware that her heart was beating faster than it should have been.

"Because we're going snowmobiling," Eli answered blithely. "You and me."

The thought thrilled Brynne; she realized she was hungry for fresh air and countryside. It never even occurred to her to refuse that blunt, offhanded *arrogant* invitation.

CHAPTER FOUR

Brynne hadn't ridden a snowmobile in years, and she'd *never* ridden one seated behind Eli Garrett, with her thighs pressing into his and her arms clasped tightly around his middle.

The streets of Painted Pony Creek were practically deserted, though folks smiled and waved from windows and doorways, looking as pleased as if they knew some benevolent mischief were afoot, and they were part of it.

Brynne waved back, when she dared let go of Eli long enough to make the gesture, but mostly she *didn't* dare, because she was breathless, delightfully, deliciously *terrified*, certain that the roaring machine racing over the snow would suddenly pitch and roll, sending both its riders flying.

Overhead, the sky was winter blue and cloudless, and the sunlight sprinkled diamonds over rooftops and yards and the snow-laden branches of trees.

The machine sped on, past the park and the library and the sign that read, "Welcome to Painted Pony Creek, Montana, Population, 5718," and then they were streaking through the open countryside, zigzagging around the craggy old trees in Ben Jackson's apple orchard, weaving around obstacles such as boulders and fallen logs.

They raced over drifts of snow, traveling alongside the freshly plowed highway, and Brynne reveled in the whole experience—the speed, the indescribable freedom, the icy nip in the air, the glorious beauty of the intricate, ever-changing tapestry that was Montana at her natural best.

Brynne clung to Eli, exultant, startled by the joy she felt, skimming over the land she'd been born to, and had always loved, and had somehow forgotten.

Presently, they passed through a stand of timber and emerged at the top of a small rise, overlooking the shallow valley that cupped the town and its surroundings gently, loosely, like the palm of a giant hand.

Eli shut off the snowmobile engine and turned to look at Brynne over one broad shoulder. "You doing all right, city girl?" he asked, with a twinkle in those hazel-green eyes of his.

"I'm doing just fine," Brynne managed, though in truth, she was quite overwhelmed. And quite sure she hadn't had so much fun since—well, she couldn't have said exactly when, because she'd been focused on emotional survival for so long, taking the next step, and the one after that, and trying not to look beyond the present moment.

So many feelings, all of them electrified and hopelessly tangled.

Eli swung a leg over the snowmobile and stood, offering Brynne his hand. She took it, rose awkwardly from her seat, stumbled a little and righted herself.

Or, rather, Eli righted her, catching her by her elbows when she fell against his chest. Her legs felt wobbly, as though they might not support her, and Eli's fingers tightened slightly, as if he'd sensed that.

Time stopped as they stood there, facing each other, and the sweet silence of a fresh snowfall was all around them, something mysterious and holy.

Brynne's heart pounded, and she hoped Eli would kiss her. Hoped he wouldn't.

He didn't. He just smiled a slight, crooked smile and traced the outline of her right cheek with a gloved thumb.

In that instant, Brynne very nearly kissed *him*. She felt compelled—not just tempted, but *compelled*—to throw her arms around Eli's neck, stand on tiptoe and plant a long, wet smacker right on that expressive mouth of his.

Everything within her seemed to thrum, like the sound of distant drums pounding out some urgent message.

She felt herself blush, and Eli smiled again, as if he knew why.

She, Brynne Bailey, who had sworn off men for the foreseeable future, especially if those men happened to be cops, was as taut as a wire. Her sexuality, in hibernation for so long, rose, stretched and *roared* within her, like a tigress ready to mate.

More than ready to mate.

If he'd guessed her thoughts, Eli was gentleman enough not to remark on them. Still holding her elbows, he set her a little away from him, or so it seemed to Brynne, though she was sure neither of them actually moved.

"Want to meet my dog?" he asked, tilting his handsome head to one side and regarding her thoughtfully.

"Why not?" Brynne managed, going for a light tone and falling just shy of the mark. "I probably should be getting back to the café, though. Lots to do to get ready for New Year's Eve—it's only a few days away, you know..."

Prattling.

Was she prattling?

"Up to you," Eli said, with maddening alacrity. A part of Brynne wanted him to throw her over one shoulder, caveman style, carry her somewhere warm and private, lay her down on something soft, and make love to her until she absolutely lost her mind.

The more sensible part of her, the one that counseled immediate flight, was gaining ground, though not very fast or very forcefully.

"I guess I could meet your dog," Brynne allowed, feeling stupid and, at the same time, brazen and bold. "Briefly."

Eli remounted the snowmobile, and Brynne climbed on behind him.

If she'd been conscious of his proximity, his heat and the hardness of his muscles, before, she was ablaze with it now.

Now that they had a destination in mind, Eli drove more moderately.

They descended the rise and burrowed across the road and a long, winding driveway, following the trail Eli had probably forged earlier when he'd decided to zip on into town and collect her from her mundane life.

His house was sturdy looking, built of logs, and a thin trail of smoke rose from the chimney, an etching against the too-blue sky.

He pulled up alongside the detached garage, shut the snowmobile off again and stood. He did that so gracefully, like a cowboy getting off a horse.

This time, when he offered his hand, Brynne ignored it.

She was feeling fitful. Flustered.

And the last thing in the universe she wanted was for Eli Garrett to see that he'd gotten under her skin.

Poor phrasing, she thought, with another hard blush.

Reckless in her disgruntled state, Brynne swung one leg over the long padded seat and went to stand, only to topple forward and land on her hands and knees in the deep snow.

Unlike before, Eli didn't catch her.

He laughed, crouched and looked into her snow-splattered face with dancing eyes. "Good one," he said.

"Shut up," Brynne said in response, struggling to get up.

Eli laughed again. "Are you really this independent, or just stubborn?"

Brynne's high dudgeon dipped low, all of a sudden, and she laughed, too. "Both, I think," she admitted.

The dog she'd ostensibly come to meet was yipping joyfully on the other side of a cyclone fence, wearing a track in the snow as he dashed six feet in one direction, then six feet in the other.

"That's Festus," Eli said, standing and unceremoniously pulling Brynne up after him. "Festus, meet Brynne Bailey."

Brynne stood, trying to brush snow off her flannel-lined jeans and the front of her warmest jacket. "Hello, there," she greeted the dog. Approaching the fence, she put out a hand for him to sniff. "I own a really bossy cat, but I hope you and I can be friends anyway."

Festus gave a gleeful yip and wagged his tail frantically as Eli opened the gate and stepped back to let Brynne precede him.

Reaching the back porch, they kicked the snow off their boots, and then they were inside, in a small but well-designed kitchen, streaked with bars of sunshine from the windows and skylights.

"Nice," Brynne said.

Eli acknowledged the one-word compliment with an

equally brief nod. "I'll build up the fire and make some coffee. You'll be warm in no time."

She was already warm, despite spending at least an hour in the freezing cold, buffeted by icy winds. The echo of Eli's body still pulsed along the length of her arms and the inside of her thighs; it was a wonder she wasn't sweating like a wrestler under hot lights.

"I'm fine," she said nervously. "Really."

Eli started toward the next room, paused as he passed her and spoke gently. "Relax, Brynne. I didn't bring you here for any reason other than to warm up before I drive you back to town in my truck."

Brynne averted her eyes, bit her lower lip.

She was relieved.

She was *disappointed*.

When Eli moved on and busied himself stoking the embers in the living room's Franklin stove, she took off her jacket, draped it over the back of one of the kitchen chairs and leaned down to pet Festus.

"I think I'm in love," she murmured, gazing into adoring canine eyes.

She thought Eli was out of earshot; turned out, he wasn't.

"I know I'm hot," he teased, "but isn't it a little soon?"

Brynne laughed, in spite of, or maybe *because of*, her jittering nerves. "Egomaniac," she replied. "I was talking to your dog."

"Damn," Eli replied, moving to the sink, where he rinsed out and then filled the carafe from his coffee maker. "Decaf or high-octane?"

"*You* drink decaf?"

"No," came the answer. "I was counting on you to ask for regular."

"Do you ever say anything serious?" Brynne inquired.

He paused, turned to look at her. They were half a room apart, but something invisible arced between them.

"How about this? I'm sorry I treated you the way I did, back in the day. I was a kid, but that's no excuse. It was wrong, and I regret it."

For a few long moments, Brynne couldn't speak. When she did, all she managed was a lame, "It's okay."

Eli filled the carafe with water, filled the plastic tank on the coffee machine, and set it on the burner beneath to catch the fragrant brew.

"It wasn't, though," he replied quietly. "It *isn't*. You were way out of Reba's league, and you deserved a lot better than the treatment you got from me."

"Eli." Brynne spoke softly. "I'm over all that. It was all so long ago, and besides, Reba was a force of nature. She was way more experienced than I was—more outgoing, more everything. And you weren't the only guy to fall for her, re-member?"

He sighed, approached the table, pulled back a chair for Brynne and waited until she sat down. With a rueful sigh, he answered, "Oh, yeah. I remember. She'd gotten to my best friends, too. Made fools of the three of us." He grinned, a little sadly. "Not that we didn't deserve exactly what we got."

Eli drew back a chair of his own, sat across from Brynne.

He seemed to be keeping his distance, and though he was probably just exhibiting good manners, Brynne would have liked to sit closer to him, risky as that might be.

"What do you want me to say?" Brynne asked, not un-kindly, but out of genuine concern.

The coffee began to bubble and steam, filling the room with the corresponding aromas. Festus sat beside Brynne's chair, resting his muzzle on her knee and watching her with unconditional adoration.

She smiled, relaxing a little, and ruffled the dog's ears.

"I want you to say you accept my apology," Eli said.

"I think I already did, when we had this discussion yesterday, in the café."

"You were pretty busy making it clear that you don't date cops."

Brynne drew a deep breath, released it slowly. "It might be more accurate to say I don't want to *get serious* about one."

"Been there, done that. Right?"

"Right."

"It was that bad?"

Brynne sighed. "Not always. There were good parts— like his children, Davey and Maddie. I miss them every day of my life."

Eli merely nodded, pushed back his chair and went to the counter to fill two mugs with coffee. "Do you use sugar or cream?"

"Artificial sweetener, if you have it."

"I don't."

Brynne smiled again. "Of course you don't."

He frowned, pretending to be offended, as he set the mugs on the table. "What is that supposed to mean?"

"It means," Brynne said pointedly, drawing out that last word a little, "that you're a man living alone, and you take your coffee black. And, most likely, when you entertain, the kitchen isn't the focal point of the evening."

Eli sat down again, cupped his hands around his coffee, gave a ragged chuckle. "That's a flattering take on the situation," he said, "but the only woman who spends any time around here is my sister. Sara comes out to cook 'a decent meal' a couple of times a month, and brings the kids with her."

Brynne was oddly relieved to hear that, though she knew Eli wasn't claiming to be celibate. He was too good-looking and too unabashedly masculine for that.

"I'm not involved with anybody right now," he went on, surprising Brynne more than a little with the frankness of that statement. "Not romantically, anyhow." A pause. "What about you?"

Brynne looked down at her coffee, considering her reply. "I'm in the recovery phase," she said.

"You've been back in the Creek for a while now," Eli pointed out. "Six, eight months?"

She blinked back sudden, unexpected and totally unwanted tears. "There's no time limit," she said, somewhat defensively.

He reached across the table then, laid one strong hand over hers, lightly. His palm and fingers were warm, and calloused.

That last part surprised Brynne a little, since, dangerous though it might be at times, Eli's job didn't involve manual labor.

She turned his hand over in hers, examined it. Ran the pad of her thumb gently over a callus.

Eli supplied an answer without being asked. Was the man psychic, or just incredibly perceptive for a member of the opposite gender?

"I work with horses when I can. Over at Cord's place."

It wasn't a surprising thing to learn, especially not in rural Montana, where horses were part of the lifestyle, but Brynne found it interesting. She loved horses herself, though, growing up in town, she hadn't been around them much and, truth to tell, they made her a bit nervous.

"I didn't see a barn or a corral when we came in," she said, in a questioning tone.

"My job doesn't really allow for a setup of my own," Eli replied, sounding sad.

"Maybe you'll take up some other kind of work, or retire or something," Brynne speculated, but she was uncertain and it showed.

"I'll always be a cop, Brynne," he said, with a certain finality. "It's always possible that I'll lose an election at some point in the future, but if that happened, I'd end up working with one of the state agencies."

"You wouldn't even *consider* doing anything else?" She was over the line, pressing the issue this way, but she couldn't seem to help herself.

He sighed. "Like what?" he asked mildly. "This is Painted Pony Creek, not Boston. Opportunities are limited."

Brynne lowered her eyes briefly. "I'm sorry," she said quietly. "The way you earn your living is none of my business."

"It's okay, Brynne," he told her. "There are things I'd like to ask you, after all."

She stroked Festus's furry head as she reflected on that statement. Presently, she said, "I think I can guess what you'd like to know."

He chuckled, sat back in his chair and folded his arms. He was wearing a worn flannel shirt over a T-shirt, and even through his clothing, his leanly muscular chest and shoulders were clearly defined. "I'm sure you can," he answered.

And then he waited.

"Go ahead," Brynne said, after a few moments.

"What do you have against cops? Too many traffic violations? Police brutality?"

Brynne smiled, in spite of herself. "Neither of those things," she answered. "As I'm sure you know, the Creek being the small, tightknit community that it is, about the man I lived with in Boston."

"Bad breakup?"

"The worst."

A brief silence fell.

Eli broke it. "Carly told me a few things," he said. "Nothing too personal."

"He was a cop, and he cheated. Big-time."

"So you concluded that all cops cheat? That's a little drastic, don't you think?"

"It's not that. Clay was nearly shot once. His partner *was* shot, and she nearly died."

"It's a dangerous job, Brynne," Eli allowed. "Nobody's denying that. But *anybody* can get into an accident, or be the victim of a crime. And anybody can cheat." He paused, grinned again. "Why just last winter, old Mrs. Drummond down at the library tripped over a toy in the storybook section and broke a hip. Dangerous work, being a librarian. I'm pretty sure she was faithful to her husband, though. She and Henry were married for almost seventy years."

Brynne made a face. "I saw Mrs. Drummond just last week. She came in with her Bible study group, and she was certainly spry for someone who'd broken a hip."

"My point exactly," Eli said, though it was anything but exact, since getting shot in the course of a convenience store robbery was in no way the same as falling and breaking a hip. "Life is deadly. In fact, *none* of us are getting out of here alive, so we might as well take our chances and be as happy as we can be."

This time, he did have a point, but she didn't have to acknowledge that.

Brynne looked down at her wrist, realized she hadn't put on her watch that morning. "I need to get back to the restaurant," she said.

"Right," Eli confirmed, rising from his chair.

He took their empty mugs to the sink, rinsed them out, set them on the drainboard.

Festus, sensing his master's imminent departure, left Brynne to stand near the back door. He whimpered pitifully.

Eli shook his head, but the love he felt for his dog was touchingly visible in his voice and in his manner.

"Mind if Festus comes along for the ride?" he asked.

Brynne smiled and shook her head. She was already starting to love that dog herself, which was crazy. "Not at all," she answered.

Eli's truck was parked in the garage, and he backed it out while Brynne and Festus waited in the yard. The snow came up to the dog's chest, but it didn't slow him down; when Eli got out and opened the rear door, Festus bounded over and jumped into the back seat.

The animal's joy was infectious, and Brynne, full of delight, couldn't help laughing.

She was about to round the truck and climb in on the front passenger side when Eli came to stand before her. He laid his hands on her shoulders and she tilted her head back to look up at him.

"No matter what else happens, Brynne," he said, "can we be friends again? Like we were before—well, before?"

She smiled into his eyes. "Yes," she replied. "We can be friends." A pause. "I had a wonderful time today, Eli. Thank you."

He curled his right index finger and used it to lift her chin.

"Now that we're out in the open, where you won't feel cornered, I think I'd like to kiss you."

"I think I'd like that, too," Brynne admitted, her voice very soft.

Eli bent his head then, brushed his cool, firm lips across hers, very lightly.

A charge shot through Brynne, radiating from her middle, filling her, turning her head to mist and at the same time sending roots of fire through the soles of her feet, coursing deep into the good earth.

When Eli kissed her in earnest, she soared.

Her arms wrapped themselves around his neck, and she stood on tiptoe.

Their tongues sparred briefly, and then the kiss ended.

Eli held her at a slight distance, breathing heavily, his head tipped back so he gazed at the blue, blue sky.

Brynne stood dazed, a little alarmed, grateful that Eli's grip on her shoulders was firm, holding her upright. Her arms remained around his neck.

"Whoa," he said, after a few tense moments. "That kiss was a little more than friendly."

Brynne actually laughed, partly with amusement, partly with relief. Nodded.

He turned her around, steered her past the back of the truck and around to the passenger door. He opened it for her, hoisted her inside.

"What on earth—?" she murmured.

"Gotta get you out of here pronto, Bailey," he said, addressing her as he had in high school, before time and Reba Shannon ruined what they'd had going. "We're *way* too close to my bed for our own good. Or mine, at least."

With that, he closed the truck door and walked around to his own side.

Festus, fidgeting in the back seat, pulled a sneak attack and licked Brynne's cheek exuberantly.

She laughed again. "Stop it, silly dog," she chided, but she gave his ears a good ruffle, rewarding him.

Eli climbed into the truck, snapped his seat belt on, and gave Brynne a look until she remembered to put hers in place, too.

"Sorry," she said, with a ridiculous little giggle that immediately embarrassed her.

"I'd hate to have to run you in for ignoring safety laws," he informed her solemnly.

"Perish the thought," Brynne replied.

She'd called the dog silly, but at the moment, she was feeling pretty silly herself. She'd regressed to her high school self, it would seem. *Giggling*, for heaven's sake. Why, she hadn't giggled in forever.

She sat facing forward, trying to compose herself. Turn back into the adult version of herself.

They were passing the city limits—"Welcome to Painted Pony Creek, Montana"—before Eli spoke again.

"Bailey?"

"Yes?"

"You're still the most beautiful woman I've ever seen."

Brynne couldn't help being flattered. "Thank you," she said.

"That cop back in Boston?"

Again, "Yes?"

"He must be a damn fool."

The remark pleased Brynne, but she didn't let on. "Friends," she said. "Remember?"

That kiss, back at Eli's place, complicated matters, but she was determined not to get carried away. If she got involved with the sexy sheriff of Wild Horse County too quickly, she might be on treacherous ground.

She didn't love Clay anymore, but she hadn't had a remotely serious relationship since their breakup, and that meant she was probably on the rebound.

Everybody knew it wasn't wise to get too serious, too quickly, especially so soon after a broken romance.

"Friends can compliment each other," Eli reasoned. "Can't they?"

Brynne said nothing. She could have offered a compliment or two of her own, but they would be more than friendly.

Eli Garrett, she could say, if she dared, which she didn't, *you are so sexy I can barely stand it.*

The way you love your dog melts me in places I didn't know I had places.

And that kiss—dear God, that kiss.

"Bailey?"

"What?" Brynne retorted cheerfully.

"Say something."

"Are you fishing for compliments?"

He grinned, made a shrugging motion with his powerful shoulders. "Maybe," he replied. "Or maybe I just like hearing the sound of your voice."

"If I had your job, I would appreciate peace and quiet."

"You'd look good in a uniform," he said.

"Stop it," she said.

He laughed.

They were passing through town now, traffic was normal, and people were going about their usual business.

When Eli pulled into a slot in front of the restaurant, there were several old-timers gathered on the sidewalk, stomping their feet and rubbing their hands together to keep warm.

"The breakfast club has arrived," Brynne said, smiling and waving at the half-dozen men clad in overalls, heavy boots and Carhartt coats. Retired farmers and ranchers all. "Just in time for a late lunch."

Eli chuckled, waved to the group with a salute-like gesture.

Frank, one of the fry cooks, who doubled as a bartender, was just unlocking the door. He'd already turned the Closed sign to Open, and he gave Brynne a curious glance before he let the men inside.

Eli got out of the truck, came around to Brynne's side, and opened the door for her. Helped her down.

"Thanks, Sheriff," she said lightly. "I might have forgotten how to open a door for myself."

He grinned. "I'm a gentleman. Get over it."

"Come in for coffee and pie?" It was a simple, ordinary invitation, and yet offering it made Brynne feel bold, maybe even a little brazen.

"Can't," Eli said, with polite regret. "I've got to check in with the Creek's PD and then head on over to my office for a while. The battle against crime never ceases."

"Right," Brynne said, giving him a little push.

She turned, peered in at Festus sitting impatiently in the back seat.

"You're invited, too," she said. "I have another canine customer, and I'll bet you've met him. His name is Trooper."

Festus yipped happily.

Brynne smiled and stepped onto the sidewalk.

Eli opened the restaurant door for her, and the breakfast club, lining the counter now, all turned to look.

They were jumping to conclusions, Brynne knew, and

they'd share those conclusions with their wives when they got home.

Something going on between Sheriff Garrett and the Bailey girl, they'd say. *They were off someplace in the sheriff's truck, in the middle of the gosh-darned day, too. Mark my words, Doris/Ruth/ Margaret/Annie/Stella/Betty, something's going on with those two.*

CHAPTER FIVE

For Brynne, the next two days raced by, she was so busy preparing for the community New Year's Eve party, a tradition in Painted Pony Creek for over a quarter of a century.

The decorations—strings of small twinkly lights, a mirrored disco ball and large tinsel banner hung with the numerals of the coming year—were easy enough to put up; Brynne and Miranda took care of the job, taking turns on the high stepladder while the other directed placement.

Planning the menu, ordering cases of champagne and coordinating a team of volunteer designated drivers to ferry home those who'd had too much to drink took more doing.

Carly and several of her friends, including Eric Worth, decorated the stage and set up the equipment for The Gate-Crashers' performance.

Brynne liked Carly Hollister very much, and she was close friends with Shallie, Cord's wife and Carly's stepmom. And she couldn't help noticing Eric's strong resemblance to his uncle—Eli Garrett.

She hadn't heard from Eli since their magical snowmobile ride and their talk inside his sparsely furnished log house, though he'd been in her thoughts almost constantly ever since.

Her mind said, *Proceed with caution.*

Her body had a whole different thing in mind, and caution wasn't part of it.

She blushed, standing there in the middle of her very popular restaurant, supervising the setting up of three long buffet tables.

The bell over the front door jingled just then, and everything quickened in Brynne; she even caught her breath, hoping Eli would appear, snowflakes dusting his hair and resting on the shoulders of his uniform jacket.

Instead, his sister, Sara, Eric's mom, bustled in, shivering with the cold.

Sara was lovely, with her long, dark hair woven into a single plait, her deep gray eyes, her enviable bone structure. She and Brynne had become friends after Brynne's return to Painted Pony Creek.

Today, Sara wore trim jeans, a red turtleneck sweater, boots and a beautifully tailored leather jacket with fringe.

Smiling, she took off the jacket and hung it from one of the pegs near the door. Then she dusted her ungloved hands together and said, "Sorry I was late—Hayley's going to a sleepover tonight and she couldn't find the pajamas she wants to wear. Major crisis, loads of drama."

Brynne laughed, and the two women embraced briefly, the way old friends do. "Still stuck on chapter twenty-three?" she whispered, since Sara's alter ego, Luke Cantrell, was a closely guarded secret.

"Nope," Sara answered, with a grin. "I figured it out. Had to throw in another body, though."

Again, Brynne laughed. Shook her head. She'd loved Sara's debut novel and looked forward to the sequel with genuine excitement.

She wanted to ask about Eli—he and Sara were fairly close, after all—but she didn't want to seem too interested.

Which was silly, of course, because she *was* interested.

Very interested.

But very scared, too, because she'd made a major mistake before, falling for a man too quickly, and she'd been shattered by that man's betrayal.

She reminded herself that she needed to proceed with caution. Maybe date a few other men, older ones, for instance. In their eighties, perhaps.

Or she could just resign herself to being single and adopting more cats.

Heaven knew that would be safer.

She pushed these thoughts aside, though she knew they would be back, probably when she least expected—or wanted—them.

For now, for this one magical night, she would pretend she wasn't afraid to love, *really* love, a man who wore a badge.

Had Eli told his sister about the hours he and Brynne had spent together, zooming over drifts on his snowmobile, talking quietly at his kitchen table?

Probably not. It probably wasn't a big deal to him—just time he'd spent with a friend.

Brynne wanted to be more than a friend to Eli—*much more*—and that terrified her. The last time she'd loved a man, she'd gotten her heart broken, and the recovery—not over even now, she suspected—had been long and difficult.

She was too old-fashioned, that was her main problem.

She was sexually attracted to Eli, no doubt about it, but she wasn't the type to surrender her body and withhold her heart.

Or was she?

She'd given Clay *everything*, fallen for him heart and soul.

No, she definitely couldn't risk loving again. Not now. But if she saw Eli again, spent time alone with him, and he decided to seduce her—well, she might not be able to resist him.

Was that so terrible? She wasn't a nun, after all.

She was older now, she reminded herself silently, and hopefully a little wiser.

Anyway, Eli hadn't called, stopped by or even texted, so maybe she'd misread the signals. Maybe he'd decided they were better off as friends.

If so, he was probably right.

Brynne resigned herself to her life as it was—blessed, but lonely.

By 2:45 that afternoon, the setup was finished, though the cooks were still busy in the kitchen, with Sara helping, preparing the food that would fill the buffet tables when the restaurant, closed for the day, would reopen.

Brynne excused herself and went upstairs to the privacy of her apartment. She had a video call scheduled for three o'clock straight-up.

Davey and Maddie Nicholls would be calling.

After giving her cat some treats, primarily to keep him quiet, Brynne brewed a cup of tea, set it on her kitchen table, beside her laptop, and began to pace, stopping every few moments to consult her watch.

Finally, she plunked down in her chair and booted up her computer.

The screensaver was a dramatic panorama of the Boston

skyline at night, very similar to the view from her old apartment, the one she'd shared with Clay.

She considered changing it—there were millions of images to choose from, of course—but then the call came through.

Davey's youthful, handsome face appeared on-screen, grinning broadly. Maddie, a little younger, and bearing a close resemblance to her mother, leaned in beside him, beaming into the camera.

"You're early!" Brynne said, delighted.

Davey looked briefly uncertain. "Is that okay? Were you busy?"

"I'm never too busy to talk to you two," Brynne replied sincerely.

Both kids looked pleased and more than a little relieved.

"We get to stay up until midnight," Maddie announced. "Dad said we could see the New Year in, just like grown-ups."

"Not like grown-ups," Davey corrected, with mild distain. "They drink booze and stuff." He made a face. "And they *kiss*."

Brynne chuckled. "Someday soon, Davey Nicholls, you'll *like* kissing."

"Yeah," Maddie said, elbowing her brother. "You'll start kissing girls all the time."

"Yuck," Davey said, and shuddered for effect.

Maddie picked up the conversational ball and ran with it. "We get pizza. Davey and me and the babysitter, I mean."

"That's good," Brynne said, dealing with a pang of—what? Loneliness? Regret?

"Dad wants to say hi," Davey said.

Brynne didn't get a chance to prepare herself—suddenly, Clay was standing behind his children, leaning down to look into the camera.

He was still devastatingly handsome, with his sandy-colored hair and irresistible eyes.

"Hey, Brynne," Clay greeted her, his voice husky.

He was wearing a white cable-knit sweater and jeans, and his hair was still damp from the shower. She could see the little ridges left behind by his comb.

"Hey," Brynne said, automatically. She waited to feel something, but all that came was a sense of being mildly startled, as though someone had hidden around a corner and then jumped out at her.

"How's Montana treating you?" Clay asked.

Brynne thought of Eli, and their snowmobile ride. She would never forget the sensation of wild freedom.

She smiled. "Just fine," she replied.

"Ask her," Maddie put in, tilting her head back to look up at her father.

"Yeah," Davey agreed. "Ask her, Dad."

Clay sighed heavily. "The kids have spring break in a couple of months. I told them you're probably really busy, but—"

Brynne's heart began to pound. She waited, holding her breath.

Davey rolled his eyes in exaggerated frustration. "We want to come out there and visit you, Brynne. Maddie and me."

Tears smarted behind Brynne's eyes, happy ones. She could live with never seeing Clay again, but she'd missed those children with all her heart.

"A visit would be wonderful," she said.

The kids cheered so enthusiastically that Clay had to quiet them down with a few mock-stern words.

"Are you sure about this, Brynne? We're kind of putting you on the spot here—"

"You're not putting me on the spot, Clay," Brynne replied,

perhaps too quickly. Too eagerly. "I would *love* to have Davey and Maddie visit. I have plenty of room, and there are lots of things to do out here in the Wild West."

"Can we ride horses?" Davey asked, eyes wide. "And go fishing?"

"Absolutely," Brynne said, blinking rapidly to hold back tears that would only confuse the children.

"Thanks, Brynne," Clay put in, his voice hoarse again. "We'll be in touch about the arrangements closer to spring break. In the meantime, well, have yourself a very happy New Year."

"You, too," Brynne said.

And then he was gone.

Brynne waited to feel that tearing-away sensation common to breakups, even after some time had passed, but it didn't come. All she felt was exuberant anticipation—Davey and Maddie were coming to visit, at long last.

She could barely wait.

The call went on for about twenty more minutes, while the kids told Brynne about their school, their friends, the things they'd given and received for Christmas. Once again, they'd thanked Brynne for the books she'd sent as gifts.

When it was over, when goodbyes had been said and the laptop screen showed the Boston skyline again, Brynne reached for her teacup, took a sip and realized the stuff had gone stone-cold.

She smiled, carried the cup to the sink, emptied it and placed it on the top rack of the dishwasher. Since she took most of her meals downstairs, it often took days to fill the machine.

It was still early, and the preparations for tonight's big celebration were complete, for the time being. Around six, when the doors opened for business and the first crop of celebrants showed up, she would be there to greet them, the consummate hostess.

She had a special outfit for the occasion, an off-white, somewhat clingy dress covered in tiny faux pearls and crystals, designed to shimmer glamorously in changing light. She planned to pin her chin-length hair up, leaving a few wisps and tendrils to dangle in strategic places, and she would wear her best earrings, diamond-and-pearl studs her folks had given her for college graduation.

She would spritz on some perfume and even put on makeup. Mascara, eye shadow, a very light dusting of blusher.

As for shoes, well, she'd chosen a pair of sexy heels, a close match to her dress.

It was more effort than she would usually have made, even for New Year's Eve, but she was a businesswoman, she told herself. She had to maintain a certain image, even in remote Painted Pony Creek.

She was dressing up for the community in general, *not* Sheriff Eli Garrett.

Okay, not *just* for him.

Eli might not even show up, given that there would be plenty of drunk drivers on the road on this night of nights. Bailey's would be packed, but places like Sully's Bar and Grill would do plenty of business, too, and that meant both the small local police department and the sheriff's people would be on high alert.

Since the big snowstorm, there had been a significant thaw, but according to the weather forecast, the temperature would drop below freezing as the evening went on, and stay there. That, of course, meant the roads would be icy and thus dangerous, even for sober people.

Like Brynne's crew of volunteer drivers, for instance.

She closed her eyes and offered a brief, silent prayer for the safety of everyone concerned.

Then she went to the refrigerator, took out a cucumber, whacked off two slices with a chef's knife and returned what was left to the vegetable crisper. She'd cried a little, during the video call with Davey and Maddie, though she was fairly sure they hadn't noticed, and she hadn't slept well the last few nights, worrying about the New Year's Eve bash.

Thinking about Eli.

Going back and forth. Should she get involved?

Or shouldn't she?

She'd kick off her shoes and lie down for a while, cover her eyes with the cucumber slices and, hopefully, emerge from her rest restored.

The moment she'd stretched out on her bed, Waldo leaped up to join her, landing in the middle of her stomach like a medicine ball.

Brynne gasped aloud, then laughed.

The cat curled up beside her, purring contentedly.

And Brynne, who hadn't slept properly in several days, dropped into a deep and dreamless slumber, cossetted by the sweet darkness of oblivion.

Waldo awakened her some two hours later. He was sitting next to her head, nibbling away at one of the cucumber slices.

Brynne bolted upright, sure she'd overslept. Maybe even missed the party.

Clarity soon returned, however. There was light at the bedroom window, though it was growing dimmer by the minute.

A glance at her bedside clock reassured her further—five thirty. She still had an hour and a half to shower, get dressed and do her hair and makeup.

Nothing to worry about.

Except that her phone, resting on her bedside table, made a dinging sound. A text had come in.

Eli?

Suddenly, Brynne's heart was racing again.

She picked up the phone, opened the text feature, and squinted at the message.

You're still beautiful, it read. *Clay.*

A lump formed in Brynne's throat. She considered replying that she wouldn't be accepting any more texts unless they concerned Davey and Maddie, then decided to simply ignore the message entirely.

She sat up, legs dangling over the side of the bed, and sighed.

No getting around it; she was disappointed.

She'd hoped Eli had been the one to contact her.

A certain peevish irritation troubled Brynne for the next few moments.

Was that it? One measly—okay, transcendent—snowmobile ride?

No calls?

No texts?

What did you expect? she asked herself, annoyed. *He asked you out—or tried to—and you said no. "I don't date cops," you said. Well, guess what, Brynne Bailey? You're a fool. And a coward. And—*

"Enough," she said aloud. It was New Year's Eve, and the restaurant was about to fill up with hungry, thirsty people in the mood to celebrate. She could spare neither the time nor the energy to sit around castigating herself.

She couldn't help her feelings, but she didn't have to chase them down the nearest rabbit hole and through the inevitable maze of things she should or shouldn't have said.

It was almost New Year's, after all. A time for new beginnings and second chances.

Who knew what might happen?

Bailey's was pulsing with laughter, music and people when Eli dropped by around 7 p.m., on his dinner break. He wasn't dressed up, since he was technically on duty, but he was wearing his newest uniform, having picked it up at the dry cleaner's earlier in the day.

So far, it had been a quiet night, so Festus was riding shotgun. With a pang of guilt, Eli had left the mutt in the SUV, with a couple of windows rolled partway down so he'd have plenty of air; as an ordinary dog, a civilian so to speak, he wasn't legally allowed to enter any public establishments, particularly restaurants.

Festus had whimpered a little when Eli left him—he'd had to park several blocks from Bailey's, since every space was full. Once Eli had promised him what amounted to a doggy bag, the critter sighed and curled up in the passenger seat, as if to snooze.

Now, a minute or two later, Eli was about to step inside the restaurant. He'd make sure everybody was behaving themselves—most of the rowdy action was likely to bust out over at Sully's, rather than here—but municipal police, like the sheriff's department, were chronically understaffed, so it couldn't hurt to keep an eye on things.

The glass in the restaurant's front door was fogged over, and the people inside looked like colorful smears—except for one, that is.

Brynne was standing near the counter, chatting with several of her customers as they perused the extensive offerings at the long line of buffet tables.

Eli's breath caught, the way it did sometimes when he rode out alone, just him and the horse, and stopped to admire a sweeping view of timber and plains, a herd of deer or elk, a sunrise or sunset.

She was wearing an ivory-colored dress, shimmering with shining beads of some kind, and her platinum blond hair was done up in a loose bun, with some slippage going on around her cheeks and the nape of her neck.

Her smile was so radiant that it nearly threw Eli back on the heels of his boots.

"Come in or go out, Sheriff," one of the older men called jovially. "You'll freeze us all to death, standing there with the door open!"

The remark drew Brynne's attention, and Eli, a grown man, the very competent sheriff of an entire county, damn it, instantly regressed to age fourteen. Testosterone, never in short supply, surged through him, and he wouldn't have been surprised by an instantaneous outbreak of acne.

He stepped inside, closed the door behind him, looked around. Wondered how many of these small-town and country folk had noticed that he'd been staring at Brynne like a damn fool.

Which he probably was. Brynne had made it pretty clear, after all, that she didn't date cops.

Maybe she was just messing with him. Paying him back for dropping her, back in those thrilling days of yesteryear.

Suddenly, he was filled with misgivings.

Still, he was about to approach her—more like, he was *drawn* to her, as though magnetized—when his nephew interrupted.

Eric looked very young and more than a little worried. "Eli? Can I talk to you for a second?"

Eli was concerned, but he was also relieved. A distraction would give him time to get his act together before he encountered Brynne directly.

"Sure," he said. "What's up?"

Eric glanced around, clearly reluctant to talk in the midst of a crowd. Whatever was bothering him, it was important— at least, to the boy.

"Mind if we go outside?"

Eli slapped his nephew lightly on one shoulder. "It's cold out there," he said, with a grin he hoped was reassuring, "but okay. Let's go."

Eric nodded. "I'll get my coat," he said. "Carly's got it, over at the band's table."

"Make it snappy," Eli urged, watching Brynne now.

And she was watching him. Looking a bit worried.

Eli moved his shoulders in a semblance of a shrug and gave Brynne what his niece and nephew called an IDK look. Sara had had to explain to him that IDK was text-speak for "I don't know."

Kids. They were changing the freaking language with their acronyms and invented words. Pretty soon, plain old everyday English would be reduced to things like WTF—Eli rather liked that one, actually—and 4EVR and, of course, the ever-popular OMG.

Brynne smiled, and it was a soft, barely perceptible smile that somehow seemed scandalously private, even in that packed, noisy restaurant.

Eli's blood threatened to catch fire.

Shit, he thought. Maybe it was a good thing he was going

to be standing in the cold for a few minutes. Next best thing to an icy shower.

Eric returned, shoving his arms into the sleeves of his ski coat, clutching his phone in one hand.

He scanned the room nervously, and then Eli opened the door for him and they went outside.

The wind bit into Eli's neck, and he raised his jacket collar against it.

Folks passed them by, coming and going.

Eric, still jumpy, indicated the corner of the building, where there was no foot traffic.

Eli was pretty worried himself by then.

"Eric," he said, "talk to me."

Eric thrust the phone at him. "I got this text about half an hour ago," the boy said. His eyes were huge in his pale face.

Eli took the phone, glanced at the screen.

I'm back, and you're going to pay for how things went down last summer, you little crap-stain. Go crying to your uncle and you don't even want to know what I'll do to you, or to that pretty little sister of yours.

Eli looked up from the screen. Two minutes before, he'd had Brynne on his mind and not much else. Now he was in uncle-mode, big-time.

"Freddie Lansing?" he asked.

Eric swallowed visibly and nodded. "I can't prove it's him," he mumbled miserably. "But who else could it be? I'm not the most popular kid in school, but I don't have any enemies. At least, not that I know of."

Eli figured the boy was right.

And he was obviously scared shitless.

The Lansing kid was a bully, a thief and a real contender for a long stretch in prison, if he didn't either get himself killed or have himself a genuine come-to-Jesus moment. The previous summer, when Eric had gotten himself into trouble with the law—and make no mistake, he was responsible for his own actions and choices, no matter how young he was— he'd gotten most of his ideas from Freddie.

Freddie had gone away to stay with relatives on the other side of the state, after he and Eric and the others were arrested. Clearly, he was back in town, and the knowledge had gotten past Eli somehow.

"I'll talk to him," Eli said. "Tonight."

Eric looked almost frantic. "Don't," he pleaded. "You saw what he said about bringing this to you!"

For the second time that night, Eli rested a hand on Eric's shoulder.

The kid was trembling.

"Listen to me, Eric. You did the right thing, telling me. And you know I'll do whatever I can to keep you and Hayley safe."

"I shouldn't have said anything," Eric fretted.

"Where's Hayley tonight?" Eli asked. He thought he recalled Sara saying something about a sleepover, but there hadn't been any specific information.

"She's at Melba's house," Eric answered. "Hayley is tight with her daughter, Jill. There's a slumber party or something."

Melba Summers was working tonight, on the lookout for drunk drivers and highway accidents. The state patrol, efficient as they were, always needed extra help on booze-saturated holidays like New Year's Eve.

"The kids are alone there?" he asked. "At Melba's place, I mean?"

"No," Eric replied, his gaze jittering from here to there, as though he expected Freddie Lansing to jump out at him from behind a bush or a parked car. "Mom said Melba's ex is spending the night."

Eli sighed, relieved. Melba's ex, Daniel, was a former navy SEAL. He'd done a hitch with the FBI, too, and now he was doing private security for some billionaire headquartered in Belize. If Dan Summers was in the house, those kids were as safe as they could be.

"That's good," he said. So much for hanging around Brynne's place for the rest of his dinner break. He'd swing by Melba's, say hello to Dan, fill him in on the situation—if indeed there *was* a situation—then he'd head out to the Lansing place, on the far side of town, for a word with Freddie's parents and, if possible, with Freddie himself.

Beyond that, there wasn't much he could do, legally. The text definitely constituted a threat, but there was no proof Freddie had sent it—he wasn't the brightest bulb in the marquee, but he was probably smart enough to use a burner phone, if only to keep his present location on the down-low. Furthermore, unless Freddie actually made a move to harm either Eric or Hayley, he couldn't be arrested.

The kid came from a family of assholes, but they were assholes with connections, and Freddie's uncle was a retired lawyer, of the scum-ball variety.

Given that Eli had been the one to arrest Freddie, as well as Eric and the others, he'd have to handle this new development very carefully. The Lansings had cried foul when Eric and the other idiots who'd danced to Freddie's tune were let off with probation, fines and community service. The difference was, Freddie had an impressive rap sheet for a teenager, and that summer's crime spree didn't qualify as his first rodeo.

In fact, if he hadn't been six months shy of his eighteenth birthday, he probably would have ended up doing hard time.

"He'll know I told you about the text," Eric reiterated.

"Yeah, even Freddie is probably smart enough to make that particular leap." Eli squeezed the boy's shoulder once more, then dropped his hand to his side. "I'll handle this. You go back inside and enjoy the evening. And *stay* inside, where there are plenty of people around. Have your mother call or text me when she's ready to head on home, and I'll provide a police escort."

Eric didn't speak.

"Got that?" Eli prompted.

"Sure," Eric said. "Do I have to tell her about the text from Freddie?"

"Yes, actually," Eli answered. "But let's save that for later, when the both of you are back home."

Eric's expression was glum. "Okay," he said, drawing the word out to twice its normal length. "She's gonna freak. She'll probably send me away to boarding school or something. Or ground me again. Carly will probably start dating some other guy and I'll be SOL."

Shit out of luck.

Eli chuckled at that. "Don't borrow trouble, kid," he counseled. "You'll run into plenty without even trying."

As they reentered the restaurant, the band was tuning up, and Carly was onstage, microphone in hand. Her proud parents, Cord and Shallie, sat at a nearby table, flanked by friends, all of them beaming up at her in happy expectation.

Eric gave his uncle one last rueful glance and went to join them. He and Carly had gotten off to a rocky start, since Carly apparently didn't go for guys with criminal tendencies, but once Eric had straightened out, they'd gradually started spending more and more time together.

At last, Eli got a chance to speak to Brynne.

"I'm just here as a friend," he joked, raising both hands, palms out.

Brynne smiled. "That's too bad," she said.

Eli was once again thoroughly taken aback. He couldn't think of a damn thing to say—nothing sensible, anyhow.

"Looks like you're on duty, all right," she observed, taking in his uniform.

"Yep," he agreed, loosening up a little now. "Took time to polish my badge for the occasion, though."

That smile. Dear God, it should have been registered somewhere, if not as a lethal weapon then at least as an unfair advantage.

"I'm impressed," Brynne said, and that rattled Eli even more than the smile had because he didn't know if she was serious or pulling his leg. "Surely you can stay long enough to eat something and hear Carly sing. She's really very good, as you probably know."

Eli flung a glance toward the daughter that might have been his, but wasn't. "She's amazing," he said. Then he turned his full attention back to Brynne, which was a semi-reckless thing to do, given how good she looked. "No time, I'm afraid. I've got to check something out."

"Something to do with Eric?" Brynne asked, raising one perfect eyebrow.

Her lips glistened with a transparent pink gloss of some kind, and she smelled like wildflowers.

"Sort of," he replied.

"Which means you can't talk about it," she guessed, smiling again.

"It's no big deal," he told her, hoping that was true. "Don't go ruining your evening by worrying about it."

"Can you come back at midnight?" Brynne asked.

The sudden change in subject matter surprised Eli. "I will if I can," he said. He didn't make promises he wasn't sure he could keep, even small ones. "Right now, I'd better get going. I left Festus in the SUV, and he'll be getting impatient—not to mention cold."

Without a word, Brynne picked up a paper plate and began adding small bits of dog-friendly food to it—a tiny square of cheddar cheese, a few cocktail wieners, random party nibbles.

"These are for Festus," she announced, covering the plate with a paper napkin. "Feel free to help yourself if you're hungry. I suppose you're probably used to eating in your car."

Eli thanked her, reached for his wallet.

"Put your money away, Sheriff," Brynne ordered. "Tonight, supper's on the house."

He took the offered plate—Festus would be overjoyed—and snagged half a roast beef sandwich for the road.

"Don't forget," Brynne reminded him. "Midnight."

CHAPTER SIX

When Dan Summers answered the door at his ex-wife's place, he pretty much filled all available space. Built like the proverbial brick shithouse, this former navy SEAL and erstwhile FBI agent stood well over six feet tall, and he must have weighed close to three hundred pounds—all muscle, no fat.

He was Black, with a shaved head and, under the right circumstances, a ready smile.

Tonight, the white dazzle of that smile made Eli blink.

"Bro!" Dan boomed. "What you got to tell me so important you go bustin' in on our party?"

He liked using street vernacular, even though he had a law degree and provided security for some of the wealthiest, most sophisticated people on the planet. During his hitch in the navy, he'd completed SEAL training, legendary for its difficulty, in one try, and gone on to train other men and women before his second hitch was up. After that, he'd gone to law school, graduated and promptly decided, according to Melba, that he'd rather fight clean.

Inside the house, a chorus of girlish voices gasped in unison at some development in a kids' movie—probably *Frozen 17* or something like it.

Eli smiled at the thought of his niece in there with her friends, having a good time. She was safe here, with Dan around and, later, Melba. Safer than she would be at home.

"Come out here, will you?" Eli said. The volume on the TV was high, but he didn't want to take the chance of being overheard.

Dan lumbered out onto the porch, ducking his head slightly as he passed through the doorframe. "Man, it's frickin' *cold*. I hope you're not planning on givin' an oration."

Eli chuckled, albeit grimly. Then he told his friend, as concisely as he could, about Freddie Lansing, the trouble he'd gotten in last year, Eric's involvement and, finally, the threatening text his nephew had received earlier.

Dan gave a low whistle of exclamation and rubbed his huge hands together. "That little bastard tries to hurt any of these kids, tonight or any other time, I'll crack his empty head like a walnut."

"You going to be in town awhile?" Eli asked, shivering himself. According to the most recent weather report, there was a Chinook coming—*Chinook* being a native word for an early thaw, but the temperature seemed to be stuck at fifteen degrees.

"Depends on whether Melba kicks me out or gives in to my manly charms," Dan answered, grinning. "She divorced me for having a dangerous job. Now that she's a deputy sheriff herself, I might be able to talk some sense into the woman. Get her to take me back. We ought to be raisin' our kids together, man."

"I hope you succeed," Eli said honestly. He liked Dan, and

he certainly liked Melba. As a Black woman in law enforcement, serving with distinction, she was opening doors not only for female minorities but for many other people, as well.

Dan arched an eyebrow, dropped his voice to a loud whisper. "You watch your back, Sheriff," he warned good-naturedly. "One of these years, Melba's going to run against you." A pause. "And if you tell her I said that, I'll deny every word."

Again, Eli chuckled. Offered a casual salute. "She'll probably win by a landslide," he said. He shifted slightly on his feet, ready to be on the move again. He wanted to talk to Freddie and/or his parents before it got any later.

Couldn't have the Lansings complaining that Sheriff Garrett was harassing them with late-night visits.

Besides, he was bound and determined to get back to Bailey's—and to Brynne—by midnight.

It was probably too soon to get lucky, but he'd settle for another kiss like that last one, following the snowmobile ride.

"Nobody gonna hurt these children on my watch," Dan stated, serious again now. "How 'bout we meet up over at Sully's one night soon? Have us a couple of beers and shoot the breeze?"

"I'd like that," Eli said.

Then he turned and made his way down Melba's porch steps.

Ten minutes later, he was turning into the long driveway leading up to the Lansing place.

The property wasn't run-down, at least not in the sad way Russ Schafer's Painted Pony Creek Motel had been, before Cord and Shallie decided to help fix the place up so they could board some of their horse-training students there, but it wasn't the kind of place that made a person feel welcome, either.

Floodlights blared from tall poles and parts of the roof, giving the impression of a prison yard at night. Fred Lansing, Sr., Freddie's dad, fancied himself a modern-day minuteman, ready to defend his freedom against an oppressive government.

He was a bitter, angry man, chronically unemployed, and his wife, who worked as a supermarket cashier, was a meek little thing, plain and quiet and noticeably jumpy.

Eli suspected Fred of abusing the poor woman—hell, maybe Freddie did, too—but there was no proof. Unless Gretchen Lansing filed a complaint, or one of those losers went after her in front of witnesses, there wasn't a damn thing he could do about it.

That galled Eli, made him want to turn in his badge and drive a truck for a living.

Since the Lansings kept dogs—a pair of pit bulls they probably mistreated—Eli made sure the small canister of mace on his service belt was easily accessible and started up the walk.

It hadn't been shoveled, and there were patches of ice to navigate.

The windows were all dark, but that didn't mean nobody was home.

Fred, Sr., was a vigilant man; he would know when a rig turned off the highway onto his land. By his reasoning, a pack of savage liberals might invade at any moment, day or night, holiday or none.

Eli stepped around a sorry-looking Christmas tree, still sporting a few baubles and dripping tinsel, lying forlornly on the walk at the base of the porch steps as though it had been flung out the front door.

He was on the porch, about to knock, when the lights came on inside, a door opened and Fred Lansing stood in the gap, scowling.

"What the hell do you want?" the little man growled.

"Happy New Year to you, too, Fred," Eli replied lightly. "Is your boy around, by any chance?"

"Why do you want to know?"

"We'll get to that," Eli answered. The two pit bulls came to flank their surly master, growling low in their throats. "I'm here to see Freddie. We can talk tonight, or I can have him brought in for questioning bright and early tomorrow morning. What's it going to be, Fred?"

"It's New Year's Eve, you know," Fred muttered. "He's not here."

"Hot date?"

Fred colored visibly at the jibe. They both knew Freddie Lansing was considered patently undesirable by every woman and girl in the county; his reputation preceded him. He was homely as hell, with his bad teeth and virulent case of acne, and if the boy hadn't been an intractable prick, Eli might have felt sorry for him.

Told him to see a good dentist and a dermatologist.

Trouble was, Freddie's real problem wasn't his looks. It was the rot slowly eating away his soul.

There were misguided people in the world. There were bad ones. And then there were the ones who were just plain evil, and proud of it. Guys like Freddie would dance on the brink of hell itself and laugh as they plunged into the flames.

Fortunately, Eli hadn't encountered all that many Freddies over the course of his career, and he was grateful.

Out in the SUV, Festus began to bark.

Eli turned, pressing one hand against the frame of the Lansings' screen door so Fred couldn't use it to knock him off his feet, and turned his head.

Freddie was sitting on the hood of Eli's rig, grinning garishly in the blazing illumination of his father's floodlights.

Seeing the kid there unnerved Eli a little. He was a creepy sight, hunching his shoulders and beaming like a crazy man.

"I can handle the sheriff, Dad," he called to Fred.

"I'm coming out," Fred insisted.

"Shut the dogs in," Eli instructed the older man, still holding the screen door closed.

Fred swore, spoke to the pit bulls and, when Eli allowed him to pass, stepped out onto the rickety porch, the door firmly closed behind him.

When Fred would have followed Eli down the steps and through the hard-crusted snow to the SUV, Eli gestured for him to lead the way.

He didn't turn his back on men like Fred Lansing, or their sons.

As Eli and his father approached, Freddie slid down off the hood of the SUV with a telling scraping sound, still grinning. The little bastard had probably keyed the paint.

Inside the rig, Festus was still barking.

"Quiet," Eli told the dog.

"You shouldn't leave a nice animal like that alone, Sheriff," Freddie drawled. "Somebody might feed him poison, or cut his throat." He paused to shrug expansively. "You just never know."

It was literally all Eli could do not to grab Freddie Lansing by the lapels of his army surplus coat, hoist him off his feet and fling him hard into the grillwork of the SUV, but he knew, from long experience, that losing his temper would put him at a real disadvantage, sooner rather than later.

Still, he didn't have to let the veiled threat pass, either.

"*Somebody* who hurts my dog—or anybody else's—might

just find himself crawling around on the ground, looking for his teeth."

Freddie gave a rough guffaw, but the glint in his eyes was at once predatory and wary. "Why, Sheriff, was that a threat?" he asked in a singsong. "You heard that, didn't you, Dad?"

"I sure did," Fred, Sr., blustered. He was a wiry little man, probably quick in a fight and stronger than he looked.

Eli kept him in his peripheral vision, took his phone from his coat pocket and held it up for both men to see. "Would you like me to play back the part of this conversation where you mentioned poisoning my dog or cutting his throat?"

Freddie sighed. He must have known Eli had been recording the conversation from the get-go, but he didn't seem overly concerned. "Let me guess, Sheriff Badass. You're here because your girly little nephew got a text and figured it was from me. Bet he wet his pants."

"I'm not here to play word games with you, Freddie. I *know* you sent that text." He paused, drew a deep, calming breath and released it slowly. "Let's be clear. If you try to hurt Eric or Hayley—or any other kid in my county—I will *personally* reach down your throat and drag your innards out through your mouth. Then I'll stomp them to a pulp. You got that?"

"Now, see here—" Fred, Sr., interrupted. "You're an officer of the law, and you just threatened my boy, right in front of me. I'll file a complaint! Get you fired!"

"Give it your best shot, Fred," Eli said smoothly.

"This is wrong!" Fred, Sr., bellowed.

He was right. It was. And at the moment, Eli didn't give a rat's ass.

"You can't do a damn thing to me," Freddie gloated. "Not until *after* I get what I want. But then it will be too late, won't it, Sheriff?"

Again, Eli suppressed a furious urge to do this kid real harm. Pound him into the frozen ground like a fence pole.

"We'll start with a restraining order and a call to your probation officer," Eli said calmly. "One wrong move and you'll be back in custody—and this time, they'll throw you in with the big boys."

He'd gotten to Freddie, at last. He knew that by the flicker of fear in Freddie's colorless eyes, though it was quickly gone.

"Guys like you, Freddie—guys who threaten little girls, never mind hurt them—well, they just don't do well in the general population. What's your new name going to be? Nancy? Maybe Susan?"

Freddie went to lunge at Eli then—exactly as Eli had hoped he would do—but caught himself just in time. Spread his hands wide and said pitiably, "This is harassment, Sheriff."

Eli was still seething, still fighting for control. He couldn't remember the last time he'd been this pissed, this triggered. "No," he said evenly, "this is me being very, very patient. You need to understand; there's a whole other side to my nature."

"I *understand* that they'll take away your badge and maybe even throw you in prison if you do a damn thing to me," Freddie spouted. "And I don't think cops do all that well behind bars, either, now do they?"

A strange calm descended over Eli, almost blissful. "I'm not going to prison, Freddie," he said quietly. "But you, with your rap sheet and your bad attitude, you're just angling for a nice long stretch in the joint. Keep pushing. That's all you've got to do."

"Okay," Freddie said, spreading his hands again. Trying to go around Eli, make his way toward the house. "I was just trying to shake the kid up a little, that's all. I didn't mean no harm. Not really."

"Cut the crap, Freddie. I meant everything I've said to-night, and a few things I *didn't* say."

"Is that the end of your sermon, Sheriff?" Freddie sneered, though he made no move to pull his arm free.

Out of the corner of his eye, Eli saw Fred, Sr., take a step toward him.

Instinctively, he sent Freddie hurtling into his father, and they both staggered, nearly losing their footing.

Festus was barking again, leaping anxiously back and forth between the passenger and driver's seats.

Eli glanced back over one shoulder, saw the pit bulls bounding toward him, tongues lolling.

He yanked open the driver's side door and climbed inside, just as the dogs arrived. One slammed into the windshield, Cujo-style, while the other struck the door Eli had just slammed.

Festus went berserk, snarling and trying to squeeze himself through the six inches of open window available to him on the passenger side.

Eli pulled him back by his collar and buzzed the window shut.

Fred, Sr., and his spawn were all but doubled over, laughing, and Gretchen stood on the porch, a small figure.

Had the dogs simply gotten past her when she opened the front door, or had she deliberately turned them loose?

No telling.

Eli started the SUV, honked the horn cheerfully and drove slowly away from the whole scene.

He'd made his point.

If the Lansings wanted to think they'd scared him off, let them.

He'd be back the day after tomorrow, when the courthouse had reopened for business, with a restraining order.

Brynne kicked off her fancy high heels at a quarter to twelve, and perched herself on the one vacant stool at the counter, clapping along with the crowd as Carly finished a particularly sweet song, one of her own composition, all about winter weather and sunlight on snow.

The lyrics made Brynne think of the time she'd spent with Eli a few days before, onboard his magic carpet of a snow-mobile, and her heart quickened at the memory.

Her gaze strayed to the door, for the thousandth time.

No Eli.

Inwardly, Brynne sighed, though she didn't let her smile slip.

Her customers had paid for a cheerful evening and they were going to get one.

The crowd had thinned considerably over the last couple of hours as people left to see the New Year in at home, or simply to go to bed. Those who remained were waiting for the traditional song and the official arrival of midnight, complete with kisses and confetti and noisemakers.

It was ironic, Brynne reflected, that with all these people around, she would essentially be celebrating alone when one calendar year ended and another began.

Well, what else was new? She'd been on her own since the breakup with Clay. Nobody to kiss under the mistletoe at Christmas. Nobody to kiss tonight at the stroke of midnight.

Not, of course, that there was any guarantee Eli would kiss her even if he did show up on time, but a girl could hope in the privacy of her own heart and mind.

Carly left the stage to take a breather before the evening's big finale and crossed to where Brynne was sitting, feet dangling.

"Thank you," the girl said. "For letting us perform tonight. It's been great."

Brynne reached out, took one of Carly's hands and gave it a light squeeze. "Thank *you*," she replied. "You and The GateCrashers always draw a crowd. Tonight was very profitable." She'd paid the band earlier, during a break. "For all of us, I think."

Carly smiled. "I only get to spend half of my share," she confided, with mock regret. "Dad and Shallie insist I save a major chunk of everything I earn singing, even though I've made a boatload of money from my YouTube channel. It isn't as if I can't afford college with no help from anybody."

Brynne laughed softly. "Not many young people can say that, Carly," she said. "You should be very proud of yourself."

The girl's shoulders moved in a shrug-like gesture. "It's been fun," she replied, as though she'd had little or no part in her own success. "I've been lucky—found myself a dad and two fantastic uncles."

She'd also lost her mother, Reba, to cancer, been left alone with a greedy stepfather and his girlfriend, and made her own way across country to arrive at the back door of Sully's Bar and Grill not that long ago, looking for her biological father.

Brynne, though certainly not friends with Reba, had been the one to break the news of her death to Cord Hollister, who had passed the word to J.P. and Eli.

Despite the fact that Reba had virtually stolen Eli from her, back in high school, Brynne had secretly felt sorry for the other girl. Oh, she'd had plenty of resentment, too, but even in her teenage years, she'd known how lucky she was to have two loving parents, a good home and a lot of friends.

Reba, arriving alone, working at the Painted Pony Creek Motel, partying like the proverbial rock star, clearly hadn't been blessed with a home and family, loving or otherwise.

"You *have* been lucky," Brynne agreed. "And so have I."

Carly smiled, nodded. Excused herself to return to the little stage occupied by the rest of the band.

A few more songs followed, each one drawing cheers from the dwindling but determined audience.

Brynne suspected she wasn't the only one watching the clock, though her reason was probably different from theirs.

Once again, she sighed.

And then it happened. At two minutes before midnight, the restaurant door swung open and Eli entered, looking both weary and frazzled, both of which were unusual for him.

He was usually so self-possessed.

As soon as he was inside, the door closed behind him, he searched the room, found Brynne. Held her gaze.

Her heart jumped.

He was pale with exhaustion

They simply stared at each other for long moments, across the crowded space between them.

Then Brynne slid off the stool, stood on her shoeless feet and waited.

Eli came to her.

"You look terrible," she said.

He quirked a grin. "Thanks. You, on the other hand, look fantastic."

Brynne blushed. She'd heard that particular line many times, from many different men, but coming from Eli Garrett, well, it was different.

She didn't speak, because she couldn't.

"Festus is in the SUV," he said. "Is there any way I can

bring him inside without getting you in trouble with the health department?"

Brynne studied him briefly, feeling troubled by his mood. What had happened since he'd left the place earlier?

"Come in through the back way," she said. "I'll be watching for you."

Eli nodded, looking grateful and worried at the same time.

"Eli," Brynne said, taking one of his hands, much as she had taken Carly's a few minutes before, "What's wrong?"

"Nothing you need to worry about," he said.

"Not good enough, Sheriff," Brynne countered gently. "I meant it when I said you look terrible, and I want to know why."

He dredged up a smile. "Okay," he replied, "but later."

The countdown had begun, led by Carly, who held the microphone.

Cheers erupted a second after she'd shouted, "One!"

And Eli took Brynne in his arms, gazing straight into her eyes, while she looked up at him in hopeful wonder.

When he kissed her, the earth swayed on its axis.

It was as if they'd both sprouted wings and soared into the dark night sky to seek out hidden stars and claim them for their own.

"Happy New Year, Bailey," Eli said gruffly, when the long, *long* kiss ended.

"Same to you, Garrett," Brynne replied.

He laughed.

The noise surrounding them was deafening, and yet they might have been entirely alone in a silent place, for all the attention they paid the others.

Twenty minutes later, when virtually everyone had shaken

Brynne's hand, thanked her for a great evening and/or kissed her on the cheek, the restaurant was finally empty.

Except for herself and Eli, that is.

They stood facing each other, close together, swaying ever so slightly from side to side, in response to music they could feel but not hear.

Streamers dropped from the ceiling.

Confetti covered the tables, the counter and the floor.

The buffet table was a mess.

All of it, Brynne decided, could wait.

"Go and get Festus," she said. "I'll head upstairs and shut Waldo—my cat—in my bedroom. Meet you out back in about five minutes?"

"Five minutes it is," Eli agreed. "Lock the door behind me."

Again, Brynne felt a niggle of unease. Of course she locked the doors when the restaurant was closed, but she'd never had cause to feel afraid, either in Bailey's or anywhere else in town.

She nodded, locked the door behind Eli and turned to survey the happy wreckage left behind by visiting celebrants.

The chafing dishes on the buffet table were mostly empty and covered by their lids, but some of the flames beneath them were still flickering.

Brynne extinguished the tiny fires quickly, then hurried upstairs to her apartment.

Waldo was curled up in an armchair in the living room, and he was plainly disgruntled when Brynne scooped him up, carried him into her bedroom, installed him on the window seat and dashed for the door, shutting it swiftly behind her.

Waldo meowed loudly in protest.

Ignoring her furry friend, Brynne went back to the stairway, and descended as far as the landing, where there were two sets of steps, one leading to the restaurant's kitchen and one to the outside door.

Brynne opened the latter, braced herself against the rush of cold air and the sight of Eli waiting on the small porch with his dog.

"Come in." It seemed deliciously clandestine, admitting Eli to her home under cover of darkness.

He hesitated, looking down at Festus, who panted cheerfully at his side, barely able to restrain his canine glee at encountering Brynne.

She bent to ruffle the dog's ears in greeting.

They entered, and Eli stopped to turn the dead bolt before following Brynne up the well-worn stairs.

Festus slipped around her and scuttled to the top, where he turned to watch the humans approach.

"I want to know what's going on," Brynne announced, the moment they were all in her living room. "I know it has something to do with your nephew. He's a nice kid and I'm worried."

Eli sighed, looking around. "Nice place," he said.

"Thanks," Brynne replied. "But don't dodge the issue. What's happening?"

"Sit down," Eli said, gesturing toward the nearest chair. "Please."

Once Brynne was seated, he took a seat on the edge of the couch, laced his fingers together and studied the floor.

Festus trotted down the hallway toward Brynne's closed door, and Waldo raged from within.

Some welcome.

"All right, I'm sitting. Tell me, Eli."

He told her.

He explained the trouble Eric and a few other kids had gotten themselves into the previous summer—she remembered the incidents, since the Creek was a small community and Eric's mother, Sara, was a friend—then he mentioned the text.

Finally, he described his visit to the Lansing place, earlier that night.

"You think Freddie or his father would actually hurt Eric—or Festus?" Brynne asked, horrified.

"Yes," Eli said bluntly.

"Can't you arrest them or something?" She was a little frantic, grasping at straws.

"I can't charge either of them unless they actually commit a crime, Brynne. This is America."

"You've warned Sara?"

"I'll speak to her when I leave here," he said. "She probably won't appreciate getting a visit at such a late hour, but this isn't something I can discuss in a text or a voice mail."

So, he didn't expect to stay the night.

Brynne was both relieved and disappointed.

She wanted Eli, wanted him powerfully—and soon. But she knew she wasn't ready, knew she had to proceed with caution.

Damn it.

"I'm sure Sara will want to know exactly what's going on, no matter how late it is," she said.

Festus returned from his diplomatic mission, a failure. With a doggy sigh, he plunked himself down near Eli's feet and rested his muzzle on his forepaws.

"I hate to scare Sara," Eli said, "but the fact is, Freddie Lansing is dangerous and so is his father."

"Surely not Gretchen," Brynne said. "I see her at the supermarket all the time. She's such a meek little thing."

"Appearances can be deceiving," Eli pointed out wearily. "I'm pretty sure she sicced the family dogs on me tonight.

They're pit bulls, neglected if not outright mistreated, and they would have torn me apart if I hadn't been able to get back into the SUV a second before they got to me."

Brynne shuddered. "Those poor dogs," she murmured.

Eli gave a chortle, and his mood seemed to improve slightly. "Gee, thanks," he teased.

"You know what I mean," Brynne retorted earnestly, though she was smiling now. Glad to see that Eli wasn't quite as glum as he had been a moment before. "Pit bulls get a bad rap. If they're raised properly, with love and good training, they are no more vicious than any other breed."

"True enough," Eli allowed. "Unfortunately, the Lansings didn't get the memo."

"Isn't it a crime, turning dogs like that loose on someone?" Brynne asked. "Can't you charge them—the Lansings, not the dogs—with attempted assault or something? You might have been killed!"

Eli bent to stroke Festus's long, slender back. "I wouldn't have been killed. Hurt, maybe, but not killed. I would have shot the dogs."

Brynne felt a chill. Here it was, the reason she didn't date cops. The dangers were innumerable, and sometimes it was impossible for an officer to escape unharmed.

Sometimes, they were horribly wounded.

Or killed.

"Brynne," Eli said.

She realized he'd read her expression, seen the fear churning up inside her.

She began to cry.

She wasn't the weepy type, but after such a long day, this was too much.

Eli stood, took her hand and drew her gently to her feet.

Then he took her into his arms, held her tightly, rested his chin on top of her head.

He didn't chide her for being silly, as Clay had done, more than once, nor did he ask her not to cry.

He simply held her, rocking her very slightly from side to side.

And she did the most dangerous thing of all: she let herself lean into Eli Garrett, into his courage and his masculinity and his strength.

She was in big trouble.

CHAPTER SEVEN

"Do you ever sleep?" Sara demanded, as she opened her back door to Eli and his sidekick, Festus. She was wearing a red zip-up bathrobe and fluffy slippers, and her dark hair hung in loose spirals around her shoulders.

She'd scrubbed off her party makeup and probably brushed her teeth.

Since it was after one in the morning, Eli supposed he was lucky she hadn't already turned in.

"I've been known to sleep, on occasion," he replied.

Sara stepped back to let her brother into her spacious kitchen. She smiled warmly and patted Festus on the head as he passed.

It was obvious that the dog was a welcome guest. Eli himself? Maybe not so much.

"Is this about Eric?" Sara asked, once she'd shut the door. She moved to the counter, started building a pot of coffee. "He's been weird tonight. Sort of jumpy."

Anyone else would have served decaf at that hour, Eli supposed, but Sara was a writer and she ran on caffeine.

Eli stood, constitutionally incapable of sitting while a woman stood. "Yes," he replied. "It's sort of about Eric, and sort of not."

Sara left the coffee maker for the sink, where she filled a bowl with water and set it down for Festus.

The dog lapped thirstily, then plunked down on the floor to wait out whatever human interaction was taking place.

Sara stood with her hands on her slender hips. She was a beautiful woman, strong, smart and successful, and yet again, Eli reflected that it was a real shame that she'd decided never to take a chance on another man. Zach Worth had single-handedly soured her on the whole male gender.

"If that boy is in trouble again, I swear I'll lose my mind," she said. Her gray eyes, weary with the lateness of the hour, flashed with conviction.

"Sara," Eli said. "Sit down."

He pulled back a chair for her, and she sat.

Eli took a seat across the table from her.

The coffee maker hummed and chortled on the counter.

"That might not be the worst idea you've ever had. Sending Eric away for a while."

Sara paled slightly. Lowered her voice when she spoke again. "Oh, my God, Eli—is he in some kind of danger?"

"Yes," Eli replied, because there was no sense in beating around the bush. If Freddie Lansing got an opportunity to hurt Eric or Hayley, he'd do it, not just because he wanted revenge for the events of last summer, but to get back at Eli for giving him a hard time tonight.

Sara got up, filled two cups before the coffee maker had finished its noisy work and brought them to the table.

"Tell me," she said. "Tell me *everything*, Eli."

So he did.

He told Sara about his exchange with Eric, back at Bailey's, and the text the boy had shown him. Then he went on to describe the encounter with Freddie and his father, out at the Lansing place.

Sara sat in silence, stoic and pale. She was used to fending for herself, with what little help she would allow Eli to give her, but this development had obviously shaken her. And with good reason.

When he'd given his account, he took out his phone and played what he'd recorded during the confrontation with the Lansings.

Sara closed her eyes and swayed slightly, and Eli reached out to steady her. At the mention of Hayley, she winced.

"Listen to me," Eli said gently, once the recording was over, "I'm going to do everything I can to keep Eric and Hayley safe, and anybody else he goes after, too, of course. The more I think about it, though, the *less* I think it's a good idea to send either of the kids away from the Creek."

Sara nodded bleakly, thrust the splayed fingers of one hand through her hair. Sighed. "If Eric and Hayley are away from Freddie, they'll be away from *us*, too. And nobody can protect them the way we can."

"I can think of one person who can," Eli said, very quietly. He knew Hayley was at the slumber party over at Melba's place, but Eric was home. He might be just out of sight, listening in.

Sara's forehead crumpled slightly as she frowned. "Who?"

Eli considered his answer solemnly before he gave it.

"Dan Summers," he said at long last.

Sara's eyes widened. "*Melba's ex-husband?*"

"Yep."

"But he—they—"

"Whatever happened between Melba and Dan on a personal level is their business, Sara." He paused, took a sip of his coffee. "He's in security. I can't be around 24/7, but he—or his crew—can."

"Melba says—"

"Sara, I don't give a rat's ass what Melba says. Like I just said, that's between the two of them."

Sara narrowed her eyes. "She *said* he cheated on her."

"Come on, Sara! I know that's a sore spot with you, after Zach and all the asshat tricks he pulled, but that has *nothing* to do with Dan's ability to keep Eric and Hayley safe until I can nail Freddie Lansing and, if necessary, his weasel of a father, too."

Sara huffed, unwilling to back away from her point. "It says something about Dan's honor," she insisted.

"It might not even be true, Sara. Maybe it's speculation on Melba's part—have you ever considered that? And even if it is true, even if it's *gospel*, it doesn't mean Dan can't protect a couple of kids from a piece of shit like Freddie Lansing."

"Okay," Sara said, drawing out the word. She still looked unconvinced.

"Listen, for all I know, Dan isn't available—he might have previous commitments. But it's worth it to ask him, don't you think?"

"He'll be expensive," Sara mused.

"Yeah," Eli said, with a semblance of a grin. "My guess is, he's *very* expensive. But with some help from your alter ego, Luke Cantrell, not to mention the money you inherited from our grandparents, I'm pretty sure you can afford Dan's going price, whatever it is."

"Of course I wouldn't cheap out on something like this," Sara snapped. "We're talking about my *children* here!"

"I didn't think you would," Eli told her gently. "I'm texting you Dan's number right now. Call him in the morning."

Sara braced her elbows on the tabletop and buried her face in her hands. "My God, Eli, I am *so scared*."

"There's a place out beyond scared," Eli reminded her. "I'll meet you there."

This paraphrasing of one of Rumi's poems was a sort of code between them. One of them, most likely Sara, had come across the verse and begun amending it to fit whatever challenge they happened to be facing at the time.

As kids, they'd used it often.

There's a place beyond heartbreak…grief…disappointment. I'll meet you there.

Sara lowered her hands, lifted her chin. Her steel-gray eyes were brimming with tears she was again too proud to shed.

"Right," she said. "I'll see you in the land of kick-ass and take names, little brother. Don't be late."

Eli stood, then leaned down to kiss his sister on the forehead. "Oh, I'll show up, all right. You can count on that."

He carried his cup to the sink, set it down.

Sara rose from her chair, too. She crossed the room, pushed aside a picture on the wall and began punching in numbers on the door of the little safe behind it.

"I can spend the night, if you want me to," he offered.

Sara opened the safe's door and took out a Glock with what appeared to be a gold-plated handle.

"We'll be fine," she replied, expertly checking the magazine for ammunition. "For tonight, anyhow, Old Bessie and I will manage just fine."

"Good God," Eli growled, startled. "Put that thing away."

Sara laughed, but there wasn't much humor in the sound. "Not a chance. I'm legal, Sheriff—permit to carry, concealed or otherwise."

"When did you—?"

"I've been going out to the gun range for months now, little brother. If you paid attention to anything besides your job, you'd know that."

"You could have mentioned that you'd taken up a hobby," Eli challenged wryly. "Is the safety on?"

"Of course it is," Sara retorted briskly. "I'm not stupid."

"What if Eric or Hayley find that thing and mess with it?" Eli, like many cops, was of the belief that most women—and men, for that matter—were better off without a handgun, simply because so many things could go wrong.

For instance, the assailant might take it away and use it against its owner.

When it came to firearms, Murphy's Law was the rule rather than the exception.

Eli was rattled. "Suppose you *think* there's an intruder in the house and you fire that thing and then find out you've maimed or killed one of your kids?"

"That isn't going to happen."

"That's what they all say."

"Stop being such an old lady, Eli. You're willing to have Dan Summers living under this roof—a human *lethal weapon*—but you're afraid of a little peashooter like this?"

"Sara."

She set the gun carefully on a sideboard. Leaned back against it like an old-time gunfighter against the bar in a saloon.

"I'd recommend you don't sneak in here and steal any more

spaghetti casseroles from the freezer," she said. "Especially not when you're just coming off a late shift."

Eli was not amused. "You're taking this whole Luke Bible thing too seriously," he accused. "You are *not* a fast gun on the side of truth, justice and the American Way."

"Oh, but I am," Sara said. "And I've got the multi-book contract to prove it. A couple of training certificates from the gun range, too. I'm downright deadly."

"That's what I'm afraid of," Eli snapped.

"I'm within my rights here, Dudley Do-Right. Not a goll-derned thing you can do about it."

Eli rolled his eyes. "Call Dan first thing tomorrow. And try not to shoot the meter reader or the UPS man, okay?"

"Tomorrow—which is actually today—is a holiday. New Year's, remember? No hapless service people will come within range."

"Shit," Eli said. "Another damn holiday."

"You still coming by for roast beef dinner?" Sara inquired, as though they hadn't been discussing carnage. "Seven o'clock sharp. Bring a bottle of red wine. In fact, bring several."

"Right," Eli replied. He was beaten, and he knew it, but he wasn't going to let this gun-thing slide. Cops and soldiers needed semiautomatic weapons like Sara's, but women in wooly red robes and fluffy slippers?

Not so much.

Seeing that his master was on the move, Festus roused himself from his light slumber and got to his feet, though he'd probably been alert since the mention of roast beef.

"Lock up behind me," Eli said.

"Well, duh," Sara replied. Shades of their younger years. They'd been as close as any brother and sister, but they'd had their differences, too, naturally.

They were there for each other, in good times and bad.

He ignored the jibe. "Good night, Sara," he said, with more gravity than the sentiment probably required.

"Good night, Dudley," Sara said.

Eli laughed then, in spite of himself, and made for the door, Festus at his heels. The moment they were outside, he heard the dead bolt engage.

On the drive home, Eli thought about Freddie Lansing, and Sara's gun, and what it would be like around her place if she hired Dan Summers or some of his crew.

He knew precisely what Melba had told Sara about her ex-husband that made her hesitant to hire him, the cost notwithstanding.

Dan billed himself as a security agent, and he was that.

He was also a mercenary, and a damn good one.

More Jesse James than Matt Dillon.

Eli approached his SUV cautiously, not only because it was late, but because that was his policy. If some asshole—like Freddie Lansing—got the jump on him, that would be his fault as much as anybody's.

The area was clear, and he and Festus got into the rig.

Eli backed out of Sara's driveway, onto the road.

After circling the block a few times, just in case, he headed for home.

By the time he got there, he was thinking about Brynne Bailey, not Freddie.

He was careful, just the same.

Parked in the yard instead of the garage, under the glare of one of the security lights, and whistled for Festus to jump out of the SUV on the driver's side.

The dog's hackles rose instantly, and a low growl rumbled in his throat.

"Easy," Eli said, unsnapping his holster cover in case he needed his service revolver.

Festus, usually obedient, ignored Eli's command to be quiet and sprang toward the yard, baying as he ran.

"Hold on," Eli half shouted, but the dog didn't listen.

He scrambled after Festus and found him straddling a prone figure on the ground.

"It's me," Eric cried, laughing and turning his head back and forth in a fruitless effort to keep the dog from licking his face. "It's me, Uncle Eli—don't shoot."

Eli swore furiously, edged Festus off the kid with a motion of one leg, and yanked his nephew to his feet by his lapels.

"What the *hell*, Eric? Are you *trying* to get yourself killed?"

"Exactly the opposite," Eric replied, dusting the snow off his jacket and pants and grinning like the damn fool he apparently was. "I came to spend the night here. Thought it would be safer for Mom, since Hayley's at Melba's and Mr. Summers is there, too."

"How did you get out here?"

Eric had his driver's license, but he didn't own a car. Sara wanted him to get a job and buy one for himself—practical life lesson and all that.

Eli respected her logic, especially after the crap Eric had pulled last year. The kid had made strides, for sure, but that didn't mean he was out of the woods.

"Carly dropped me off. I've been waiting awhile."

"Your mother thinks you're at home, tucked up in your little bed. Call her, right now, and let her know where you are." Eli stomped up the back steps, unlocked the door via the keypad on the porch wall and went inside. "And *whatever* you do, you idiot, don't go waltzing in there without announcing yourself when you decide to go back, because Calamity Jane might just blow your dumb ass to kingdom come."

Eric, so nervous earlier in the evening, was almost cavalier now. "Mom's a crack shot, all right," he said, following his uncle into the darkened house.

Eli flipped on the kitchen lights. He knew nobody was lying in wait inside—his dog and his gut, in that order, would have alerted him otherwise—but he was careful anyway.

He was letting Freddie Lansing get to him, and that pissed him right off. He had the upper hand in this situation, as long as he kept his head.

"Did you call Freddie out about that text?" Eric asked. He was crouching alongside Festus now, one arm looped loosely around the dog's neck, and the cockiness was gone, replaced by uneasiness.

Eli removed his coat, hung it up, took off his service belt and secured his weapon in a gun safe bolted to the kitchen counter. "Yes," he answered, at length. "Call your mother."

Sara wouldn't be asleep, Eli was pretty sure of that. More likely, she was sitting bolt upright in one of the living room chairs, with that Glock resting on her lap.

If the situation hadn't been so serious, Eli would have smiled at the image.

"She'll be mad," Eric said. "Because I left without telling her, I mean."

"Your problem, not mine." Eli opened the refrigerator, inspected the contents—as usual, he was overdue for a trip to the supermarket—and settled for the last slice of packaged cheese.

Before Eric could reply to that, his cell rang in the pocket of his jacket.

"Crap," he said, frowning at the screen. "It's Mom."

Eli merely grinned, grabbed a can of beer, popped the top and closed the refrigerator door.

"I'm all right," Eric said, into the phone. "I'm at Eli's place…*yes*, I know how worried you are… *I'm sorry*, okay?"

Sara's voice came through the phone speaker as an unintelligible hiss, but it didn't take a linguistics expert to get the general drift. Basically, she was tearing the kid a new one, not so much out of anger as out of fear.

She must have gone to Eric's room to check on him, say good-night if he was awake, and found it empty. Eli guessed the boy had gone home from Bailey's with Sara, waited a while, then sneaked out to meet Carly, who must have, in turn, sneaked out to meet *him*.

The girl would be in Dutch with Cord and Shallie if they'd caught her.

"Okay, yes," Eric complained, rolling his eyes at Eli to show how put-upon he was, having Sara for a mother. "I know I'm grounded—of course I didn't hitch, Carly brought me—wait, you won't tell her mom and dad, right?"

Eli, who had been leaning against one of the kitchen counters, washing that lonely slice of cheese down with beer, set the can aside and extended one hand.

"Eli wants to talk to you," Eric told his mother, sounding relieved.

"Did you know about this?" Sara demanded.

"Of course I didn't," Eli replied reasonably. "Eric was waiting in the yard when I got home. Festus thought he was a burglar and knocked him off his feet. I guess his plan was to lick the kid to death."

"Sometimes I really hate being a parent," Sara sighed, having simmered down a little. "I should have been a nun. Or a spinster librarian."

"Now, Luke," Eli teased, "I just can't picture you as either one of those things."

Sara laughed in spite of herself. "How many times have I asked you not to call me 'Luke'?"

"Not enough, apparently," Eli replied. "Go to bed, sis. Get some sleep. I'll bring the happy wanderer by in the morning. For tonight, he'll be fine on my couch."

"I could strangle Eric," Sara confessed. She sounded exhausted now, and close to tears. "When I went to say goodnight and he was gone—"

"I know," Eli said, his voice gruff and as gentle as he could make it. "We're all tired. Let's all call it a day and let tomorrow take care of itself."

"Good idea," Sara replied, albeit reluctantly.

"And, Sara?"

"What?"

"Put that frigging Glock back in the safe."

"Not gonna happen, Sheriff. Tonight, it goes into the top drawer of my nightstand."

Eli closed his eyes for a moment, out of weariness and frustration. Arguing with his sister was like pushing boulders uphill.

"Has anybody ever told you that you are one stubborn human being?" he grumbled, after taking a final swig of beer.

"Runs in the family," Sara retorted.

Eli unclamped his back molars. "Good *night*, Sara."

"Good night," Sara replied, almost merrily. "And, oh, yeah, happy New Year."

Eli didn't reply, and there wouldn't have been any point in doing so, because his sister had already ended the call.

He handed the phone back to Eric.

"Can I borrow a charger?" the kid asked. "And maybe some sweatpants and a T-shirt to sleep in?"

Eli sighed and shook his head. "In the future, if you're going to hit the road, you might do a little planning first."

Eric was standing now, shrugging out of his coat, kicking off his heavy boots. "Yeah," he said. "I shouldn't have left Mom alone. I got scared and I sort of freaked out and called Carly to pick me up. I thought you'd be home by the time we got here."

Eli laid a hand on the boy's shoulder as he'd done earlier in the evening, when Eric had shown him Freddie's text. "Trust me, buddy. Your mother can take care of herself and about half the population of the Creek, single-handed. You screwed up tonight, though—no question about it—besides scaring the hell out of your mom, you probably got Carly in trouble with her folks."

Eric deflated visibly. "Yeah. She already texted me that Cord grounded her when she got home."

Eli went into the second bedroom, where he kept his computer and a few packed bookshelves. After switching on the light, he took blankets and a pillow from the closet and tossed them to Eric.

"Make up your bed on the couch. I'll get my spare charger and some duds you can sleep in."

"Eli?"

Eli, already in the corridor and headed for his own room, paused without turning around. "What?"

"Do you think I'm a coward?"

Inwardly, Eli sighed. He wasn't sure he had another philosophical conversation in him; it had been a long damn day. Still, this wasn't something he could put off, without taking a chance on messing up his nephew's self-esteem.

He turned around, met Eric's anxious gaze. "Being scared doesn't make you a coward, kid," he said. "Fear has a purpose—it can save your life. Cowardice is letting fear overrule your common sense. You did the right thing by showing me that text, if that's what you're getting at."

"I guess. I wouldn't have a chance against Freddie in a fight, though."

"Maybe we ought to do something about that," Eli said. He was on the move again. If he didn't get to bed, he might fall asleep standing up, like a horse. "We'll discuss it tomorrow."

Eli entered his bedroom, took a spare pair of sweats from one drawer and a T-shirt from another and tossed them to the kid, who was standing in the doorway.

Though he was holding the folded blankets and a pillow, Eric managed to catch the clothes.

"There are some extra toothbrushes in the bathroom cabinet," Eli finished. "Help yourself."

Once the boy had completed his nightly routine, he settled himself on the couch, with Festus keeping him company.

Eli took a quick shower, put on a pair of sweatpants afterward, brushed his teeth and headed for bed.

He didn't lie down so much as collapse, but, not surprisingly, sleep eluded him, at least for the first fifteen or twenty minutes.

He wasn't thinking about the Lansings and the danger they represented, or about Sara, home alone with a Glock in her nightstand drawer, or about what he'd say to Dan Summers the next day, when he intended to outline the need for professional security.

No, Eli was thinking about Brynne.

About their midnight kiss.

It had been electric.

He thought about their conversation afterward, in her apartment, and the way she'd felt in his arms, all soft and warm and welcoming.

He'd wanted nothing more than to lead her to the nearest bed and make slow, sweet love to her. To caress her silken skin, run his fingers through her hair, bury his face in the curve of her neck.

And a few other places.

He knew she'd wanted him, too. Knew she would have arched her back and gasped his name as she received him.

In the cold silence of his otherwise empty bed, Eli bit back a groan.

Brynne wasn't like other women he'd known, and not just because she was so beautiful. He sensed that, beneath that fragility, that desperate need to proceed with caution where any romantic entanglement was concerned, she was strong as steel.

With Brynne, casual sex wasn't an option—never had been.

Not that Eli had anything against casual sex; he'd indulged in it plenty of times, starting with Reba Shannon. That had been irresponsible, of course, but after that crazy, hormonal summer, his eighteenth year on the planet, he'd always taken precautions.

He thought back to the time before Reba, when he and Brynne had "gone steady"—an old-fashioned term, these days. For most kids, it meant swapping class rings, doing a lot of necking, and pairing up for movies, dances and the like. Maybe a burger and fries, if the funds were available.

He and Brynne had done plenty of kissing and plenty of hand holding, too, but things had never gotten hot and heavy between them. God knew, he'd been as horny as any other kid his age, but he'd enjoyed a special kind of intimacy with Brynne.

She told him her secrets.

Shared her dreams.

As much as he'd wanted Brynne, Eli hadn't pushed for more than she was willing to give.

And he wouldn't push her now.

He'd wait, if it killed him.

Which he figured it might.

He lay sprawled on his back because lying on his stomach would have been like straddling a fallen fence post.

He considered taking another shower, this time a cold one, and decided he didn't have the energy. He'd just have to suffer for a while.

So he closed his eyes, and the next thing he knew, it was morning, and his phone was moving around like a Mexican jumping bean on his bedside table.

"Sheriff Garrett," he said, out of long habit.

"It's Melba," came the response.

Eli sat up, wide-awake. "What?"

"We need you out at the Painted Pony Creek Motel, pronto," Melba answered. "Specifically the lot behind it."

"I'll be there in fifteen minutes," Eli said, throwing back the covers on his bed and getting to his feet. "What's going on?"

"You're not going to like it," Melba said. She was smart as hell, and one of the best cops Eli had ever had the privilege of working with, but she could get on his last nerve when it came to getting to the point.

"Try me," Eli barked, out of bed, pulling on a pair of jeans. Then he yelled, "Eric! Get up *now*!"

"Ouch," Melba complained.

"Talk to me, damn it."

"Well, Sheriff," his new favorite deputy replied matter-of-factly, "we've got ourselves a body out here."

CHAPTER EIGHT

Brynne watched from her apartment's front windows, coffee cup in hand, as several police cars sped past, streaks of light and sound.

It was almost a parade, she reflected on the calm surface of her mind, although there was certainly nothing celebratory about the scene. Beneath, where the deeper waters ran, Brynne's spirit churned with alarm.

Where was Eli? That was her most urgent thought.

As rapidly as the vehicles moved, she saw and registered each insignia—the Creek's small municipal force, the Montana state police, the sheriff's department—not Eli's SUV, but one of the cruisers.

Where was he?

The two rigs bringing up the rear moved at a slow, solemn pace: the van marked Wild Horse County Coroner and the ambulance.

No lights, no sirens.

No hurry.

Brynne bit her lower lip and pressed her face closer to the breath-fogged glass, straining to see farther down the street, but the window frame and the sign next door—Nellie's Nails—blocked her view.

And that was when the first what-if struck her.

What if the call all those police were answering was "officer down"?

And what if that officer is Eli?

What if he's been shot or stabbed or God knows what else in the line of duty, and that coroner's van is for him?

Sickness surged, scalding, into the back of Brynne's throat and, for a long and treacherous moment, she actually thought she might faint.

She set her cup down and grasped the wide windowsill until her head stopped spinning and her breathing slowed enough to rule out hyperventilation.

At her feet, poor Waldo wailed piteously, aware of her distress and frightened by it.

Brynne scooped the cat up, a dizzying process all by itself, and snuggled him for a few moments. "It's okay," she murmured. "Everything's okay, little guy. I promise."

Waldo probably wasn't convinced, given that his ruff was damp with Brynne's tears by that point, but he stopped yowling at least, and that was a mercy.

As she showered, she wondered who she could call—Sara? Melba Summers? Connie Sue Hildebrand, the day receptionist at the sheriff's headquarters?

Brynne hadn't come to a decision even when she was dressed in her "day off" outfit of jeans and an old college sweatshirt—Bailey's was closed on New Year's Day, though the cleanup crew was downstairs, making plenty of noise as they worked.

Figuring one of them might know what was happening, she hurried down to the restaurant's kitchen, where the commercial dishwashers were running at capacity, and steam from the sinks coated every surface in condensation.

There were no people in evidence, so Brynne proceeded to the dining and bar area, up front.

Her crew—three waitresses and two cooks, all being paid double time—were standing on the sidewalk, huddled against the cold, talking on cell phones and gesturing to each other.

Again, Brynne felt sick.

A single name thrummed inside her like a second heartbeat, *Eli—Eli—Eli*.

She made it to the door, called everybody back inside where it was warm. None of them had bothered with a coat.

"What's happening?" she demanded, her gaze moving from one face to another.

The consensus?

Nobody knew.

Brynne's knees threatened to give out, and Miranda, her second mother, took her by one arm and dragged her to a chair.

"Put your head between your knees, Brynne," Miranda commanded, once she'd been seated. "Harry, run to the storage closet and get a brown paper bag."

"I'm all right," Brynne protested, but weakly. Her breathing had gone fast and shallow again, just as it had upstairs, when she'd first realized Eli's SUV wasn't in the speeding convoy.

"You're not all right," Miranda argued. And then she laid one strong hand to Brynne's nape and forced her head down. "Now do as I say."

Miranda had worked for Brynne's parents for some twenty years by the time the business changed hands. She'd helped raise the Baileys' only child, in fact, and she had a certain authority because of that.

That and her naturally bossy nature.

Someone brought a glass of ice-cold water after the blood had returned to Brynne's brain, and she sipped it gratefully, embarrassed by her behavior, by what she'd revealed.

She had a thing for Sheriff Eli Garrett.

Most likely, nobody was surprised, however. No one who had witnessed that midnight kiss couldn't have any real doubts.

When Eli's SUV finally shot past the restaurant like a belated bullet, Brynne gave a great, gasping sob of relief, and Miranda took her into her arms and hugged her hard.

"There, now, you see? That man of yours is just fine," she said.

That man of yours.

Oh, no. *No.*

She could *not* love Eli Garrett. She simply could not.

Except, she did.

She'd loved Eli in high school—okay, kindergarten, but nobody needed to know that—she loved him now, and she'd loved him for all the years in between.

She was doomed.

"About time you got here," Melba told Eli, when he reached the vacant lot behind Russ Schafer's motel.

Melba was a tall, slender Black woman, with short dark hair and golden brown eyes. She'd met Dan when they were both in the navy and kept pace with him from basic training right on through the SEAL program. They'd married while Dan was in law school and Melba was walking a beat on the mean streets of a major city, had two kids—both girls—and split up when Dan graduated and entered the FBI.

Evidently tired of city life—and possibly because she needed a place to hole up and lick her wounds—Melba had eventually returned to the Creek, her hometown, with her young daughters, looking for work.

She'd purchased her late grandmother's house, where she'd been raised, applied for a job with the sheriff's department, gotten it, and had rapidly proved her worth. She was smart and fit and so far beyond *competent* that there wasn't a word for it.

Once, when she and Eli were on a long, boring stakeout together, Melba, who usually played her proverbial cards close, had answered the question Eli had wanted to ask, but hadn't.

"I don't know that any woman ever loved a man more than I loved Dan Summers," she'd said quietly, almost brokenly. "But nothing was ever enough for that man. He aced the SEAL program, so he had to get a law degree. That didn't suit him—he graduated at the top of his class and had job offers from all over the country, you know—it wasn't *exciting* enough. So when he joined the FBI, I figured it was time to get off that merry-go-round because he wasn't ever going to stop reaching—reaching for the next thing. He couldn't just settle down someplace, work a job he could be proud of, be a husband and a father. Oh, *hell* no, not Dan Summers! He was too big a hotshot for that.

"Well, I wanted to be a cop—that's all I ever wanted to be, besides a wife and mother—and do right by the people I was hired to serve and protect. So I came on home to the Creek, and here I mean to stay."

"You were a SEAL, Melba. A woman. Isn't being a deputy sheriff kind of anticlimactic after that?"

Melba had laughed her smoky, torch singer's laugh. "Anticlimactic?" she'd mocked. "Isn't it just like a man to think of everything in terms of *climaxes*?" She'd paused then to enjoy her own joke for a while. "I have two growing girls to care for, Eli. And getting that right is challenge enough for me."

"Over here," Melba said, snapping Eli back to the present moment and the lonely expanse of hard ground behind the motel.

He followed her lead, though it was unnecessary because a gang of forensics people crowded around the body.

The victim was—had been—a young woman, probably in her early twenties. She wasn't wearing a coat, but her outfit—jeans, a long-sleeved blue T-shirt and a pair of knockoff Uggs—was intact.

A small, tidy bullet hole told the tale: she'd been shot in the throat. Her dyed blond hair spilled around her face, congealed blood nearly obliterating the color.

Eli's stomach rolled, and he swallowed hard.

Looking at this girl, a stranger, he felt sick, not just with revulsion, but with sorrow. Sorrow for all she'd miss out on, dead at such a young age, and beneath that dark emotion lay an even darker one—a cold, quiet rage.

"We're catching this case," Melba informed Eli briskly. "Outside the city limits and all that. The Staters are just sharing their resources."

Eli knew all that without being told, but he didn't point that out. Melba was thorough, and she liked to make sure all the boxes were checked.

He stepped closer to the body and crouched, careful not to touch anything. The coroner and the state's people were finishing up, moving away.

He studied her.

She looked vaguely familiar, somehow, and yet he couldn't place her.

"Any ID?" he asked Melba.

"Nope," Melba replied.

"Who found her? When?"

"Cord Hollister," came the answer. "He and Russ Schafer came out here early this morning. Said they were thinking this thaw might hold long enough for them to get the bulldozers in. Clear some space. Maybe even dig a few foundations. They were walking around and Russ literally stumbled across this poor girl."

Eli stood, shut his eyes for a moment, imagining the shock of that discovery. Russ, the son of two alcoholics, and Shallie Hollister's foster brother, had been working hard over the last several months to get his act together.

Russ had never been a criminal, really, just a very depressed asshole with awkward social skills. A loner by choice.

As a kid, he'd been a bully—Eli had had a run-in or two with the guy himself—but these days, he was a decent enough dude. Or so it seemed.

Russ appeared to be trying, anyway, partnering with Cord, refurbishing that old motel, striving to make something of his life, which was a hell of a lot more than Eli could have said for, say, Freddie Lansing, or that worthless father of his.

"Anybody have a guess who she was?"

"Talk to Russ," Melba said, a little sadly.

"Oh, believe me," Eli replied. "I will."

Melba caught his arm as he moved away. "Eli?"

"What?"

"Don't jump to any conclusions, okay? Yeah, Russ found the body, and that makes him a person of interest, but he was out here with Cord. A community leader, known for his integrity, and one of your best friends."

Eli didn't answer, though he acknowledged Melba's words with a crisp nod. He figured she was thinking Russ wouldn't have brought such a credible witness as Cord along if he'd killed the girl and then staged a discovery.

His reasoning varied slightly from that of his sharp deputy. Murder a girl, pretend to find her, bring along a man everyone in the county, if not the whole state, knew and respected. Be shocked and horrified.

Russ was standing near Cord's truck, and Cord was beside him, one hand resting on the man's broad shoulder. After years of obesity, Russ had begun working out, eating right. He was no Adonis, but he wasn't overweight anymore, either.

Just solid.

"Who's the girl?" Eli asked, without preamble, when he reached Russ and Cord.

Cord looked irritated, but he didn't speak.

"She—I don't know for sure—" Russ stumbled. His eyes were red and his nose was running, and he wiped it unceremoniously on the sleeve of his flannel shirt. "She looks a lot like—like my sister, Bethanne."

Bethanne Schafer, Eli knew, had run away from home years ago. As far as he knew, no one had seen or heard from her since.

"A relative?" Eli pressed, though not so abruptly this time.

"Bethanne's daughter, maybe," Russ said, snuffling again. Looking understandably miserable. "Kinda reminds me of when Carly showed up, looking so much like Reba—"

"We're going to need a cheek swab, Russ," Eli said. "Stop by the coroner's office as soon as you can manage it."

Russ merely nodded. "Can I go home now?" He watched as the paramedics loaded the body into the back of the ambulance, zipped into a bag. "I feel sick."

"Yeah," Eli replied. "You can go home."

Russ ambled off toward the motel.

Eli and Cord stood in silence for a long time, watching each other.

"Sometimes you really piss me off," Cord said, at long last.

Eli grinned, but it was reflexive, entirely lacking humor. "Is that supposed to be news? I've pissed you off plenty of times, and I'll do it plenty of times in the future." He stopped. Sighed. "I'm just doing my job, Cord. You know that. Russ found the body, and there might be a family connection. That means I have to check him out."

Cord looked mildly chagrined. "I know. But I was here, Eli. I saw Russ's reaction. He screamed like a little girl, and then he threw up in the bushes."

"Where were you at the time?"

Cord put a hand to his chest in mock cooperation. "When Russ barfed? Or when he found the body?" He didn't wait for an answer, and he remained in smart-ass mode. "Well, Sheriff, I was on the other side of the lot, making sure I had my story straight. Hiding evidence. When I'm not training horses, loving my smart, beautiful wife or grounding my impetuous daughter for sneaking out to meet *your* nephew in the middle of the night, I like to plan my next murder."

"Okay, butthole, I get your point. Here's mine. I needed to know how Russ acted when he found that poor girl lying there with a bullet hole in her throat, and you told me." A beat passed, and Eli started to walk away, paused, looked back and said, "Keep Carly close to home for a while. Something's up with Eric—he got a threat from Freddie Lansing last night, during the shindig at Bailey's, and I'm taking steps to make sure the little bastard doesn't follow through on it. I don't want Carly caught in the crossfire."

Cord's expression turned dead solemn. "You can't just say

something like that and then walk away, Eli. If my daughter is in danger, I need to know the details."

"And you will. Soon—very soon—but not now. In case you haven't noticed, I'm up to my ass in alligators at the moment— nothing like a dead body to throw a wrench in the works."

All true. It would be a long, *long* day.

Melba was waiting when Eli returned to the spot where the young woman had been killed. Everyone else was gone.

"What's the plan?" she asked, though she knew, of course.

Eli might have replied, *The usual*—an autopsy, meetings with other jurisdictions to hammer out who would handle what, interviews with Russ Schafer and anybody else with even a remote connection to the dead girl.

"First thing—we order DNA tests. If there's a match, we'll at least have something to go on as far as identifying the girl. You and the rest of the team can ask around, show pictures, see if anybody recognizes her. I can't peg her as a local, but that doesn't mean she isn't. People come and go all the time, like they do any other place."

"That will take time. The DNA thing, I mean."

Sometimes Melba, in her thoroughness, could be pedantic.

DNA tests *always* took time because every lab in the country was perpetually backed up. Sad commentary on the state of the nation, in Eli's opinion.

"Yes," Eli replied evenly. "So the sooner we get the swabs, the better."

"You remember Bethanne Schafer?" Melba asked, ignoring his statement, as they approached their vehicles, hers a cruiser, his the SUV. "She was older, so I didn't know her very well, but it was pretty clear that she and Russ and Shallie had it rough at home. Shallie was a foster child, wasn't she?"

"Yes," Eli replied. Then he smiled at the memory of Shallie

as a kid, a dichotomy of a girl: rough and tough, soft and pretty. Once, when Russ had been bullying her, she'd broken his nose with a well-aimed right hook. "Might be a good thing if you go and talk to Shallie. See if she's been in contact with Bethanne over the years. If she has, she'll know if that girl could be Bethanne's daughter. She's a little old for a runaway but, then again, she might have been on her own for a long time." He thought of Carly, a seventeen-year-old kid on the run, risking her life at every turn as she hitched her way across the country, carrying everything she possessed in a shabby backpack, looking for her dad, hoping to find a home and a family.

A chilly ache formed in his guts.

That dead girl could have been Carly.

Or Hayley.

Or one of Melba and Dan's spirited, beautiful daughters.

His fingers curled into fists and inevitably an image of Freddie Lansing formed in his mind.

Was Lansing capable of a crime of that magnitude?

Almost certainly.

Was there a connection? A motive?

Maybe. Guys like Freddie probably didn't need much of a motive. They tended to be narcissistic, easily offended, whether the slight was real or imagined. Figuratively, and sometimes literally, they shot first and asked questions later.

Or never asked questions at all.

Slow down, Eli told himself silently. He was on treacherous ground here, making a case against Lansing simply because he *wanted* a case against him, *any* case.

A completely human reaction? Yes.

In line with his personal values? No.

Eli was composed of flesh and blood, and when his family or friends were threatened, a pure and ferocious rage rose within him, pounding at his rib cage and the back of his throat, fighting, clawing to be released.

As a responsible citizen of earth, let alone a man sworn to uphold the law—to the letter—Eli resisted that part of himself with all his might. Why? Because his honor, his integrity and his dogged pursuit of justice were entwined with his deepest, truest self, and he knew that if he wasn't careful, he might become a person he didn't want to be.

In short, if he wanted to live in his own skin, with any degree of comfort, he couldn't knowingly break the law.

All the way back to town, and his office, where the lot was crowded with rigs from varying jurisdictions, Eli thought about the dead girl. Whoever she'd been in life, whatever she'd done or failed to do, she hadn't deserved to die the way she had.

As he parked, his watch, rather than his phone, indicated an incoming text.

He braced himself for a shot of Freddie Lansing's hate speech as he walked across the parking lot, heading for the office.

Instead, the message was from Sara. Dan Summers agreed to provide security, and he's moving in today. Eric is holed up in his room with Festus; says he's going to be a laughingstock, going to school with a bodyguard.

Eli smiled at that, pulled out his phone to text back. No way was he going to attempt a reasonable response on the Lilliputian keyboard the watch offered.

I'll stop by when I can, he wrote. Tell Eric I said to chill. Very busy at the moment.

Sara's reply was nearly instantaneous. We heard the sirens. Town's buzzing with speculation. What's up?

Eli opened the office door, stepped into the lobby. As if I'd tell you in a text. I'm busy, Sara. LATER.

Did Freddie Lansing do something? Is he in jail? I ran into his mother when I went to the store for groceries half an hour ago and she looked at me as though I'd just run over her puppy.

SARA. STOP. LATER.

Okay, Dudley, have it your way, but you're going to have to explain eventually.

GOODBYE.

Eli?

He put his phone away without replying.

Inside, Connie Sue Hildebrand, the day receptionist/dispatcher, was fielding calls with grim efficiency.

No, the sheriff was *not* available for comment.

No, she could not personally make any official statement.

Fortunately, the news crews from larger cities in Montana had yet to arrive, but they were on their way, for sure, and when they arrived, they would stir the present shitshow to a whole new level.

Eli sighed and shoved a hand through his hair. He looked around for Melba, remembered she'd gone to question Shallie Hollister about Russ's sister, Bethanne.

Five minutes later, the cop convention had gathered in the department's small meeting room. It was standing room only.

The discussion that followed raised a great many questions and very few answers. The municipals wanted Russ picked up for interrogation, and so did the state people. The coroner's assistant, a fiercely intelligent young Asian man named Sam Wu, stated that the autopsy was underway and he would report on the results as soon as the coroner—Alec Storm, a retired GP—had finished his assessment of the victim's condition.

Condition? Eli thought grimly. *She was* dead. *That* was the victim's "condition."

It took until noon to settle what *could* be settled, and then—finally—the crowd dispersed and Eli could breathe again.

Until the first media van pulled into the lot, that is.

As he'd predicted, the whole cluster grew into an instant crap circus, complete with flying monkeys.

Connie, a sweet-faced woman in her mid-forties, kept them at bay for a while. Eli left the department to check in with Doc Storm—Sam Wu's promise aside, no information had been forthcoming from the town's ill-equipped little morgue, conveniently located in the basement of the Sweet Rest Funeral Home. The media vans followed him.

Reporters hounded him as soon as he stepped out of the SUV, and he waved them off, ducked his head and burrowed his way to the main entrance, where Sam Wu waited to admit him, then relocked the door.

Oddly, given the circumstances, he thought of Brynne. Had it really only been *last night* that he'd kissed her? That everything in his world had been made right during those electric moments when their lips were joined and their tongues sparred?

Yes, it had. And before that kiss, he'd confronted the Lansings and damn near been torn to shreds by their dogs.

Now it was the first day of a brand-new year, a holiday for most people. Anything but for Eli and his deputies, not to mention Doc Storm and Sam Wu.

It seemed impossible that so much could happen in such a short time, and Eli wondered with a touch of sadness when he'd get a chance to breathe again. When he'd get to see Brynne Bailey, simply be in her presence, never mind when he'd get to kiss her again. Take her on a real date—somewhere fancy, like she deserved—instead of just a snowmobile ride.

He realized he was starting to feel sorry for himself, and that wouldn't do.

He was the sheriff of Wild Horse County.

A young woman, a Jane Doe, had been murdered.

And the ball was in his court, whether he liked it or not.

Brynne hadn't wanted to impose—it was a holiday, after all—but after the restaurant had been restored to order and she found herself with nothing to do, or, at least, nothing she *wanted* to do, the worry she felt simply grew too great to bear alone.

She called Sara, asked if it would be all right to stop in.

Sara, told her to come right over. She was preparing a New Year's Day dinner of standing rib roast and all the appropriate trimmings, and she'd like someone to talk to, since Hayley and Eric were in the living room playing video games with Dan Summers.

"Join us," Sara said. "I'm hoping Eli will be able to fit us in at some point, but you know how it is, with his job and all hell breaking loose."

Brynne wondered, with a whisper of shame, if Sara knew how much her friend was hoping for even a glimpse of Eli, for the smallest indication that he was all right. "What shall I bring?"

"Yourself and a few bottles of white wine," Sara answered. "Eli's bringing the red—if he remembers." She paused, sighed with benign resignation. "If, indeed, he shows up at all." A smile blossomed in Sara's voice. "What am I saying? Eli *will* be here at some point because we have his dog."

Brynne laughed, though her throat was tight to the point of aching. "Thank you, Sara. For letting me intrude."

"You are *not* intruding, Brynne. Get over here, as quickly as you can, and don't bother to dress up. I'm in sweatpants and an ancient T-shirt."

"My kind of dress code," Brynne replied, though, of course, it wasn't. Her public image had always been the pretty girl who wore the best clothes she could afford; even her jeans were expensive.

Bottom line? She was over-cautious sometimes.

Hesitant to trust.

Clay, the only man she'd ever been truly intimate with, had accused her of withholding the sacred, secret parts of herself from him.

Screw you, Clay, she thought, remembering the inappropriate text he'd sent. *You had access to my body, but you couldn't be trusted with my soul. And you proved that.*

Feeling a little better, Brynne washed her face, combed her hair and applied a touch of lip gloss. Then she spooned celebratory tuna into Waldo's dish, and left him to enjoy his feast alone.

Downstairs, behind the bar, Brynne opened the cooler and took out two bottles of high-grade pinot grigio and two of name-brand champagne. She placed these in a box and carried them out back, to her car.

Brynne drove a kit car, a careful re-creation of a 1954 MG Roadster, totally impractical in a rural Montana town, but she didn't care. She loved that bright red roadster, if only because it belied her proper-to-the-point-of-untouchable image—another idea of Clay's.

He'd actually called her that, in the heat of their last argument. *Untouchable.*

That had been his excuse for cheating with his ex-wife.

And it had been pure bullshit.

She opened the small trunk and placed the box of wine inside, slammed the lid. Then, with furious motions of one arm, Brynne cleared the windshield of her car, loving it more than ever.

It was fast and it was beautiful.

It was also a middle finger to Clay and to anyone else who judged Brynne on the basis of her appearance and her quiet personality.

A strange, violent joy possessed Brynne as she slipped into the driver's seat, extracted her keys from her purse and turned the ignition.

The engine, too big for such a small vehicle, gave a satisfactory roar.

She backed out of her short driveway, careful not to overturn the garbage cans placed at the curb by her cleanup crew, and pointed herself in the direction of Sara's house.

Minutes later, she pulled into the wide circular driveway of a modest but beautiful brick house, with an old-fashioned porch and white shutters at the many windows.

Given Sara's success as Luke Cantrell, creator of Elliott Starr, a Clint Eastwood–style lawman and inveterate seeker of justice, the casual observer might have wondered at the relatively small size of the place.

Brynne knew, as did Sara's other friends, that the simplicity of that house was a reflection of Sara's nature. She lived well, but possessions weren't that important to her; she val-

ued her children, her brother, her friends. She wrote because
she was a born storyteller, and she confided to Brynne more
than once that she sometimes felt a little guilty, being paid so
well for something she would have done for free.

Sara, by her own admission, had been making up stories
since the age of ten, at first to create refuges for herself, imaginary places where life was kinder and far more interesting,
then because she'd grown to love writing so much that she
couldn't stop.

Stories followed her, haunting her, demanding to be told.

Brynne got out of her car and went around behind it to
collect the wine.

Dan Summers burst out of the front door, startling her.
Beaming that infectious smile of his.

"Let me get that," he said. "You go on inside, where it's
nice and warm. Sara's waiting for you in the kitchen."

Brynne laughed. "Well, happy New Year to you, too, Dan."

The grin broadened. "Hurry up," he said. "Eric's been
handing me my ass at *World of Warcraft* for an hour. I need to
get back in there and try to save my honor as a man."

"I'm hurrying," Brynne answered, smiling. Halfway up the
walk, she turned and called over one shoulder, "Are Melba
and the girls joining us?"

Instantly, the grin was gone from Dan's handsome face.

"She's busy," he said. "And the girls are with their grandmother."

The sadness Brynne saw in Dan Summers was as big as the
man himself, maybe bigger.

Brynne wanted to reassure him, but she wouldn't have
known what to say.

Melba was a police officer, a deputy sheriff. And whatever

was going on in the Creek at the moment, she'd be in the thick of it. Totally absorbed. Totally committed.

Just like Eli.

CHAPTER NINE

The body rested on a cold steel slab, hidden beneath a sheet.

Dr. Alec Storm, suited up in scrubs, was washing his hands at a large sink when Eli left the open doorway to enter the room.

The tile on the floor of that small, cramped space reached halfway up the walls. There was a drain beneath the autopsy table where Jane Doe lay, and the whole setup—especially the competing smells of disinfectant and death—made Eli feel faintly nauseous.

He'd seen his share of bodies, naturally, but it wasn't something he'd ever gotten used to; each one was unique, of course, with its own tragic or merciful story.

This girl's obviously fell into the former category.

"Hello, Eli," Alec said, with a sad smile. "I'd wish you a happy New Year, but that would clearly be inappropriate at the moment."

Eli nodded in response to the doctor's greeting. "Sorry to drag you away from your family on a holiday," he said.

Alec was drying his hands, tossing the paper towel into the nearby trash bin, pulling on latex gloves. Growing up, the man had been Eli and Sara's physician—*everybody's* physician, since he'd been the only doctor in town until about ten years ago, when the local hospital had been built.

After that, three other MDs moved to the Creek and set up their practices—one of them was Alec's eldest daughter, Marisol. She'd taken over for him when he retired.

Alec hadn't adjusted to retirement straight off. He'd gone through a second divorce—the first had been the break with Marisol's mother—and, by his own admission, taken to drinking too much, too often.

When the next election year rolled around, he'd run for coroner, unopposed since his predecessor had died of a heart attack six months before and nobody else wanted the gig. He'd been doing an excellent job ever since, having slowed way down on the booze and found himself a live-in girlfriend named Isabel.

"Sam and I have taken various samples, but that's about all I can tell you. I've been dodging calls from people who can't get through to you ever since we came back from the scene."

Eli wanted to protest that he hadn't been avoiding calls, but he knew Alec hadn't meant anything by the term. He was a very direct man and Eli understood that because he was the same.

"What is it with the media?" he countered. "What part of 'no comment' do they not understand?"

Alec chuckled grimly. "Reporters don't get very far if they have any comprehension of the word *no*, Sheriff. They just keep asking until they get some kind of answer, preferably one that fits their personal and professional biases."

It was rhetoric, Eli knew, so he didn't reply.

Sam Wu showed up then, clad in surgical duds now, and frowned at Eli. "Are you here to observe?" he asked moderately. He was young, a freshly minted pathologist serving an internship, and he wasn't out to make friends.

Eli admired Sam's reserve.

"No," he said, keeping his distance from the autopy table, not out of revulsion, but because he didn't want to contaminate anything that might turn out to be evidence. "I just wanted to ask if there's any sign of sexual assault."

"Nothing visible," Alec said. "We did a rape kit, just in case, but if I had to guess, I'd say this attack was motivated by something else. It was violent—no question of that, considering the bullet wound—but we haven't found any overt signs of struggle. No defensive wounds, nothing unusual under the fingernails. Just a few light bruises on the victim's right upper arm." The doctor drew a breath, expelled it with the force of frustration. "Meaning, obviously, that somebody grabbed her—most likely, she tried to walk or run away and the assailant moved to stop her."

"The full report isn't finished, but as far as I know, the CSIs didn't find any footprints," Eli said, thinking aloud rather than imparting information. "There's a lot of brush on that lot, but still—"

Sam opened the steaming autoclave on the far side of the room and began plucking surgical instruments from the inside, using tongs, placing them on a sterilized metal tray. "Are you open to wholesale speculation, Sheriff?" he asked. "What I have is mostly intuitive, but I have a good track record when it comes to hunches."

"That's true," Alec interjected. "If I'd listened to Sam, I would have won a shitload of money on last week's NFL game."

Sam chuckled, shook his head.

"Right now, I'll take anything. We've got eff-all."

Sam nodded, setting the tray of scalpels and other wickedly sharp tools on a smaller table near the one where the body was laid out. "I think someone talked that girl into meeting them in a fairly remote place. Maybe they promised her drugs, or money. Maybe there was blackmail involved. It's all guesswork, but I'd bet my custom-made gaming computer that she was there of her own free will."

"It makes as much sense as anything else I've been able to come up with," Eli said, thoroughly discouraged. He'd thought of all those possibilities himself, but he still had to wonder where Jane Doe's coat or jacket was—among other questions.

It was January in Montana, and thus it was bitterly cold. Nobody went around coatless in weather like that, not even young women too foolish—or too desperate—to realize that clandestine meetings in isolated places could go south in a heartbeat.

"I'll leave you to it," he said, when neither Sam nor the Doc offered further comment. They wanted to get on with their grisly work, hurry home for a holiday dinner.

Once again, Eli's stomach rolled.

"I'll be in touch the moment we have anything solid," Alec told him, not unkindly. "The specimens are tagged and ready to go to the lab in Kalispell tomorrow—Sam will drive them up there himself." A brief silence fell. "Oh, and Russ Schafer called about twenty minutes ago, said he'd be in Marisol's office tomorrow to have a swab taken."

Eli nodded again, and left.

He'd accomplished nothing by this visit—wondered, in fact, what in the hell he'd *expected* to accomplish.

He was irritated with himself, spinning his metaphorical wheels.

And Eli Garrett hated wasting time.

He climbed into his SUV and radioed Melba.

"Have you spoken to Shallie?" he asked without preamble the instant she answered.

"Yes," Melba replied, sounding as discouraged as Eli felt. "The last Shallie heard, Bethanne was in rehab, on her third or fourth go-round. She did time for drug- and alcohol-related crimes—was married at least once—Shallie doesn't think there were any children, but there are some pretty big gaps in Bethanne's history, so who knows?"

"Nothing on social media?"

"I've scoured all the major sites, and the answer is basically no."

"'Basically' no?"

"Bethanne was pretty active online, back in the Myspace days, but she's nowhere on the Book of Faces. Same with Twitter and Instagram and all the other virtual hangouts."

"Helpful," Eli said.

"Don't kill the messenger," Melba answered lightly.

Eli chuckled, but it was a grim sound, lacking even a trace of humor. "Sorry."

"I'll bet."

"Dan says you're planning to run against me," Eli said, wishing in the moment that she *would* run for sheriff, come the next election year—and win.

Melba didn't miss a beat. "Dan Summers is full of sheep-dip. If you haven't figured that out, *Sheriff*, maybe I *should* give you a run for your money."

"Today, I would hand you this job on the fabled silver platter."

"Fortunately for me, you can't," came the crisp reply.

Eli laughed again. Still no amusement. "Damn it," he half growled.

"What's the next step?" Melba wanted to know. She wasn't much for light banter, though she could certainly hold her own in that—or any other—arena.

"In your campaign for sheriff?"

Melba made an eloquent sound of dismissal. "That's two years away, Eli, and you're still a pretty popular guy in this county. I *meant* what's the next step in the investigation?"

Eli sighed heavily. "I'm headed out to the Painted Pony Creek Motel to ask Russ Schafer a few questions. Make sure he doesn't forget to go in for a swab."

"Yesterday," Melba reflected aloud, "that poor girl was still alive."

"Maybe," Eli allowed. "She could have been out there for a day or two, though. Weather this cold keeps a body pretty fresh."

"Where was her coat?" Melba asked, still musing aloud rather than seeking an answer.

"I've been wondering that, too. If she drove out to that lot, she could have left her coat or jacket in the car. She might have been in a hurry to confront whomever she was meeting." He paused. "Of course, that begs the question, what happened to the car?"

"Exactly," Melba said. Then, after drawing in an audible breath, she asked, "Why don't you call it a day after you talk to Russ? Go over to your sister's house and enjoy a nice dinner with your family."

"I'm planning on doing that," Eli answered.

"Brynne's there," Melba informed him.

Had everyone in the whole damn town seen him kiss Bailey the night before and drawn their own conclusions?

Evidently.

"So is Dan," Eli retorted. "Join us? At Sara's place, there's always room for one more."

While waiting for an answer, he shifted the SUV into Reverse, checked his mirrors and backed out of his parking space in the funeral home's parking lot.

"Sara invited me," Melba admitted.

"Bring the kids," Eli suggested generously.

"They're at my mom's, over in Silver Hills. She'll bring them to school in the morning."

Eli was rolling toward the edge of town, and the highway that would take him to Schafer's run-down motel. The place always made him think of Norman Bates, of *Psycho* fame, sitting in a rocking chair, dressed up in his mother's clothes.

"All the more reason to get out of the house," Eli said.

"I'm not *in* the house, Sheriff. I'm in your office, trying to find some trace of Bethanne Schafer."

"Go home, Deputy. Swap the uniform out for civvies and head on over to Sara's place."

Melba said nothing, but the space between them was charged with—what? Annoyance? Challenge?

"What's the matter, Summers?" Eli chided. "Are you chicken?"

Melba huffed. "Schoolyard tactics, Sheriff," she accused. "I expected more from you."

"You *are* chicken," Eli pressed, with a chuckle.

"You know damn well I'm not," Melba replied coldly.

"Not when it comes to muggers and bank robbers and druggies, maybe, but you are sure as hell one hundred percent scared of Dan Summers."

Melba sputtered, clearly on the verge of telling Eli—boss or not—what he could do with his taunts, but not quite able to bring herself to do it.

"Or are you afraid of *yourself*, Deputy?"

"With all due respect, Sheriff," Melba answered moderately, "go piss up a rope."

Eli gave a husky guffaw, and the release of tension was downright restorative. "Thanks for that," he said. He wasn't talking about the suggestion; he was talking about the reason to laugh.

"Unless you've got something to say that's related to Jane Doe, boss man, this conversation is *done*."

"Well, then," Eli answered, in a teasing drawl, "if that's the case, over and out."

Melba was no longer on his frequency.

Roughly ten minutes later, Eli pulled into the gravel and grass parking lot in front of Russ's motel.

He'd done some renovations, with financial help from Shallie and Cord, but the place still looked as though it had been dragged into the twenty-first century by its gutter pipes.

Russ's car, a rust-bucket sedan, was the only one in sight, and the motel's vintage sign, equally rusty and very weatherworn, was either shut off from inside or simply too tired to light up.

Shallie had grown up here, with Russ and Bethanne and their folks; in those days, she and Reba had hung out together, working for next to nothing, cleaning rooms whenever some hapless customer showed up.

Reba had left town the night of the bonfire, when he and Cord and J.P. had found out, simultaneously, that they'd been played, big-time, and Shallie had taken off soon afterward, only to return to Painted Pony Creek last year, looking to lay a few ghosts to rest.

She'd succeeded in that—found the mother who had abandoned her, right here at the Bates Motel, when she was two years old. They had a decent relationship now, mother and daughter, and Shallie and Russ were on fairly good terms, too.

Shallie and Cord had connected through Cord's work, and look at them now. Happily married and hoping to start a family soon.

Eli felt a stab of envy.

He hadn't thought all that much about having a wife and family of his own, at least, not until Brynne Bailey had come home to the Creek. Before that, he'd had plenty of women— more than he'd had time for, actually—but he hadn't allowed any of them to get too close.

When Brynne came back, things had shifted. He'd lost interest in casual dating, casual *anything*, and he'd been forced to acknowledge, if only to himself, that when he let himself slow down enough to consider his life, he was lonely as hell.

At first, he'd taken the attraction to Brynne lightly. After all, what red-blooded man *wouldn't* be attracted to a woman as smart and sweet and beautiful as she was?

Eli brought himself back to the present moment.

Seeing that Russ had placed a paper Closed sign on the inside of the front door, which lead into the office, he knocked. Then knocked again, more forcefully this time.

Russ appeared, looking rumpled, a large smear of a man smudged onto the fogged glass in the door.

Reluctantly, he opened up.

"I didn't kill that girl," he said, before Eli could speak.

"I'm not saying you did," Eli replied succinctly, "but I need to ask you some questions just the same."

"Okay," Russ said, stepping back so Eli could enter the building, "but I don't have a lot of time. I'm invited over to Cord and Shallie's place for dinner."

"So am I," Eli replied. "I probably won't make it, though, because my sister is expecting me." *And because Melba told me Brynne will be at Sara's.*

The inside of that office smelled musty, though it was probably clean enough. The carpets, curtains—the very walls—were just plain *old*, past their prime.

In Eli's unsolicited opinion, it would have made more sense to bulldoze the whole place, sell all that wood and wire and rebar for salvage, and rebuild.

The whole idea was to provide a place for Cord and Shallie's students, all prospective horse-whisperers, to stay while they went through the six comprehensive weeks of the program. Like the clients who hired Cord to work his magic and train untrainable horses, the students tended to be well-heeled, used to comfortable if not luxurious accommodations, and even with renovations the property would still be haunted by its troubled past.

Russ led the way past the battered old reception desk to the living quarters in back.

The living room probably looked pretty much the way it had when the original owners, Russ's drunken parents, were alive. The furniture was dated, and the carpet was the color of sliced avocado.

The TV, which still had knobs instead of buttons, sported an actual antenna flagged with tin foil. The volume was way down, but Russ had clearly been watching the news.

Eli watched himself on-screen, leaving the office, waving off reporters, climbing into his SUV.

In the next shot, a young man with an orange cast to his

skin and ridiculously white teeth was shoving a microphone into Connie Sue's angry, tight-lipped face.

Finally, there was a sweeping image of the field behind the motel and the crime scene, complete with yellow tape fluttering in the chilly breeze.

"No need for sound," Russ lamented wearily. "They're all saying the same thing, that nobody will tell them anything."

"Typical," Eli said.

"Have a seat," Russ replied, with a nod. "You want any coffee? I've got instant."

"No, thanks," Eli replied, moving a stack of newspapers from one of the couch cushions to sit down. "I wouldn't mind some water, though."

Russ moved into the adjoining kitchen area, which resembled a museum diorama depicting the last quarter of the twentieth century, with its harvest-gold appliances, red-and-black-checkered tile floor and white metal cabinets.

Eli rubbed his eyes, giving his beleaguered brain a chance to assimilate the jumble of textures and colors.

He heard the fridge open and close, and then Russ was back in the living room, offering a bottle of water.

The liquid was cold, and pure, and it flowed into Eli like a magical elixir, clearing his brain, strengthening his muscles, boosting his energy, which had begun to flag at some point without his noticing.

Russ sank into an ancient recliner on the other side of the coffee table, the surface of which lay hidden beneath a variety of clutter—junk mail, old copies of *TV Guide* and *Reader's Digest*, generic books of crossword puzzles, candy wrappers and a few coffee mugs, none too clean.

One of the reasons Eli had been glad to receive bottled water, instead of a glass from the tap.

"You taking your meds, Russ?" Eli asked thoughtfully, not as a gibe, but out of real concern. The man had made a lot of strides lately, but he'd suffered for years from chronic depression on a scale few people were made to endure.

"Yes," Russ said, sounding more resigned than defensive. "I'm on some new stuff. Takes a while to kick in."

"Stick with it, okay?"

Russ made a *harrumph* kind of sound. "Trust me, I will. After what happened out there—" He cocked a meaty thumb over one shoulder to indicate the lot where he and Cord had stumbled across the body. An event guaranteed to eff-up a man's day. "I might just double up on the happy pills."

Eli was through making small talk. "Russ, if you have any idea who that girl might be, I need you to tell me. Now. There's a family resemblance, I'm told, and that can't be a coincidence."

Russ startled Eli a little by practically bolting from his chair. He crossed the room, rustled around in stacks of stuff on top of a bookshelf and came to stand just on the other side of the coffee table, holding out a framed photograph.

Eli took it, examined the face behind the dust-coated glass.

"That's my sister," Russ said. "She was sixteen when that was taken. It was the year before she would have graduated, if she hadn't run away."

Bethanne had been a pretty girl, at least when this picture was taken, even with mild acne scars, cat-eye glasses and crooked teeth. Her hair was dirty blond and badly cut, and her eyes, a soft shade of blue, revealed a depth of sorrow few sixteen-year-olds ever encounter.

Eli felt a pinch at the back of his heart, looking at her. His memories of her were vague. "Was she a good student, Russ? Did she have friends?"

Russ sighed, and the sadness in that sound rivaled the hopelessness so visible in Bethanne's time-faded eyes. "Let's just say, she tried hard in school. The folks didn't place a lot of importance on things like that, as you probably already know. As for friends, who can say? Bethanne spent a lot of time by herself, maybe by choice, maybe because nobody else wanted to hang out with her. Shallie was the smart one in this family, and God knows, she was good-looking. Still is."

Eli was still holding the photo, still searching that face for some indefinable clue. "Can I keep this for a while? I'll have it scanned and then give it back."

"No need," Russ said. "I can print out a copy right now."

"Thanks," Eli replied, following Russ into a nearby room, which was much cleaner than the one they'd just left, and outfitted with some very nice equipment two powerful computers.

"I'm guessing you didn't hear a shot?" he ventured, while Russ approached one of the desktops, tapped a few keys, and scrolled through a steady stream of photos in search of Bethanne's image.

Russ didn't look around. "No," he replied, "I didn't. But I might not have paid much attention even if I had—lots of grouse-hunting goes on around here."

True enough.

Presently, Russ selected a picture and pressed print.

Handed the copy to Eli.

"I appreciate it," Eli said.

"Sure," Russ said, returning to the living room and dropping into his chair with a force that threatened to snap the framework.

"That's quite a set-up you've got in there," Eli observed, cocking a thumb in the direction of the computer room.

"I use one for gaming," Russ told him. "I mostly code on the other one. Taught myself."

"Impressive," Eli replied honestly. He'd underestimated Russ, and he was sorry for that. "I'm fairly literate, as far as work stuff goes, but I still have to ask my nephew to translate a lot of things."

"I didn't kill that girl, Eli," Russ repeated, out of context.

"Okay," Eli said.

It wasn't a challenge. It was an invitation to say more.

"What motive would I have?"

"What motive does *anybody* have? Murder never really makes sense, not to most people."

"Then there are the exceptions," Russ said, with resignation.

"You ever have any trouble with Fred Lansing or his boy, Freddie?" Eli asked, probably because those two had been at the back of his mind ever since he'd laid eyes on Jane Doe lying there on the hard ground.

Russ looked up, surprise in his eyes. "Nothing recent," he said. "Why?"

"Let's just say I have my reasons for asking. Their place isn't far from here, right? A mile or two, maybe?"

"They're not the best neighbors," Russ conceded, with a nod, "but in all fairness, they could probably say the same thing about me."

"Any boundary disputes? Problems with trespassing?"

Russ thought for a while, then shook his head. "Way back, my mom had a few nasty run-ins with Gretchen—Mrs. Lansing. They were friends, once upon a time, drinking buddies, more like, but then they had a falling-out over something—I don't remember what, if I ever knew, since Mom had anger issues."

"Gretchen Lansing was a drinker?" Eli asked, surprised. He'd probably exchanged less than half a dozen words with the woman in his whole life, and he didn't pay much attention to gossip.

Maybe he ought to re-think that approach.

"Oh, yeah," Russ said, with emphasis and a roll of his eyes. "Third time around, Dutch McKutchen, your late predecessor, ran her in for drinking and driving—this was way before your timed—she did six months in the old county jail." The facility was closed now due to lack of funding. Prisoners in the Creek cooled their heels in the town's two-cell hoosegow until they were either released or transferred. "Guess that turned her around because she hasn't kicked up that kind of dust since then, to my knowledge anyhow. Doesn't even drive these days—Fred takes her to and from work. Freddie did, too, until Judge Farley pulled his license for driving without insurance."

It occurred to Eli that Russ knew a lot about the Lansing family, for a disinterested neighbor. "If you'd seen our Jane Doe with Freddie," he ventured carefully, "would you be scared to say so? Afraid of reprisal?"

"No," Russ said firmly. "I'm not stupid—like practically everybody else around here, I know Freddie's a grade A asshole, and bone-mean to boot, but if I knew they'd been together, him and that girl, I'd say so. That way, I wouldn't be the number-one suspect in a murder investigation."

"That's reasonable," Eli said. Then he sighed and stood up, the half-finished water bottle in one hand, the framed photo under his arm.

Russ didn't rise from his chair; in fact, he looked a little gray around the gills, and his large body gave the impression of a punctured raft with a hole in it, slowly deflating.

"Don't forget the swab, Russ. Marisol's office, first thing tomorrow morning."

Russ nodded, sighed. "You know it'll come back positive," he said. "I've never seen that girl in my life, but it's uncanny how much she looks like Bethanne. Nobody's going to believe I didn't know who she was."

"Being related doesn't mean you're the killer," Eli reminded the other man. "It doesn't mean you're a liar, either. Try not to make a big thing out of this, Russ. My main objective here isn't to charge you with murder—I'm trying to find out who the girl is, that's all. That might be the whole puzzle, right there. If we know who she is, we can find out who she hung out with, and at that point, I think we're going to know who killed her."

"What if it was a stranger?" Russ asked, almost plaintively. "What if she *was* Bethanne's kid, and she was trying to get here for some reason? What if she was in trouble and she was hoping to find some kinfolks here? Somebody who would help her, take her in?"

"All that's possible, of course," Eli said, feeling sorry for Russ and doing his damnedest not to let it show. "Statistically, though, most victims are murdered by someone they know. Random crimes happen, obviously, but in general, killing another human being requires some strong emotions, usually a combination of them. Revenge. Jealousy. Rejection. That kind of thing."

"Right," Russ said wearily, hoisting himself up from his chair. "Guess I'd better get spiffed up for Shallie's New Year's get-together," he said. "You think she'd understand if I begged off?"

"Yeah," Eli said quietly, "I think she'd understand. But you

ought to go, Russ. Get out of here for a while. Give yourself
a breather from everything that's going on."

"You sound just like Shallie. Cord, too. As far as they're
concerned, taking action is the cure for everything." Russ's
grin was feeble, but it was a grin, and some of the light had
come back into his eyes. "Suspected of first-degree murder? Simple—go out and ride a horse for hours. Better yet,
teach it a few tricks, like how to walk on water or perform
in *Swan Lake*."

Eli smiled. "If anybody could get a horse to walk on water,"
he said, "it would be Cord Hollister."

With that, he gave Russ a half salute in farewell and left
the Painted Pony Creek Motel for more cheerful destinations.

He drove back through town, not stopping at the office,
and headed out to his own place. Without Festus there to
sound the alarm, he supposed he was vulnerable to some kind
of surprise attack, but he wasn't too worried.

He was ready for a fight, if one should come his way.

Ready for *something*.

Without shutting off the SUV, he took out his phone,
tapped into the app controlling the security cameras covering both entrances to his house, scrolled through until he
saw himself leaving that morning, in great haste, with Festus
frolicking at his heels, probably expecting a game of Frisbee
to break out at any second.

There was nothing else, which was a relief.

He'd dropped Festus off at Sara's, like a kid at day care, and
hastened to join Melba and the others at the murder scene.

In the interim, zip.

Maybe Freddie and the folks were sitting down to a holiday
dinner right about now, like normal people, having slept in
after a late night, waiting for the ball to drop in Times Square.

Whatever. It was broad daylight, and Freddie and the old man probably did most of their dirty work under cover of darkness.

Besides, they were cowards, which meant they were more likely to go after Eric or Hayley or even Festus. Maybe Sara.

That would prove to be a mistake, considering she and her family had Dan Summers for a bodyguard.

And then there was Sara's Glock.

Eli went inside the house, scanned his surroundings, the way he always did, then stripped and took a hot shower. When that was done, he splashed on some cologne—fancy stuff recommended by his sister—and dressed in jeans and a beige Henley shirt, open at the throat.

Then, hair combed and left to dry on its own, teeth brushed and mouthwash swished, he proceeded to the kitchen in search of the red wine Sara had requested.

The cabinet was empty.

No surprise there; Eli was a beer man, and he rarely drank wine. Kept it on hand only for pizza nights and spaghetti dinners, when Sara and the kids were over.

He sighed, tossed his keys, caught them.

After he secured the house, resetting the alarm system and checking the app to make sure the cameras were still operating, he walked to the SUV. He would normally have driven his truck, since he was technically off the clock, but today, he wanted the official rig and all the equipment it contained close at hand.

He drove back into town, passing the turnoff to Sara's place, and made his way to the town's one real supermarket. He parked and got out of the rig, scrolling through his phone in search of Sara's text, the one where she'd asked him to bring red wine.

He found it, went inside the store and grabbed a cart, one of the smaller ones, meant for shoppers who weren't there to stock up for the next faux-Armageddon, but just to pick up milk, bread and eggs.

The wine had a whole aisle to itself, both sides stacked high.

The selection was overwhelming.

Eli tracked down the ones he knew Sara favored, laid them in the cart, where they rattled annoyingly, until he braced them with half a case of good beer.

Rolling toward the checkout lines, which were surprisingly clear, he spotted none other than Gretchen Lansing at one of the tills, and headed her way.

Small and mercilessly freckled, with mouse-brown hair that rested limply across her low forehead and left her ears exposed, Gretchen greeted him with a poisonous look.

After running the first bottle across the scanner, she set it down with an eloquent *thump*.

Eli suppressed a grin. "How's your day going, Mrs. Lansing?" he asked.

"'Bout like you'd expect," she said, still glaring.

Eli wondered if Gretchen Lansing treated every customer to the stink eye, decided that she was probably civil to most folks, if only to keep herself gainfully employed. Being the sheriff, and thus antagonistic toward her son and husband, he was beneath contempt.

"I'm sorry to hear that," Eli finally replied. She hadn't exactly *said* she was having a bad day, but then, she didn't need to say it.

Gretchen lowered her voice, looked briefly around for eavesdropping managers, and spat, "I'll just bet you are, Sheriff. You *leave my boy alone*, you hear me?"

"Or what, Mrs. Lansing?"

"Just leave him be!" Gretchen hissed. "He's trying to make a fresh start!"

Eli ignored that. "Does Freddie have a girlfriend?" he asked.

Color flooded Gretchen's pale face, throwing her freckles into sharp relief. "No," she snarled, "he doesn't. And if you think you're going to pin anything on him, you're dead wrong!"

"Now, why would I try to 'pin anything' on poor Freddie. He's such a good, upstanding citizen, after all. Just like you and Fred."

For a moment, Gretchen looked as though she might spring across the counter, like some small, wiry, weasel-like creature, all teeth and claws and most definitely rabid.

Eli was reminded of a time when he was a kid, and he and J.P. and Cord had come across a young raccoon up in the foothills, where cottonwoods rustled among close stands of fir and pine.

Thinking the animal was hurt, he'd reached out, meaning to pick it up off the ground, where it lay sprawled and stunned.

In the space of a heartbeat, that raccoon balled himself up and came hurtling at Eli with the force of something fired from a giant slingshot, bowling him over, leaving him flat on his back, with cuts stinging all over his arms and chest and the wind knocked right out of him.

He'd had to have stitches, and a series of rabies shots.

Now, years later, standing in a supermarket, he couldn't help drawing the obvious parallels between that critter and Gretchen Lansing.

Not much difference, for his money, except that she probably wasn't rabid.

"I'll be out to your place sometime tomorrow with official notification of the restraining order I mentioned to your husband and son last night. Make sure Freddie's around because I've got some questions for him. Got that?"

Gretchen finished ringing up his order and then bagging the four wine bottles, each one carefully wrapped, all without saying a single word.

Her thin lips were pressed together hard, and her gaze skirted Eli's.

"In the meantime," Eli went on, putting away his debit card and gathering up his purchases, "I'd like to wish you a genuinely happy New Year."

CHAPTER TEN

Brynne found Sara in her kitchen, at the epicenter of holiday chaos.

Sara's young daughter, Hayley, was seated at the table, carefully sprinkling coconut flakes onto a white layer cake, while her friends, Melba and Dan's daughters, Jill, twelve, and Carrie, nine, supervised.

Eric and Dan could be heard all the way from the den, on the other side of the house, shouts of jubilation alternating with bellows of protest as they battled it out on their video game.

Sara smiled a greeting and rolled her eyes. "Sit down and make yourself at home, if you dare," she said.

Brynne laughed, though she felt a familiar pang of loneliness as she shed her coat and hung it from one of the pegs next to the back door. She couldn't help comparing this happy cacophony to the silence of her apartment.

"What can I do to help?" she asked.

Dan had left the wine she'd brought on a nearby counter.

"You could pop those bottles into the wine cooler," Sara replied, stirring something in the giant bowl she held. She was wearing a colorful cobbler apron over her jeans and bright green sweater, and she looked about twelve years old.

"Mom," Hayley said, backing away from the cake to consider it solemnly. "Does this look okay?"

"It looks fabulous," Sara said. "Thank you."

Hayley resembled her mother, with her dark hair and gray eyes, and she seemed to have inherited Sara's good disposition. "Can we go to my room and watch a movie?"

"Use the TV in the living room," Sara replied, setting the bowl down, opening the oven door and bending to peer inside, her long braid dangling. The lovely aroma of roast beef filled the steamy room. "This is a holiday and I don't want you holed up in your bedroom all day."

The three young girls trooped out of the kitchen, and Sara heaved a great sigh, though she was smiling.

Brynne had slipped three of the four bottles she'd brought into the built-in cooler, a small under-the-counter refrigerator with a glass door, but she waggled the fourth enticingly. "Shall I pour?" she asked.

"Please do," Sara responded. "Every year, when New Year's rolls around, I wonder why I don't just spend the day in my bathrobe with my feet up."

Brynne took two glasses from the rack affixed to the underside of the cupboard above the cooler and reached into a drawer for the corkscrew. "Why don't you?" she asked, as she began the process of opening a lovely bottle of crisp, dry white. "The holidays seem to get more hectic every year—first, there's Thanksgiving, and all the attendant fuss, then, too soon, it's Christmas, and even *more* fuss. A week after that, we're staying up until midnight, and finally—"

"We're cooking a roast beef dinner and hoping we can get everybody fed before half the guests are crowded into the den, watching the big football game," Sara finished.

Brynne handed a glass to Sara, then filled one for herself. "You do it all because you love your family and your friends and you want your kids to have great memories to look back on. You're a wonderful mother, Sara."

To Brynne's surprise, her friend's eyes filled with tears and she sank into a chair at the table, nearly thrusting her elbow into the coconut layer cake in the process.

Brynne immediately set her own glass down and rested a hand on Sara's shoulder. The other woman was trembling a little.

"Sara," she said, "what is it?"

"I don't want to spoil the holiday by telling you," Sara replied, with a sniffle. She picked up her glass and took a resolute sip.

Brynne sat down, pulled her chair closer to Sara's. "Tell me what?" she asked, though she had a pretty good idea what the problem was. The night before, Eli had told her about the threatening text Sara's son, Eric, had received from Freddie Lansing.

She knew, too, that Dan Summers was there as a professional, rather than a friend, although he was certainly that, too.

For all that, Brynne knew that the choice to discuss the problem was Sara's to make, not hers or Eli's. Plus, on the off chance that Eli had spoken out of turn, she didn't want to throw him under the bus.

Sara spilled the story Brynne had expected to hear, but with greater detail.

She'd hired Dan Summers to live in her house until the

Freddie Lansing threat had been resolved. He would be accompanying Eric to school, while one of his crewmen, scheduled to arrive that afternoon, would watch over Hayley.

"What about you?" Brynne asked, thinking what an outrage it was that Sara, the sister of the county sheriff, had to go to such lengths to protect her family, while Freddie, that punk, was free to come and go. "Who's going to keep *you* safe, Sara?"

Sara blinked away her tears, took another sip of wine, savored it for a moment and swallowed. "Well, *I* am," she said, sounding surprised.

Brynne laid a hand on her friend's forearm. "*Sara*, Freddie Lansing isn't a schoolyard bully, he's a *grown man*. He might try to hurt you!"

Sara's jawline tightened, and her gaze strayed to a small painting hanging on the far wall. It was Brynne's own work, a simple watercolor still life featuring a plain crockery bowl filled with fruit.

"I almost wish he would," Sara said.

Brynne knew there was a safe secreted behind the painting and, now, she had a pretty good guess what was inside, besides the usual jewelry, passports and other important documents.

"Sara," she breathed, alarmed. "Do not tell me you have a gun, right here in this kitchen."

"Okay, I won't tell you," Sara said, straightening her shoulders and looking quietly determined.

"Could you really shoot someone?" The idea made Brynne slightly ill. She hated guns, had always hated them, although Clay's experience in that Boston convenience store, where he'd nearly been shot, right along with his partner, had caused her to hate them even more.

"If they broke into my home, intending to harm my children or anyone else who might be around? You're damn right I could, Brynne. In a freaking heartbeat."

Imagining herself in such a situation, Brynne realized that she herself could kill someone. It was a chilling insight into her own nature.

"Are you judging me?" Sara asked, without rancor.

"No," Brynne answered promptly. Honestly. "I'm just scared of guns, that's all. *Really* scared of guns."

"That just shows you're a sane human being," Sara replied, resting a hand on Brynne's, probably to communicate that she wasn't offended by her horrified reaction to Sara's apparent willingness to pick up a firearm with intent to kill. "I'm no expert—not like Eli or Dan, anyway—but I've had the best available training. And as long as there are people like Freddie Lansing in the world, I'm going to keep my skills polished to a high shine."

Brynne swallowed. "Here's hoping you never have to use those skills, Sara."

Sara tapped the rim of her wineglass against the rim of Brynne's. "Here's hoping," she agreed. She paused thoughtfully, and the noises from the den and the living room seemed to recede into the distance. "Maybe you should learn to shoot, Brynne. My instructor at the range is marvelous. Or Eli could teach you."

Brynne shivered. "Why would I do that?"

"Maybe so you wouldn't be so afraid of guns," Sara suggested lightly. "Or if, God forbid, you needed to protect yourself."

Brynne was about to change the subject, out of pure desperation, when the back door opened and Eli entered, nearly tripping when Festus shot past him and headed straight for the next room, barking with delight.

"He's a party animal," Eli said dryly, setting the bulky bags he carried on the end of the counter and closing it behind him with a motion of one foot.

"Hysterical," Sara remarked, though she got up, went to Eli and kissed him smartly on the cheek.

Brynne was staring at him, and he was staring back.

Brynne swallowed. "Hello, Eli," she said.

His voice was husky. "Hello," he replied.

"Now *that*," Sara interjected with a laugh, "was some snappy repartee. Remind me not to use it in any of my books."

Eli shrugged out of his uniform jacket, found a place for it on the crowded row of pegs where other coats hung. To Brynne, he looked exhausted, and that pressed a bruise into the center of her heart, the size of a thumbprint.

"I was just trying to convince Brynne that she ought to learn to handle a gun," Sara announced lightly, reaching for her wineglass.

"You're already drunk?" Eli teased good-naturedly. "At this hour?"

"I'm serious," Sara said.

"So am I," Eli replied. "It's a lousy idea."

"You could teach her," Sara pressed, opening the oven for another peek at the roast. "Or Zeke could give her lessons. He's my instructor, and he is one handsome hunk of Montana man."

Eli sighed, though there was a glimmer of amusement in his tired eyes. "Zeke *is* a good-looking guy. He's also gay."

"No!" Sara cried. "*Really?*"

"Disappointed, Luke?" Eli chided.

For once, Sara had nothing to say.

For Brynne's part, she was enjoying the brother-and-sister exchange, wishing, not for the first time in her life by any means, that she had a sibling, someone to joke with, bicker with, love unconditionally and be loved the same way in return.

Of course, Sara and Eli's relationship was probably unusual. Even rare.

Why? Because everything about Eli was rare. He was no ordinary man.

And Sara was no ordinary woman.

Brynne felt rather shallow by comparison to either one of them.

Eli moved to stand briefly beside Brynne's chair, and his hand brushed across the back of her left shoulder, light as a spring breeze. "Don't listen to my sister," he said. "She thinks she's that cowboy detective she writes about."

With that, he left the room.

Brynne heard Hayley greeting him in the living room with a gleeful, "Hey!"

"Hey, yourself," he replied audibly.

Brynne sat very still in her chair, still recovering from the jolt that had raced through her at his touch. Her feet seemed bolted to the floor.

"Guess you're finally over Clay Nicholls, that scumbag," Sara said gently, with a smile in her voice.

To her own surprise, if not Sara's, Brynne suddenly began to cry, though silently. Her shoulders shook and her nose ran and when Sara produced a box of tissues, she snatched up a handful and buried her face in them.

"Oh, Brynne," Sara said, her tone tender now. "I'm so sorry. I shouldn't have opened my big mouth."

Brynne recovered quickly, mainly because she didn't want anybody else to see her shedding ridiculous tears, like a schoolgirl ditched on prom night.

She knew a thing or two about that.

"I'm all right," she insisted, not quite meeting Sara's eyes, though she could feel her friend's gaze probing, however kindly, into things she didn't want to reveal. "It's just, well, all the stress of getting the restaurant ready for last night—"

"Right," Sara agreed, though she was only being polite, and Brynne knew it. "Relax, Brynne. Have another glass of wine, and then we'll get dinner on the table. And I'll be a model of tact from now on." She paused to cross her heart. "I promise."

Brynne laughed, in spite of herself.

"What?"

"You, a model of tact," Brynne replied. "I can't picture it."

Sara laughed, too. Then she leaned forward and hugged Brynne.

Before either of them could say anything, a ruckus erupted in the general vicinity of the front door.

Both women left the kitchen, Sara untying her apron as she went.

Melba Summers had just arrived, wearing a soft, formfitting red dress and strappy high heels. Since she was rarely seen in anything but a uniform, she made quite an impression.

She was carrying a covered bowl in the curve of one arm, and she beamed at her daughters as they rushed her, shrieking in delight.

"What are you two doing here?" Melba asked, in genuine surprise. "You were supposed to be spending the night with your grandmother!"

"Dad made arrangements with Grandma and had one of his men pick us up at her place," Jill said, bouncing happily on the balls of her feet. Like her sister, Carrie, Jill would grow up to be a stunner; they both resembled Melba. "We got to ride in a *Hummer*!"

Just then, Dan filled the doorway to the den, taking in his ex-wife's wildly curly ebony hair and knockout figure and looking as though he'd just been poleaxed. Eli stepped around him, a slight grin curling one side of his mouth.

"Hello, Deputy," he said. "Lookin' good."

She made a face at him, but her eyes were bright with mischief.

Melba searched the room for a safe place to land her gaze and found Sara. "I brought Waldorf salad," she said, almost shyly, holding out the bowl she carried.

Sara hurried to take the bowl and make her guest comfortable. "I'm assuming my brother told you Dan would be here," she said in a loud whisper, slanting a challenging glance at Eli.

Eli raised both hands, as if in surrender. "I told her," he swore.

Dan looked flummoxed. "I just wanted us all to be together," he said, addressing Melba directly. Brynne wasn't sure he was aware, just then, that anyone else was in the room. "You know. Start the New Year out right."

Something softened in Melba, a visible relaxation of small muscles and wary thoughts. "Dan Summers," she said, "you know I don't like it when you involve the girls in your business. Hummer or no Hummer, I don't trust any of those people you hire from God knows where to look after our daughters."

Dan puffed out his cheeks, collapsed them again by expelling a loud breath. "If we're going to argue," he said, "could we do it later? In private?"

Melba looked mildly chagrined. "Yes," she replied quietly.

"If the sheriff and I don't get called out in the meantime, we can talk in private."

"Take that and run with it, old buddy," Eli advised his friend, laying one hand on Dan's broad shoulder.

Summers was, Brynne thought, the biggest man she'd ever seen. He had to duck his head just to pass through doorways. He was also a man very much in love with his former wife; that was painfully obvious.

Was Melba still in love with him?

If Brynne had to hazard a guess, she'd say yes. The very atmosphere seemed to pulse around those two.

"Let's get dinner on the table," Sara said.

She turned to head back into the kitchen, and both Brynne and Melba followed quickly.

The moment Dan and Melba were in separate rooms, the house seemed to exhale.

The food was probably delicious, but Eli, seated directly across Sara's dining room table from Brynne, was barely aware that he was eating. It was as though all his senses had melded into a single, laser-sharp focus, trained on her to the exclusion of their surroundings.

The insight was vivid and very strange, unlike anything he'd ever experienced before, a glimpse into the past, the present and the future, all at once. If it hadn't been so real, and so beautiful, Eli would have been terrified by the sheer emotional power crackling between them.

He wasn't a psychic, didn't even believe in such things. He was a just-the-facts-ma'am kind of man, a cop with sharp professional instincts, honed by time and practice, and he believed in what he could see, touch, hear, smell and taste.

This was something new, something beyond the way he'd seen her as a girl back in high school.

In a flash, Eli saw the essence of Brynne Bailey, her goodness, her strength, her compassion, the very fabric of her finely woven soul. She was multifaceted, like a living gem, and he saw these facets clearly—Brynne as a human being, as a woman, as a wife and mother, even as an artist, the owner of a business. He saw her as a daughter, too; as an infant and as a very old lady.

He saw all that and much, much more, between one heartbeat and the next, and he knew he would need days, if not years, to sort these impressions.

Eli snapped out of his trance only because he dropped his knife and fork, sent them clattering onto his china plate.

Everyone at the table turned to look at him.

"You all right?" Dan asked. He sat beside Eli, one chair over, and yet the two of them might have been different planets, orbiting around separate suns.

No, Eli thought.

"Yes," he said, literally tearing his gaze from Brynne, who had been watching him with some degree of alarm, like everyone else at the table. "I guess my mind went wandering there for a minute."

"No wonder," Melba commented, from her chair beside Brynne's. "You've got a lot to deal with, between Jane Doe and—" She paused, swallowed a sip of water; like Eli, she wasn't indulging in wine or whiskey today. "Sorry. No topic for the dinner table."

Hayley, Jill and Carrie sat at the foot of the table, pretending not to listen and taking in every word, while Eric, squeezed in between Brynne and Melba, was, as they say, all ears.

"We know what's going on, Mom," Jill said. "There was a murder, out at the Painted Pony Motel. It's all over the web."

"Maybe Freddie did it," Eric put in. "I wouldn't put it past him."

Eli narrowed his eyes, studying his nephew. Why hadn't he thought to ask Eric for more information about Freddie? The kid was certainly in a position to know, having hung out with the punk for the better part of last summer.

"What makes you say that?" he asked.

Eric shrugged, mighty casual now that he was safe in his own home, surrounded by protective adults. "Freddie's mean. That isn't exactly red-alert stuff."

"Did he—or does he—have a girlfriend, by any chance?"

Jill, Hayley and even Carrie gave a collective, "Ewwwww!"

"He was always messaging girls online," Eric replied, reaching for the mashed potatoes and slopping a spoonful onto his plate, which he had already cleared once. "I don't know if he ever met any of them."

"Freddie isn't on social media," Melba said. "I checked."

"He's on the dark web," Eric responded, as though that should have been obvious.

And it should have been.

A chill trickled down Eli's spine, pausing at every vertebrae. "Are you?" he asked pointedly.

Eric looked insulted. "*No*," he said. "Do you think I'm some kind of creep?"

"I wondered, for a while there," Eli said moderately, remembering the kid's previous escapades.

Eric colored, from the base of his throat to his hairline. "I'd *never* go on the dark web," he said. "It's full of terrible things. Besides, Mom would *kill* me!"

"With my bare hands," Sara confirmed, watching her son very closely now.

Eli turned his attention to Dan, though he was still hyper-aware of Brynne, who looked more than a little frightened.

"You must have people who know how to navigate that cyber snake pit."

"Of course I do, myself included," Dan said, slightly affronted. His gaze slid to Melba, who skirted it, probably embarrassed, as Eli was, by the oversight. "First place we look, when we're dealing with the worst of the worst."

Eli cursed silently, pushed back his chair.

Melba immediately followed suit.

"Eli," Sara said, in the big-sister tone she reserved for certain rare occasions, "this is a holiday. We're in the middle of a family dinner."

Dan got up, too, but in a resigned way. He was obviously reluctant to leave a full plate—his second—to surf a scummy sea of ugly information.

Just the thought of it made Eli long to take a shower.

And then lose himself in the sweet, shimmering light that was Brynne.

Sara sighed, aware that she'd lost the battle, if not the war. "Use the computer in my office," she said. "I don't want any trace of this dark-web crap on the kids' system." Her gaze landed on Eric's face, then Hayley's.

In Sara's modest office, furnished with a simple desk, a Mac desktop with two monitors, and floor-to-ceiling bookshelves, jam-packed, Dan eased into the adjustable leather chair and reached for the wireless mouse.

One monitor flared immediately to life; the image was a family photo—Sara, Eli, Eric and Hayley posing near the chutes at the Creek's annual rodeo.

Eli was comforted by that picture, which had been taken by either Cord or J.P. a couple of years back, but he was also reminded of how very much he had to protect.

"Password," Dan said. The chair creaked under his weight as he turned to look at Sara, who was standing in the office doorway by then, with Brynne peering over her shoulder.

The man had eyes in the back of his head.

A handy trait, in his business.

Sara recited the string of letters and numbers.

"Too easy," Dan scolded. "I could have guessed that in about five seconds."

"Then why didn't you?" Melba demanded, standing just behind her ex-husband and a little to the left.

"Damn it, woman," Dan breathed. "Would it kill you to cut me some slack here?"

Eli chuckled at this, and received a scathing Melba-glare for his trouble.

Dan's enormous fingers danced over the keyboard with amazing delicacy.

Presently, he said, "We're in."

Eli went to the door, gently but firmly easing Sara and Brynne backward, into the hallway. "And you two are *out*," he said.

With that, he closed the door in their faces, then went back to his place opposite Melba. Dan was like a human mountain between them.

Eli fixed his attention on the monitor screen.

Dan was still clicking away on the keyboard, and as various images flickered by, Eli realized they were traveling deeper and deeper into patently evil territory.

He shuddered involuntarily.

They were on the devil's playground now, a place where even angels probably feared to tread.

Presently, the image of an old barn filled the screen.

Eli recognized it, and so did Melba.

They both drew in their breaths.

"This," Dan said, "is Lansing's home page."

"I thought that pile of scrap wood had been torn down years ago," Melba said, and gave a little shudder of her own.

"Me, too," Eli replied.

"Want a virtual tour?" Dan asked, unflappable as always.

"Yes," Melba said, without conviction.

Dan clicked on the barn's sagging doors, and they swung open.

"This guy might be a crap-wad," he remarked calmly, "but he knows how to code. Too bad he's on the wrong side."

There were no bodies inside that pixilated structure, at least, none that were in camera range, just long, dust-speckled shadows, cobwebs and what looked like an army cot shoved up against one wall.

"Is this in real time?" Melba asked.

Dan shook his shaved head. "He could stream from there, if he wanted, but these images are still shots, edited to flow together."

"What's that? In the corner?" Eli leaned in, tapped a fingertip against a bulky shape.

Dan zoomed in, and the undefined shape crystalized into a navy blue backpack, clean and fairly new looking. The zipper pull was still shiny, and there were no tears or stains to be seen.

Eli straightened, looked over at Melba, who was looking back at him.

"I have another set of shoes in the car," Melba said.

"Good," Eli replied.

"I'm going with you," Dan stated, about to shut down Freddie's freaky website and stand.

"Stay here," Eli said. "See what else you can find."

Dan growled in protest, turning in the chair to glower at Melba and Eli both. "I don't like the feel of this. You two need professional backup."

"We *are* professionals," Melba retorted.

Dan looked furious, but he must have known, more than most, that it was futile to argue with Deputy Melba Summers when she was in cop mode.

Which was most of the time.

"That's right," Eli agreed, already on his way to the door.

Brynne and Sara were lurking outside, and they barely managed to get out of the way without being bowled over by the dynamic duo.

"Get your shoes," Eli barked. "We'll take my SUV."

Melba pulled off her heels, tossed them aside and ran for the front door.

"For heaven's sake," Sara sputtered. "What's going on?"

"I don't have time to answer that," Eli replied, sprinting after Melba. "Dan can fill you in."

Brynne stood with her mouth slightly open and her eyes enormous in her pale face. Eli paused just long enough to plant a kiss on her forehead and give her shoulder a squeeze, hopefully reassuring her.

With a couple of minutes, Eli and Melba were in the SUV, speeding along the back road that ran behind Sara's house toward the opposite end of town.

Melba, buckled in, shifted awkwardly in the passenger seat, trying to pull on one of her sneakers.

"Are you sure this is an emergency?" she asked, somewhat after the fact.

They weren't using the lights or the siren, but, yeah, Eli read this as an emergency. He wanted to search the inside of that barn, get there before the backpack disappeared.

He said as much.

"Don't we need a warrant?" Melba pressed.

"Not in this case," Eli said. "That barn is part of the original McCall homestead. It's on J.P.'s land."

Melba blew out a loud breath, making her bangs dance on her forehead. "Why did I think that old eyesore had been torn down years ago?"

"Probably because it should have been. The McCall place is big, and parts of it are pretty remote. Most likely, J.P. forgot all about it, just like the rest of us."

"But Freddie Lansing has been using it as a sort of hideout."

"I hope to God that's *all* he used it for," Eli replied, as they shot past the city limits and onto the county highway.

"Do we need backup?"

"I doubt it," Eli answered, "but it wouldn't hurt to give J.P. a call, let him know we're headed for his place and why."

Melba nodded, punched in the number as Eli reeled it off, and waited. "Hey, J.P.," she said, after a few moments. "This is Deputy Summers. The sheriff and I are on our way to that old barn on your land—yeah. Wait a second." She turned to Eli, eyebrows slightly raised. "He says he'll meet us there. Is that all right?"

Eli gave a raspy chuckle. "No," he said, "it isn't all right. But that won't stop J.P."

Melba relayed that information, then ended the call.

"He just laughed," she said.

"Of course he did," Eli answered.

They zoomed on, reaching the gate to the McCall place within minutes.

Probably because J.P. had been alerted, it stood open.

The tires rattled loudly as they crossed the cattle guard onto J.P.'s property. He co-owned the ranch with his two older sisters, neither of whom lived on the place, though they kept a vested interest.

J.P. managed the various enterprises ownership entailed, including mineral rights and several thousand head of cattle.

Eli didn't slow down as he passed the spacious ranch house, a long, low structure of brick and wood, where J.P. lived alone, except for his dog, Trooper.

He was waiting at the base of his paved driveway, behind the wheel of the ancient white pickup truck he used strictly for ranch work, Trooper riding shotgun, and as soon as Eli and Melba passed him in the SUV, he pulled out behind them.

J.P. wasn't a cop, but he'd had Eli's back for as long as he could remember, as had Cord, and it was good to have him around.

Once they left the ranch road for the glorified cow path that led toward the original homestead, and the barn, the going was teeth-rattling rough.

"Sorry," Eli said, glancing at Melba.

She jutted out her chin. "Worry about yourself, Sheriff. I'm fine."

"You do realize that we're on the same side, right?"

Melba sighed. "I'm still mad at Dan," she confessed.

"Why?"

"Because he's so damn smart."

"You'd rather he was stupid?"

"No, I'd rather he was the slightest bit *humble*."

Eli gave a loud guffaw at that.

A good thing, because it would be a while before he laughed again.

CHAPTER ELEVEN

The body swayed gently between shadow and light, surrounded by shimmering dust motes. The scents of mildewed hay, mice and death mingled in the cold air inside the old barn.

Eli swore, and Melba released a small cry of startled dismay.

"Shit," J.P. said, standing behind them.

"You have a knife in your truck?" Eli heard himself ask, as the initial shock of finding another body—the second in as many days—began to subside. "Get it."

While J.P. ran for his truck, Eli slipped on a pair of gloves from his pocket and looked for something to stand on.

The rafters in that barn were high, and the rope was long, though not long enough to be accessible to a man standing on the ground. A pillowcase covered the head like a mask, but Eli knew who this was.

It was Melba who located a dusty trunk sheathed in cobwebs, pushed up against a far wall; the two of them hauled it into the center of the space as J.P. rushed back in with the requested knife.

Before Eli could scramble onto the trunk, J.P. did it. He moved with the practiced ease of a rancher's kid all grown up.

As the body turned in slow half circles, he swore. Almost lost his balance on the trunk, which threatened to splinter beneath his weight.

With a few slashes of his hunting blade, a relic of his time in the armed forces, J.P. cut the body down.

Clad in a long, filthy coat, worn sneakers, jeans and a plaid flannel shirt, the dead man landed just this side of the trunk, toppling forward to land facedown on the hard dirt floor.

"Freddie Lansing?" Melba asked, even as Eli crouched, turned the corpse over onto its back and reached for the pillowcase.

"Yes," Eli said. He would have been a liar if he'd said he wasn't relieved, but he also knew that this situation was the start of a major crap-show.

He pulled the pillowcase away, revealing Freddie's purple, bloated face. His tongue protruded, a classic response to strangulation, and his eyes bulged.

Melba was on her way to the SUV to call for backup and the coroner.

She returned after a few minutes.

"Alec and Sam are on their way," she said. "I told Alec it looks like a suicide, and he asked if he ought to roust one of the state's CSI teams."

Eli, standing beside J.P., was looking around the chilly space, chinked with blue sky and sunlight, comparing it to the images Dan had opened up on the dark web, back at Sara's place.

"What did you tell him?"

Melba looked extremely out of place, in her bright red holiday dress, and she was shivering. Realizing for the first time that she must have forgotten her coat in the rush to get to this place, Eli took off his uniform jacket and laid it over her shoulders.

"I said he was probably the best person to make that particular call," she replied. "If Freddie Lansing didn't take his own life—and I don't see any reason to believe otherwise—then Alec will be able to tell us."

Eli nodded, mildly distracted. He squinted, found the cot he'd seen online and then the backpack. Went for it.

"What can I do to help?" J.P. asked quietly. He was standing with his booted feet apart and his arms folded. Like Melba, he'd forgotten his coat, but he didn't look cold.

"Go back to the gate," Eli suggested, carrying the backpack outside, into the sunshine. J.P. and Melba followed. "Point Alec and the others in the right direction."

"Got it," J.P. said, and headed for his truck. On his way, he turned, tossed Melba a grin and remarked, "I like your uniform, Deputy Summers."

Eli gave a grim chuckle, and Melba pretended she hadn't heard what J.P. said.

The wind was brisk now, and without his coat, it bit into Eli's hide like row on row of shark's teeth.

He set the bag on the hood of the SUV, examined the outside for any kind of identification, but there was nothing beyond a partial orange price tag bearing part of the word "clearance."

Melba drew nearer, as intrigued as Eli was. Had been since they'd spotted the backpack in Freddie's website photos.

He'd been in a hurry to get out here, to this isolated, lonely place, not because he'd expected to find another body—he hadn't—but because of this canvas bag, with its shiny new zipper. He'd known it had a story to tell, an important one.

And he hadn't been wrong.

Inside were a pair of wrinkled jeans, a crumpled blue hoodie, some dingy underwear and—bingo—a cheap wallet, pink, with rhinestones glued to the flap. Many had already fallen away.

Eli fumbled a little, trying to open the wallet, and Melba took it from him, opened it, drew in an audible breath.

"Here's our girl," she said, handing Eli a driver's license.

The DMV photo was a few years old, and the young woman's hair was short, instead of long, brown instead of blond, but this was definitely the person Russ Schafer had found on his back lot, shot to death, only the day before.

Her name was—had been—Tiffany Ulbridge, age nineteen, and she hailed from Lubbock, Texas.

Eli got out his phone and speed-dialed Dan Summers.

"Yo," Dan greeted him. "Find anything?"

"Sure did. Freddie Lansing, for starters, hanging from one of the barn rafters."

Dan let out a long, low whistle of exclamation. "What else?"

"ID for *yesterday's* dead body. Mind running it for me? Since you're sitting all warm and toasty and full of my sister's good cooking and we're out here freezing our asses off, waiting for the coroner?"

"You got a name, Sheriff Andy, or do I have to wait for a Howler?"

Despite the events of the last twenty minutes, Eli chuckled. It was a dry sound, and it hurt his throat a little. "Tiffany Ulbridge."

"Spelled like it sounds?"

"Yeah," Eli replied, following up with the address in Lubbock.

He could hear the rapid clicking of Dan's surprisingly deft fingers on the keyboard. "Let me guess. The info was in the backpack we saw in the pictures."

"Affirmative. Got anything?"

"Give me a minute, will you? I shifted mental gears after you and Melba shot out of here like clowns out of a cannon—the ball game's on."

Eli huffed out a sigh.

Melba pulled Eli's uniform jacket around her, a little more tightly now, as the wind picked up.

"This has been one hell of a New Year's," Dan remarked, still busy. "Makes a man dread Valentine's Day. Gotta get myself back to the war zone, where it's safe."

Eli said nothing; he just waited. He figured if Melba picked up on the gist of *this* conversation, she'd crawl right into his phone, shimmy through some wormhole in the time/space continuum and rip Dan Summers a new one.

"Okay—yeah—" Dan mused aloud. "Tiffany's been on the run from home for three years. Looks like the local PD and the home folks searched for her for a while, then gave up. I imagine our brothers and sisters in blue are as overworked and underfunded in Lubbock as they are everywhere else."

"Anything on social media?"

"Yeah," Dan said thoughtfully, "but they're not *our* Tiffany."

"Ulbridge can't be that common a name," Eli prodded.

He heard vehicles in the distance, bumping over hard ranch roads.

"I'm looking, I'm looking," Dan chided. "*Chill.*"

"Oh, I'm *chill* all right. It's a wonder my teeth aren't chattering."

Melba began to shrug off his coat, and Eli signaled her to keep it on, which she reluctantly did.

J.P.'s old truck arrived first, flanked by two deputies and Alec's van.

"Look, I've got to get off the phone now," Eli told Dan. "Keep looking. I want to know as much about this girl as I can."

"Wait. You said you found Freddie Lansing dead? That's the kid who threatened your niece and nephew, am I right?"

"That's him. Keep it to yourself, Dan. His folks have to be told before this is made public."

"Ten-four, good buddy," Dan replied. "I'll get the details later."

"Much later," Eli answered, with a sigh.

The call ended.

J.P. approached, handed Melba a woman's ski jacket, red like her dress, and she took it gratefully, wriggling out of Eli's coat and handing it back.

"Belongs to my sister," J.P. clarified, though no one had asked about the provenance of the red jacket. "One of them, anyway."

"Thanks," Melba said, donning the jacket and zipping it to her chin.

Alec and Sam were climbing out of the van, equipment bags in hand.

"Not again," Alec said.

"Sorry, but yeah," Eli replied. "It's Freddie Lansing. Looks as though he hanged himself, but you never know."

Sam, thinking his own thoughts, as usual, said nothing.

Eli led them toward the barn. The doors had been partially off their hinges for years, so the entrance was clear.

If Freddie—and maybe Tiffany Ulbridge—had used this place for a refuge of some kind, they must have damn near frozen.

The two deputies—Jake Riverton and Amos Edwards—came up behind Alec and Sam. Jake had a camera in one hand.

Melba filled the lawmen in while Eli and J.P. walked around, looking for any evidence they might find on the ground.

They circled the barn, slowly, Trooper sniffing along behind them, but found nothing other than old bottles, scraps of wood and rusty nails. Back in the day, they'd partied here fairly often with all their friends until J.P.'s dad had landed in the middle of one of their shindigs like a fox in a henhouse and sent everybody scurrying for the hills.

Everybody except J.P., Cord and Eli himself, that is.

He'd herded the three of them back to the ranch house, read them the riot act, then called Cord's grandparents and Eli's mom and dad.

All that had happened when they were fifteen—before Reba had all but tanked their friendship—and Eli remembered it fondly, even though he'd caught hell from his folks, not just at home, but all the way there.

He'd missed baseball practice for two solid weeks, nearly losing his place on the team, and that, to his mind, had represented a personal apocalypse.

The end of the known world.

He sighed, shook his head.

Went back into the barn.

Sam, evidently nimble as well as brilliant, was perched

astraddle of the rafter, examining the knot that had secured the rope.

"Is that necessary?" Eli asked Alec, in an undertone.

"Sam likes to get an overview," Alec replied. "Let the kid do his thing. He's smarter than you and I put together."

"I don't doubt that," Eli admitted, turning his attention to the coroner, who was crouching beside Freddie's body, wielding a pair of tweezers and dropping fibers, some of them minute, into an evidence bag.

"Too early for a conclusion?" Eli prompted, but carefully.

"I'm 99 percent sure it's suicide," Alex responded. "Sam checked his pockets. No note."

Eli crouched opposite Alec, thrust out another heavy sigh. "You're sure? Because I've got to pay a visit to Freddie's folks pretty soon, and they'll want to know exactly what happened."

"Can't blame them for that," Alec sighed as well.

Sam shinnied down a support beam, agile and quick. He landed on the barn floor with a slap of his sneakered feet and hurried over to the cot. Threw back the old sleeping bag atop it.

"Sheriff," he said, excited. "Guess what I just found?"

Eli, mildly annoyed, stood up and made his way over, along with J.P.

A snub-nosed .45 lay, cold and black, on the lining of the sleeping bag.

Eli silently berated himself for not checking out the cot right away. He'd seen that in Freddie's pictures, as well as the backpack.

"Don't touch it," Sam said.

Eli gave him a look.

To his credit, Sam backed off slightly. "I'll get more gloves and another evidence bag," he said.

"You do that," Eli practically growled.

Sam moved to one of the equipment bags, took out a pair of steel tongs and the promised bag. Brought them to Eli without meeting his gaze.

"Thanks," Eli half barked, snapping on the gloves and lifting the gun carefully from its resting place.

The chamber was empty.

He sniffed the barrel. The weapon hadn't been fired, not recently anyway.

He dropped the pistol into the evidence bag and handed the works over to Sam.

Then he shook out the sleeping bag, but there was nothing inside.

He wondered if Freddie had slept here often. If he'd owned the piece or stolen it.

Melba materialized beside Eli. "You think that's the gun that killed the Ulbridge girl?" she asked, very quietly.

"Yep." There would have to be ballistics tests, a check for fingerprints, etc., but Eil would have bet his best chance at re-election that they'd just found and bagged the murder weapon.

There was a degree of satisfaction in that, though the fundamentals obviously hadn't changed. Tiffany Ulbridge was still dead.

She would be nineteen forever.

"So we can be reasonably certain that Freddie Lansing killed her," Melba speculated.

"That would be my guess, but we can't afford to jump to conclusions, Deputy. The gun could have been planted, or used to force Freddie into hanging himself. Or it could have nothing to do with either scenario."

Melba huddled inside her borrowed coat, frowning. "Sometimes this job drives me crazy."

"Tell me about it," Eli replied.

At Alec's request, the deputies, Amos and Jake, who had been standing around up to that point, fetched a body bag and stretcher from the van.

Freddie's body was heavy, and it took both deputies, Eli and Sam to lay him in the bag.

The zipper made a tearing sound as Sam yanked it closed.

It was a sad finale to a young man's life, however misspent.

After helping Sara with the cleanup and thanking her for the invitation to dinner, Brynne climbed into her roadster and started for home.

Halfway there, she flipped a U-turn and, with no clear objective in mind, headed for the sheriff's office instead. While she was certainly curious—Eli and Melba had left the Worth place in such a hurry, and Dan wasn't answering any questions related to whatever the three of them had found on Sara's computer—Brynne was compelled by something deeper, something far more personal.

She *needed* to see Eli, allow her eyes and her heart and her intuition to tell her, in some small measure, how he was holding up under the pressure of this new incident, whatever it was.

Never mind that Eli Garrett's well-being was essentially none of her business; she simply had to see him, if only from a distance.

Did that make her obsessive? A stalker-in-training?

The thought made her nervous.

Then it made her laugh.

Maybe she needed therapy.

When she pulled into the parking lot, Eli was there, just getting out of his SUV. Either Melba had already gone inside, or he had dropped her off along the way.

Brynne shifted into neutral and rolled down her driver's side window.

Eli approached, bent to rest his forearms on the base of said window and smiled. He looked so weary, so beleaguered, that Brynne's heart squeezed.

"I'm not here to ask questions," she said.

He arched one eyebrow. "Good," he replied gruffly, "because I'm not here to answer any."

"Something bad happened?" Brynne asked softly.

He gave a hoarse, mirthless chuckle. "That was a question," he pointed out. "But, yeah, something bad happened. I wouldn't mind telling you about it, but I have to inform the next of kin first." He sighed. "Obviously, I'm not looking forward to that."

"Okay," Brynne said. "Eli?"

"What?"

"You could come over to my place later, if you wanted to. You could bring Festus, too."

Eli studied her solemnly for a long moment, and something flickered in his eyes. "That sounds good, Brynne. Really good."

Brynne's cheeks felt warm, despite the cold. She forced herself to hold Eli's gaze, though sudden shyness made her want to look away.

"Just to hang out, I mean. Not necessarily to have sex."

Eli actually laughed. "I'll settle for the possibility," he said. "Frankly, after the last two days, I'd settle for popcorn and a few hours of Netflix."

Brynne was still kicking herself inwardly for mentioning

sex. She felt like a foolish, virginal teenager laying the ground rules for her first date ever.

"Eli, I—"

He smiled, rested one index finger against her lips. Even that innocent touch stirred parts of Brynne that had never been awakened before. "I'll be over later, if the invitation still stands. No strings attached. No expectations on my part. If I can be with you—just you—for a while, I'll be grateful."

Brynne marveled, gazing at this man. He either had the patience of your average saint, or he was playing it cool, planning to seduce her as soon as they were alone.

Unless, of course, *she* seduced *him* first.

She had never wanted a man—including Clay Nicholls—the way she wanted this one.

"Call or text when you're off duty," she said. "I'll leave the back door open."

"I have the purest of intentions," Eli told her, looking serious, "but I have to ask—are you sure?"

"I thought we weren't doing questions," Brynne teased.

Eli straightened. Laughed again, albeit with an undercurrent of sad resignation. "You've got me there, Bailey. If I don't show up in the next couple of hours, don't wait up. This shitshow is still unfolding, and I'm not sure when I'll get a break."

Brynne nodded her understanding.

Eli leaned down again, caught her chin gently in one hand. "Consider yourself kissed," he said, and then he turned and walked toward the office, giving a backward wave as he went.

"Brynne Bailey," Brynne told herself, "you are an idiot."

Then she turned the MG around and drove away.

At home, she greeted Waldo with an impromptu cuddle, to which he objected vociferously, and then gave him his daily ration of flaked tuna.

After that, she took a long, luxurious shower, dried herself off and put on fresh clothes: black jeans, a matching cowl-necked sweater and slip-on shoes. She dried her hair and pinned it up the way she had the night before, when she dressed for the New Year's Eve bash.

Eli hadn't said so, but she suspected he'd liked the look, since his eyes had widened, ever so slightly, just before they kissed.

She'd barely slept, reliving that kiss over and over again.

And, right or wrong, smart or stupid, she wanted a hundred more just like it.

Beyond that?

Time would tell.

"I'm going with you," Melba told Eli, leaving no room for objections.

She was standing, looking very official in her uniform, in front of his desk, where he'd been filling out a preliminary report regarding Freddie Lansing's unfortunate demise.

"I guess the red dress wouldn't have been appropriate," Eli remarked, with a sigh, leaning back in his chair. He clasped his hands behind his head and stretched, tired to the bone.

"Very funny," Melba said.

"I wasn't kidding. You look good in that dress, Summers."

"If I didn't know you're batshit crazy about Brynne Bailey, I'd call you out for sexual harassment, Sheriff Garrett."

Eli winced, shoved back his chair and stood. "It's that obvious?"

Melba rolled her eyes. "Only to those of us with functional eyeballs."

"Shit," Eli said. "Do you think she noticed?"

"No," Melba said, adjusting her service belt. "She was too busy being batshit crazy about *you*."

Eli doubted that was true—he'd known Brynne for a long time—but a man could hope. "You're a fine one to talk," he pointed out. "Things are pretty hot between you and Dan, if you ask me."

"I *didn't*," Melba said. "Let's go and tell the Lansings their son is dead. I want to get this over with, and I'm sure you do, too."

There was no denying that. "This is the part of the job I hate the most," he confided, as they left his inner office for the reception area, where the night dispatcher, Evelyn, occupied the main desk.

Evelyn, a middle-aged woman and former beat cop, nodded in farewell as they passed.

Outside, they headed for the SUV.

"Dan's back at our house again, now that Freddie isn't a threat," Melba said, once they were inside, seat belts fastened, good to go.

"I'd be lying if I said I'm not glad that little shit streak can't hurt my family," Eli confessed, starting the engine. "I wouldn't have wished Freddie dead, but I'm relieved."

He *was* relieved, but for some reason, he had a niggling sense that, somehow, things were still unresolved. There was another shoe, he was sure of that, and who knew when and how it would drop?

"There's always the chance the kid might have turned his life around at some point. Found Jesus, or something," he said, as they rolled out of the lot and onto the highway.

"Fat chance," Melba said. "Look at the facts, Eli. He killed that poor girl—Tiffany—you know he did. Forensics will prove it. And if he took her life, who can say he hasn't murdered other people? Or *would have*, if he'd survived."

Eli absorbed all that, weighing it in his mind—and in his gut, which seemed to have a mind of its own. "Why do you suppose he did himself in like that? He wasn't the poster child for mental health, but this seems out of character. He had a lot of years ahead of him."

"Sure," Melba confirmed dryly. "Years he would have spent in prison for murder."

"He was a narcissist, Melba, if not a straight-up psychopath. He probably thought he'd get away with killing that girl." He paused. "If he *did* kill her. At least until the forensics people wrap up their investigation, everything we have is circumstantial."

"He did it," Melba said, with certainty. She was probably right; her instincts were good. Better than good. "But I get what you're saying—keep my theories to myself, at least where the public is concerned, until we have something solid."

"Yeah."

"Mind if I brainstorm with Dan?" she asked, gazing straight ahead, at the road.

"Go ahead," Eli said. "I plan on doing that myself, at some point."

"He's still trying to trace Tiffany Ulbridge's steps back to Lubbock, or where she was before she came here."

"Good," Eli said.

They rode in silence for a while, each thinking their own thoughts.

After a few minutes, they passed the Painted Pony Creek Motel, looking as forlorn as ever in the rapidly fading light of day, and a couple of minutes after that, they were pulling into the Lansings' driveway.

The stripped Christmas tree had been removed from the front walk and probably burned out back.

Fred's car was parked outside the attached garage, and the two pit bulls were prowling the fenced area alongside the house. If food or water had been provided, the bowls were out of sight.

"Here we go," Melba murmured, unsnapping the holster on her service belt. Although she wouldn't have admitted it under the most dire of circumstances, she was afraid of dogs. Big ones, little ones, on or off their leashes.

"Stick with pepper spray, Deputy," Eli said easily. "Leave your service revolver where it is until further notice."

Melba stiffened slightly, but she didn't say anything.

Maybe she was planning her campaign for sheriff of Wild Horse County. First order of business: assign her current boss to crosswalk duty.

Eli shoved open the driver's side door, after drawing and releasing a deep, silent breath, and climbed out of the rig.

The dogs, probably hungry, given their slatted ribs, were more curious than aggressive this time, poking their noses against the cyclone fence in the side yard, sniffing audibly.

Eli wondered if anybody ever patted them on the head, ruffled their ears or threw a Frisbee for them.

Hell, he wondered if anybody ever *fed* the poor critters.

He made a mental note to call animal control. Ask for a wellness check.

Melba gave the dogs a wide berth, even though they were behind a fence, and Eli didn't blame her. They probably could have jumped the barrier without much effort, if they'd been in the mood.

Gretchen Lansing stepped onto the porch, looking half again as unpleasant as she had earlier in the day, at the supermarket. "If this is about Freddie, he ain't here!" she all but snarled.

As obnoxious as she was, Eli couldn't help feeling sorry for this woman. The news he was about to give her was the worst a parent could expect to receive.

"Is Fred at home?" he asked mildly.

"Yes," Gretchen replied. "Not that it's any of your business."

"Can we come in?"

For the first time, Gretchen looked alarmed. She shook her head and turned her head to call back over one shoulder, "Fred!"

Eli stood respectfully at the foot of the porch steps. Melba took her place alongside him, still keeping an eye on the dogs, at least peripherally.

Fred stepped onto the porch, a little apart from his wife.

It struck Eli as odd that the Lansings weren't touching. A lot of men would have draped an arm around their partner's shoulders, or taken her hand, confronted by two law enforcement officers and all. And a lot of women would have turned instinctively to their husband.

"You're sure you don't want to go inside," Eli urged. "Sit down?"

Gretchen pressed a hand to her mouth, but her feet were firmly planted on the floorboards of her weathered porch. Once again, she shook her head.

"What's this about?" Fred grumbled. To his credit, he looked worried now, as well as recalcitrant.

Eli sighed, rubbed the back of his neck with one hand, wishing this whole thing were over. Wishing he could materialize in Brynne's living room and take quiet solace in the simple fact of her presence.

"Freddie is dead," he said. It was blunt, but it would have been unkind to draw the matter out any further. "We found him in that old barn on the McCall place. We're still investigating, but the evidence indicates that he hanged himself."

Gretchen cried out, and her knees buckled.

Fred caught her as she crumpled beside him.

"That's a lie!" he bellowed. "Freddie can't be dead! What are you trying to pull here, Sheriff?"

Melba spoke up then, her voice firm, but kind, too. "It's the truth, Mr. Lansing. We're sorry, but your son is gone."

Gretchen wailed again, and the sound chilled Eli. It was primal, despair so heavy and so dark that it was crushing her.

"We can drive you to the funeral home," Eli offered quietly. "Freddie's there, if you want to see him."

Gretchen's agony was terrible to hear, and it was continuous.

Fred, Sr., held her against his side, though, paradoxically, he seemed entirely unaware of her existence. "Freddie wouldn't have done that," he said, with desperation. "He wouldn't have killed himself!"

"I'm sorry," Eli repeated. "There will be an investigation, as I said, but it doesn't look as if there was foul play."

"Get off my land," Fred ordered, his eyes wild and covered in a sheen of tears. "Both of you! Just get off my land before I turn these dogs loose on you!"

Eli held out both hands. "Take it easy, Fred. We're going."

Melba made a beeline for the SUV, opened the passenger door and climbed inside the rig, shutting the door hard behind her.

Eli, backing slowly away from the two people glaring at him from their porch, lowered his hands. "If you need anything," he said, "or if you have any questions, call me. I'll help if I can."

Neither Gretchen nor Fred, Sr., spoke.

Eli got behind the wheel, closed the door, fastened his seat belt.

"Damn," Melba said, as he started the engine and backed the SUV into a three-point turn. "That was *awful*."

Eli nodded, said nothing. He was bothered by something about the Lansings' response to the news of their son's death, though he couldn't have said for the life of him what that something was.

CHAPTER TWELVE

Eli's text arrived at ten thirty that night.

Still invited? No pressure. I know it's late, and I'll be okay with
a no.

Brynne smiled at the message and replied immediately,
Still invited.

The reply: Be there in five minutes.

He was right on time, pulling in behind the restaurant in
his truck, with Festus riding in the passenger seat.

Brynne, standing on the small back porch, hugged herself
against the cold.

When Eli had parked and shut off the engine, he stepped
down and gave a low whistle, which prompted Festus to leap
down after him, tail wagging, tongue lolling.

Clearly, Eli had been home and changed; he was wearing
different clothes, jeans, a T-shirt and a long-sleeved wool

shirt. His Western boots were well-worn but clean, and his hair was still damp from a recent shower.

Festus rushed Brynne and was overjoyed to receive a good reception—a warm laugh and a ruffling of his floppy ears. His mismatched eyes gleamed in the dim glow of the porch light.

Eli walked toward Brynne, stood looking up at her for a moment before mounting the steps.

"You look like an angel, complete with halo," he said, and his voice was husky.

Coming from any other man, Clay included, Brynne would have written those words off as a hokey pickup line. Coming from Eli, who, in her experience at least, tended to be straightforward to the point of bluntness and utterly lacking in poetic inclinations, they were something to be pondered and cherished.

Oddly stricken, Brynne was silent.

Eli mounted the steps, closing the space between them, and bent his head, brushing his cheek—freshly shaven and smelling faintly of soap and toothpaste—against hers.

Brynne shivered, and Eli immediately wrapped her in his arms.

"You're cold," he said.

Just then, with her body in such close contact with Eli's, she was anything *but* cold. Things were melting inside her, tipping and flowing, leaving a warm ache wherever they touched.

She barely had the breath to speak. "Come in," she said, the fingers of both hands clasping the front of his shirt. Pulling.

He gave a low, ragged laugh and kissed her.

It wasn't a deep kiss, like the one they'd shared to mark the coming of a New Year, but it sparked new fires just the same.

With something dangerously close to desperation, Brynne grasped Eli's hand and half dragged him in from the porch.

She closed and locked the inside door behind them, then led the way up the stairs to the landing, where Festus was already waiting, still wagging his tail.

Inside the apartment, where it was deliciously warm, Brynne turned to face Eli, wondering if she was rushing things, if she'd gotten in over her head.

In the final analysis, she didn't care.

Tonight was all that mattered. *Now* was all that mattered.

Who even knew if there would *be* a tomorrow?

When the silence grew too long to bear, Brynne asked the first question that came to mind. "Are you hungry?"

After all, she owned a restaurant. Feeding people was what she did.

Eli's grin smoldered, right along with his eyes, as he took her in. It was leisurely, like a thirsty man taking a long, slow drink of the purest water.

"Oh, yeah," he drawled. "I am *very* hungry."

Brynne blushed, and then blushed *because* she'd blushed, revealing too much by her reaction.

Eli chuckled. "Damn," he said. "I love it when you do that."

"When I do what?" she asked, though she knew.

He didn't reply. He simply came to her, took her into his arms again.

"How many kids do you think we'd have by now, if we'd gotten married right out of college? Or, better yet, high school?" he asked.

Brynne pretended to shove him away, though her hands remained on his chest, resting lightly there, feeling the hard warmth beneath the fabric of his shirt. "I think we'd be divorced—*especially* if we'd married right after high school."

Eli's expression was one of exaggerated surprise. "Divorced? What makes you think we'd be divorced?"

"It's simple," Brynne answered lightly. "Neither one of us would have had time to become who we are. Did you know a person's frontal cortex doesn't stop developing until they're twenty-five years old?"

"Excellent reasoning," Eli replied, "but I think all that legitimate sex would have made up for an underdeveloped frontal cortex, at least a little."

"I don't agree," Brynne said, with a slight smile, "but I get that men under twenty-five—and often *over* twenty-five—don't think with that particular part of their anatomy anyway, so maybe it doesn't matter."

Eli's grin broadened. "You may have a point there, Bailey. I'll take it under advisement."

Brynne reflected in the privacy of her own mind that, right about now, she'd rather be taken under something quite different from advisement. What she said aloud was, "Take off your shirt."

Eli looked pleasantly startled. "Well," he replied, "all righty, then."

Now it was Brynne who laughed. "Your shoulders are too close to your ears, Sheriff. You need a back rub."

Eli removed his flannel shirt, tossed it over the back of a chair. "I won't turn that down," he said, reaching for one of the chairs at Brynne's kitchen table.

He turned it around and sat astride it.

Brynne stood behind him, began to work the muscle in Eli's neck and shoulders with the strong fingers of an artist and a cook.

He groaned, rested his forehead on his arms, folded across the back of the chair. He was still wearing his T-shirt.

"Hard day?" Brynne asked quietly. Of course, the question was rhetorical, since that much was perfectly obvious, given the way he and Melba had rushed out of Sara's house earlier.

His response was muffled because he didn't raise his head. "Worse than hard," he replied. "Freddie Lansing hanged himself in that old barn on J.P.'s ranch."

Brynne had only encountered Freddie once or twice, in passing, and she'd recoiled inwardly each time. She knew he'd threatened Eric Worth and, by extension, his younger sister, in the text Eric had shown Eli the night before.

Sara had filled her in on the details, explaining that she'd taken the threat seriously, and hired Dan Summers as a bodyguard.

"That's awful," she said, and she meant it, even though a part of her was deeply relieved that Sara and her children were no longer in harm's way.

Eli sighed. "I despised that kid," he said, relaxing slowly as Brynne's fingers worked to loosen rigid muscles. "But I sure as hell wouldn't have wished him dead. His folks are destroyed. Freddie wasn't much, but he was all Fred, Sr., and Gretchen had."

Brynne pressed her thumbs into a hard knot between Eli's shoulder blades. "I feel sorry for them," she replied honestly.

"Yeah," Eli breathed out the word. "So do I." He paused, turned his head from side to side, stretching his neck. "People like Fred and Gretchen confound me. They seem to *like* being miserable. I don't get it."

"They're damaged," Brynne said simply. "Most likely, they were raised by people just like them. Or worse."

"I don't know," Eli answered, between low groans of pleasure. "Makes me wonder what they were like—Fred, Sr., and Gretchen, I mean—when they were young and in love. Did they get off on making each other suffer, or what? And how the hell did they get Freddie, when the two of them are like a pair of porcupines with every quill ready to launch?"

Brynne sighed. She was sad for the Lansings—all of them— but she couldn't help smiling at the picture Eli had painted in her mind.

"You might be a writer, like your sister," she observed.

That made Eli lift his head, look back at her over one shoulder. "Oh, *hell* no," he said with force, though that devastating grin of his was very much in evidence. "Sara makes a lot of money, and she loves what she does, but if I had to sit in front of a computer screen all day and spin yarns, I'd die of boredom. Or writer's block."

"I don't think Sara *gets* writer's block," Brynne answered, feeling light-headed, as though she were trembling on the edge of a precipice, about to tumble end over end into Eli Garrett's laughing eyes. "She told me once that she'll never live long enough to tell all the stories inside her." A pause. "I used to feel that way about painting."

Eli made no comment. He stood, turned the chair around, sat down and pulled Brynne onto his lap.

She landed astraddle of his thighs, and a tsunami of heat roared through her, then pooled, pulsing, in her lower belly and between her legs.

She trembled, closed her eyes against the onslaught of physical sensations—and emotions. It would have been impossible, she thought, to untangle all the things she felt.

Eli stroked her cheeks very gently with the edges of his thumbs. "Shhh," he said, and though that made no sense, it soothed her a little.

Then she realized he was hard. *Very* hard.

So much for being soothed.

She opened her eyes, gazed directly into his. "Eli—"

"It's okay, Brynne," he said. "If you're not ready, that's okay. I'm not in any hurry, here." He paused, and an impish twinkle sparked in his eyes. "Well, actually, I *am* in a hurry, but we're going to follow your timetable, not mine."

"You," Brynne replied, "are not a normal man."

"Gee, thanks," Eli drawled.

"I didn't mean it that way, and you know it. I meant, well, you're *different*. I've never been with anybody like you."

Eli pretended to consider her words deeply. "How am I different?" he asked. "In case you haven't noticed, the flag might not be flying, but the pole is up."

Brynne laughed and swatted at him lightly, then let her hand linger on his shoulder. "I definitely noticed. *Am noticing*. You're hard and you're making me want you and yet you're telling me there's no hurry. The crazy thing is, I think you actually *mean* it."

"Okay, I'll give it to you straight." Another pause. Another grin. "Pun intended. I want you, Brynne, too much to push you into something you're not ready for. I'm not being noble—I'm hedging my bets. When we make love—and I'm pretty sure that's inevitable—I want it to be right, for both of us. Not because I've had a hard day and you want to make me feel better."

Brynne rested her forehead against his, closed her eyes again. "Could we—could we just lie down together for a while? Hold each other and see what happens? Because honest to God, Eli, right now I want so much to be held."

He kissed her mouth lightly. Briefly. "Are you the least bit particular about who does the holding?" he teased.

"You," Brynne blurted, pulling back to meet Eli's gaze. He was even harder now, pressing against her, and she feared—

hoped—that if he moved at all, she would go over the edge in a ball of flame. "I want *you* to hold me."

It happened then. Eli shifted in his chair and Brynne, straddling him in much the same way she had during the snowmobile ride, shattered, arching her back, crying out in startled release.

Eli groaned and slid his hands up under her sweater and bra, stroking her hard nipples with the pads of his thumbs.

Brynne ground against him, in glorious frenzy, and came again, harder than before, so hard that she convulsed in Eli's arms. When she'd finally finished, she collapsed against his chest, resting her head on his shoulder, her breath fast and shallow.

She was embarrassed.

She was satisfied.

And she wanted to be satisfied again. Then again.

"You know," she said, when she could speak, without raising her head to look into Eli's face, "I think I'm ready."

Eli gave a low laugh, his hands still cupping her breasts, his thumbs stirring her to want more.

Much, much more.

"You've been saving those up for a while," he said, moving to pull off her sweater, unfasten her bra and toss it aside, leaving her breasts bare to his gaze. "Let's see if you have any more tucked away."

With that, he leaned forward to take Brynne's right nipple into his mouth. He suckled gently, but hungrily, and she squirmed, her fingers in his hair.

"Eli—" she whimpered, pleading. "The bed—"

He stopped suckling only to tease her with the tip of his tongue. "Not yet," he murmured. Then he opened the snap on her jeans, eased his hand inside and found the core of her femininity.

As he enjoyed her breasts, he stroked her with his fingers, teasing her endlessly. Mercilessly.

And when the next orgasm seized her, it was so powerful that it didn't make Brynne whimper, like before. It made her *howl*.

After that cataclysmic release of tension and pent-up longings, things happened, at least for Brynne, in a dreamlike sequence.

Beyond the fact that Eli carried her to her bed, she would remember sensations, sweet chaos, an unrelenting hunger for this man she wanted so fiercely, so ferociously, and was so very afraid to love.

After the lovemaking, Eli was exhausted—this time, in a good way—but he didn't allow himself to sleep. Long after Brynne drifted off, soft and sweet in his arms, he simply lay there, holding her, reveling in her warmth and her presence.

Beyond the boundaries of that rumpled bed, the real world waited to pounce, and Eli didn't want to go back and tangle with it one moment before he had to make the shift from lover to lawman.

Not that the word *lover* covered the subject, because it didn't. It was far too casual to define what he felt for this woman.

He'd loved her for a long time, he knew that now, but tonight, when they'd joined, over and over again, with all the force of two fiery meteors colliding in outer space, new things had come into being, intangible and, at the same time, elemental.

It was as if they'd created a brand-new universe, complete

with galaxies and black holes, moons and planets, a vast, uncharted expanse that existed only between, and for, them. Exploring even a small part of this invisible but very real microcosm would take a lifetime, if not several of them.

Eli wound a tendril of Brynne's silver-blond hair gently around one finger.

He wanted to say it. *I love you.*

But he wouldn't, couldn't. Not yet.

Because, while Brynne had certainly been more than ready for lovemaking—by far the best Eli had ever had—she *wasn't* prepared to deal with the full force of his love for her.

She was still fragile. Could she still be hung up on Clay Nicholls?

Yes, she'd made love like a tigress.

But that didn't mean she'd had the same deep, life-changing experience as he'd had.

So he would wait.

He would take things step-by-step, breath by breath, heartbeat by heartbeat.

Holding himself back would be like trying to round up a herd of wild horses, single-handed, and drive them into a corral, but he would manage it.

Somehow.

Eli smiled, remembering Brynne's unrestrained responses to his touch, first on his lap in a kitchen chair, then in bed. He'd never dreamed she could be that passionate, with her cool, Nordic queen beauty.

But she'd sought him out, hurled her body against his, clawed and clutched and bucked beneath him, only to ride him minutes later, wild in her desire to give and receive pleasure.

He was sated, on a physical level, but tonight, with Brynne, he'd visited other dimensions, places that weren't places, time out of time.

I love you, Brynne Bailey, he told her silently.

She stirred in her sleep, and the softest of smiles curved her lips.

Eli lay awake until sunrise, and he savored the warmth of Brynne's presence, the clean, faintly flowering scent of her hair, the slow and even meter of her breathing.

For now, it was enough to be near her.

Something cold and damp pressed against Brynne's forehead; she opened her eyes and gave a squeak of surprise.

She was face-to-muzzle with Festus.

She laughed, sat up.

Eli's side of the bed was empty, but the scent of freshly brewed coffee and the sizzle of bacon indicated that he'd gone no farther than the kitchen.

Brynne sprang out of bed, realized she was completely naked and dashed for the hook next to the shower stall in her bathroom, where her favorite chenille bathrobe hung.

She pulled it on, tied the belt at her waist and hurried barefoot out of the bedroom and along the corridor to the living room-kitchen area of the apartment.

Eli was back in his clothes, now slightly rumpled, but she knew he'd showered, because his hair was damp and he smelled of her favorite peony-scented body wash.

He stood in front of the stove, frying bacon in her cast-iron skillet.

"Morning," he said, looking back at her over one shoulder and grinning. "You might want to call in the law—I stole this bacon from downstairs. The eggs, too."

Without waiting for a reply, he inclined his head toward

the refrigerator. "Don't you eat anything besides yogurt and canned tuna?" He made a disgusted face. "What a combination."

"The tuna is for Waldo," she said.

She paused, vaguely alarmed. Festus was present, probably hoping for a bacon rainfall, but there was no sign of her cat.

"Where's Waldo?" she asked, concerned.

Eli laughed. Shook his head once.

Brynne got the joke and laughed, too, but then she went looking for her feline companion.

She found him seated majestically on the back of the couch, apparently untroubled by Festus's presence in the apartment, but not quite ready to roll out the red carpet, either.

Satisfied that the animal had not been traumatized, she returned to the kitchen and helped herself to a cup of coffee.

"Do you always cook breakfast for women you've just slept with?" she asked, faintly surprised at her own boldness. The man had melted every muscle in her body the night before, and she still felt deliciously languid.

"Only sometimes," Eli answered, spearing slices of bacon and placing them onto a plate covered by a paper towel.

"What's the deciding factor?" Brynne asked, teasing.

Using a spatula, Eli scooped scrambled eggs from a second pan into a bowl. Carried them to the table, already set for two, along with the platter of bacon.

While doing those things, he appeared to deliberate.

Finally, as he drew back a chair for Brynne, he said, "It usually means I didn't get called out to a car wreck or a bar brawl in the middle of the night."

Brynne pretended offense, though she took the chair he offered. "Well, *that's* romantic," she replied. "Does that happen a lot?"

"Getting called out in the middle of the night?" Eli asked, purposefully missing the point. "Or sleeping with a woman I might or might not cook breakfast for?"

"What do you think, Sheriff Garrett?"

Eli laughed and sank into his own chair—the one he'd taken the night before, when she'd offered him a back rub.

Brynne blushed at the memory, not out of embarrassment, but out of residual pleasure.

She waited.

So did Festus. He sat nearby, on full alert, his attention trained on the slice of bacon Eli raised to his mouth.

"Are you asking me if I sleep with a lot of women?"

Brynne said nothing. She sensed a trap.

"Because," Eli went on, after chewing thoughtfully on a bite of bacon, "if you are, I must remind you that, were I to ask *you* if you 'sleep with a lot of men,' you'd probably hand me my head."

"I don't sleep with a lot of men," Brynne said, rather primly, though it was actually none of Eli Garrett's *business* how many partners she'd had.

"I'd already figured that out," Eli said. He gestured toward her empty plate. "Eat something."

Now Brynne's pride was stung. "Strange," she said. "I could have sworn you were having a good time."

"Brynne," Eli said, "I didn't mean you seemed inexperienced. I meant, you seemed—hungry."

"So did you," Brynne pointed out.

He reached across the table, holding a strip of crisply fried bacon in front of Brynne's lips. "Eat," he repeated. "You're cranky."

"I'm *not* cranky." She took the bacon, nibbled.

"Yes, you are," Eli said reasonably. "I'd like to know why."

Suddenly, Brynne began to cry.

And that mortified her.

"Because I'm afraid we made a mistake," she admitted, drying her eyes on the soft sleeve of her robe.

Could she *be* any less sophisticated?

"If that was a mistake," Eli replied, "I'd really like to make it again."

Brynne scooped scrambled eggs onto her plate. "What if it has lasting consequences?" she asked, between bites. She needed sustenance; last night's exertions had burned a lot of fuel.

"Such as?" Eli inquired lightly. "It's pretty unlikely that you're pregnant, since you're on birth control and I used condoms."

"I wasn't referring to pregnancy," Brynne said. "I meant, what if we both regret this?"

"Speaking for myself, I can safely say I'll *never* regret last night. It was practically a near-death experience."

Brynne lightened up; now that she had some food in her stomach, she felt better. Or was it because Eli hadn't rushed out, while she slept, leaving her to wonder if he'd given her— or their lovemaking—a second thought.

"A near-death experience?" she asked. "Really?"

"Really. Wherever this thing goes or doesn't go, last night will still be the best sex I've ever had. Period."

"Well," Brynne said, almost in a whisper, "I guess that beats flowers and a thank-you note."

Eli smiled. "You'll get the flowers," he assured her. "Maybe not the note."

She laughed, which was strange because she wanted to cry again.

She wanted to, but she didn't.

"Be careful," she said. "Doris Gilford holds a black belt in gossip."

Doris ran the only floral shop in town.

Brynne went on, "Even a bouquet of flowers will have her spamming everyone on her contact list with photo evidence that something must be going on between Sheriff Garrett and the manager of a certain restaurant."

Eli, finished with his breakfast, leaned back in his chair and regarded Brynne thoughtfully, but with a gleam in his eyes. "Brynne," he said, his tone mock-reproving, "the word is out. Has been since the midnight kiss, night before last. By now, Doris and her friends are marking their calendars so they can gloat if you wind up in the maternity ward nine months from now."

He was right, Brynne realized. She'd forgotten the way of small towns after living in Boston for so long.

An unexpected chill rippled through her, taking some of the luster off the exchange with Eli.

There was another small-town meme, too.

Deaths come in threes.

Remembering the young girl found on the lot behind Russ Schafer's motel and then Freddie Lansing, Brynne gave an involuntary shiver.

"What?" Eli asked, frowning. He was *way* too perceptive, probably because his job required him to notice nuances.

"It's only superstition," Brynne said, shaking her head.

It *was*, she knew that. And yet she'd seen it happen, over and over again.

"The death-in-triplicate thing?"

Brynne nodded. "Do you believe in it?"

Eli considered the question before answering. She liked that tendency in him, although she supposed it might be frustrating at times. "In towns the size of the Creek," he finally replied, "every death gets noticed because everybody knows everybody else. Since the human brain always looks for patterns, it's easy enough to group them into threes and call it a phenomenon."

"I suppose this means you walk under ladders and refuse to throw salt over your shoulder when you spill it," Brynne teased.

He grinned, pushed back his chair, took his plate in one hand and tossed Festus a scrap of bacon. "I like to walk on the wild side," he told her. "If a black cat crosses my path, I just keep going. Straight ahead—that's the only direction I travel in, Bailey."

With that, he carried his plate to the sink, rinsed it, along with the silverware he'd used and dropped the works into the dishwasher.

Straight ahead. That's the only direction I travel in.

"No going back?" she asked, very quietly.

He came to her, bent and kissed her forehead, then her mouth. "Everything worthwhile is out ahead," he said. "Not behind."

With that, he found his car keys, summoned his dog and headed for the door.

Brynne wanted to say so many things in that moment— *Don't go—be careful—I love you.*

But her vocal chords wouldn't cooperate.

"This will probably be another long day," Eli told her, in parting. "I'll check in later."

Brynne could only nod. If she'd spoken, she would have pleaded with him to stay there, with her, and let Wild Horse County fend for itself.

Of course, he would have refused. He had a job to do, and he took it very seriously.

He left.

Brynne remembered then that *she* had a job to do as well, and it was time she got started.

She fed Waldo, who was willing to descend from his upholstered mountain now that Festus was gone, tidied the kitchen and retreated to her bathroom for a shower.

Half an hour later, she was downstairs.

Frank, the breakfast cook, was filling orders as fast as Miranda, working solo, could take and serve them.

"So," Miranda remarked, with a twinkle, "Sheriff Garrett's truck was parked out back when I came to work this morning."

Brynne, reverting to childhood when she'd been constantly underfoot in the restaurant, according to her mother and Miranda, put out her tongue.

"You and Eli?"

"It was a robbery," Brynne said, keeping a straight face. "Fortunately, no one got hurt."

"A robbery, was it?" Miranda teased. "What was taken?"

"None of your business," Brynne responded.

Since the customers were busy rehashing the latest development—Freddie Lansing's suicide—no one picked up on the little exchange.

Speculation ran rampant: some said Freddie and the dead girl, Tiffany-something, had been dating.

A young guy who worked as a lineman for the electric company scoffed at that, said Freddie was an incel.

"What," Brynne asked, "is an 'incel'?"

"Involuntary celibate," was the reply.

She turned to Miranda, who was delivering biscuits and

gravy one table over. "I'm going to have to learn a whole new language. Forget English—nobody speaks it anymore."

"Tell me about it," Miranda replied. "My grandkids talk the same way they text. OMG. WTF—I tell them they ought to get their mouths washed out with soap for *that* one."

And so it went, until the blessed lull between breakfast and lunch.

Doris Gilford arrived at five minutes after eleven, her elfin face hidden behind the massive bouquet of yellow and white roses she carried.

"These are for you," Doris announced, coming to the table where Brynne was sitting, resting her feet and sipping coffee, and plunking down the enormous crystal vase in front of her. "From Sheriff Garrett."

Brynne took a moment to breathe in the lovely scent of all those roses—twenty-four of them, unless she missed her guess—and to hide her smile from a beaming Doris.

She was a small, round woman with dyed blond hair, hit-and-miss lipstick, and very fancy fingernails.

"They're beautiful," she said. The card was tucked inside the bouquet, in a tiny envelope.

Brynne opened the card, read it, and smiled again.

The message read, "What happens at Bailey's stays at Bailey's."

CHAPTER THIRTEEN

A week after Brynne's first and wildly wonderful night with Eli, her parents called, the old-fashioned way, reaching her by the landline in her father's old office, behind the restaurant's kitchen.

"We're coming home early," Alice Bailey announced, without a "hello" or a "how are you" to pave the way. "We'll be there in less than a week!"

Brynne closed her eyes for a moment. She loved her mom and dad dearly, but she had a pretty good idea why they were returning to Painted Pony Creek two months early; they'd gotten wind that their only daughter was dating the sheriff, and they wanted to see what was going on for themselves, up close and personal.

"Brynne?" her dad prompted. "You there, honey?"

Brynne could picture them sharing a phone receiver, their heads touching, their smiles wide. "I'm here, Dad," she said, late by a beat or two. "I'm just surprised."

"I'll call Hank and have him get the house ready," Mike Bailey said. "Hope none of the pipes have frozen."

Brynne suppressed a sigh, wondering who had clued the elder Baileys in that their daughter was involved with a man and how she could murder that person—or persons—with impunity.

Her money was on Miranda, but her parents had a lot of friends, having lived in the area for so many years, and they might have gotten the memo from any one of them. Or several.

In any case, they'd liked Eli, when he and Brynne had gone together in high school; they'd mostly kept their opinions and concerns to themselves after the break-up, though they definitely hadn't liked seeing their daughter hurt.

"It's still pretty cold up here," she said.

Mike's laugh was expansive, like him. Though not overweight, or very tall, he was barrel-chested and strong as a bull. He'd helped run the bar and restaurant for as long as Brynne could remember, but he'd worked blue-collar jobs before that.

He was a good husband and father, and he'd been a wonderful provider. He loved his wife and daughter without reservation, and often joked that he was glad Brynne had taken after her mother, not him, when it came to looks.

Alice, Brynne's mother, was tall, slender and elegantly beautiful. Brynne's blond hair and dark blue eyes came from her. Alice had been a successful model once upon a time, and given up her career without a qualm when, on a ski vacation in Montana, she'd met and fallen in love with Mike Bailey, a plain young man with a prematurely receding hairline and a soul as solid as the Rocky Mountains.

He hadn't been at the lodge to ski that fateful weekend. He'd been hired to repair and maintain the machinery for the lifts, with occasional stints as a bartender when the equipment was in good working order.

He liked to say he hadn't been smart enough to know when a woman was out of his league, so when Alice meandered into the bar during one of his shifts and asked for a dirty martini with extra olives, he'd tossed the figurative customer service manual over one shoulder and asked her out.

Just like that. He'd offered her dinner and a ride in a horse-drawn sleigh, and, as he put it, *damned if that goddess in ski pants and a parka didn't say yes, on the spot.* Six months later, they'd married, pooled their savings and bought a run-down restaurant-bar in a small western town.

They'd worked hard and prospered.

If Alice ever missed her glamorous career, not to mention the money she'd earned, she never let it show. She threw herself into her marriage, the family business, the community, and when Brynne came along, a full ten years after the wedding, both Mike and Alice had been absolutely thrilled.

They'd loved their daughter wholeheartedly, but wisely, too. She'd been cherished, but they'd taken great care not to spoil her.

She'd been taught to say "please" and "thank you" from an early age. To treat other people with respect. She'd had chores to do and, because Alice had been a gifted seamstress among her other talents, she'd helped make her own clothes.

Mike, whose father had been a farrier, had supplemented the restaurant earnings by shoeing horses, and he'd often taken his young daughter along as a "helper." She'd learned to ride eventually, though, unlike her school friends Cord Hollister, J.P. McCall and Eli Garrett, she'd never been a confident rider.

In fact, when she was nine years old and riding near the main ranch house on the Hollister place with J.P. and Cord, her horse had spooked while they were crossing the creek from which the town had taken its name, and she would have drowned for sure if Cord and J.P. hadn't fished her out of the water and hauled her to the opposite bank.

All these memories and insights came to Brynne as a single concept, rather than anything linear.

Her parents were coming home early.

And while they hadn't said as much, they *surely* knew she was dating Eli.

As it was, Brynne felt as though all her private business had been plastered on a billboard for all to see. Mike and Alice— *especially* Alice—might think things between her and Eli were more serious than they were.

They tried hard to curb their enthusiasm, Brynne's parents, but there was no denying that they were eager to see her safely settled.

Any day now, Alice might start showing Brynne pictures of wedding dresses and spectacular cakes, just as she had when Brynne moved in with Clay. She'd insist that the ceremony be held in the church she and Mike had attended since they'd come to live in Painted Pony Creek, and tour venues, far and wide, for the reception.

She'd want to measure Brynne's closest friends—Shallie Hollister, Sara Worth and Brynne's college roommate, Andrea—for bridesmaids' dresses, which, of course, she would design and sew herself.

For Brynne, who would have readily admitted that she didn't have an impulsive bone in her body, the whole experience would make her feel much as she had when she'd fallen off that horse and into the creek all those years ago—swept along by a current too powerful to fight.

"Why not stay in Arizona a little longer? Till it warms up here, I mean?" she heard herself ask.

"Because we miss you," Mike boomed.

"And we've been everywhere else we want to go," added Alice.

I don't believe you, Brynne wanted to say, but didn't quite dare. *You want to see for yourselves what's happening between Eli and me and steamroll us into getting married and giving you grandchildren.*

"I've missed you, too," was what she *did* say. That, of course, was quite true; when her parents weren't trying to marry her off to the first viable candidate, they were wonderful.

"We'd like to take over Bailey's for a while, too, dear," Alice informed her daughter. "Give you some time off to enjoy yourself. Get back to your painting."

It wasn't as if running the restaurant was Brynne's life calling, but she enjoyed choosing new dishes for the menu, greeting customers, and making them comfortable and welcome. She worked hard to maintain a festive atmosphere in the place, not just at Christmas, but all year around.

Bailey's was a refuge of sorts, a place to meet with friends and family, and it was particularly appealing in winter, when Brynne made sure every customer was greeted by warmth and light, a way of literally coming in from the cold.

"Hello?" Alice prompted, though not unkindly. Alice Bailey was *never* unkind; the idea of making that small-town eatery a kind of community center had been hers, after all. She'd been the one to keep plenty of oldies available on the jukebox, to hang bright curtains at the windows and keep a never-ending stream of coffee pouring for anyone who wanted to linger.

"Sorry," Brynne said. "I guess I'm not tracking all that well. We've had a lot going on around here."

"We heard about that poor murdered girl," Mike said. "And Freddie Lansing. Sad. That's just so sad."

"How are Fred, Sr., and Gretchen holding up?" Alice asked, with genuine concern.

Another small-town phenomenon. Fred and Gretchen were universally disliked in the Creek, if not the whole of Wild Horse County, and yet practically everyone had sent a card, most enclosing a check, or planned to send flowers when the body was released and a proper funeral could be held.

The small chapel at Sweet Rest would be packed with sympathetic folks, even knowing that the Lansings would be surly, if they greeted them at all.

"Not very well," Brynne answered, however belatedly. "I took a food basket out there yesterday, but they wouldn't answer the door. I just left it on the porch."

"Good," Alice murmured. "Good that you took them food, I mean."

"At least they didn't set those darned dogs on you," Mike remarked.

Brynne wanted to sigh, but she didn't because it might have been misinterpreted. "Animal control took the dogs a few days ago," she said. "They weren't being fed properly, and there were other signs of abuse."

"Poor animals—that's awful. When is the funeral service?" Alice wanted to know.

"Sometime this week, hopefully. Technically, Freddie's death is still under investigation."

"I guess you probably know more about that than the rest of us," Mike said mildly.

Did he think Eli told her the details of the crimes he investigated?

He didn't.

"It's all public knowledge," she replied, trying not to sound annoyed. "The dead girl has been identified, at least. She was Russ and Bethanne's cousin, apparently. Grew up in Lubbock, Texas. She and Freddie met online, and it looks like she came here to see him and try to get some money out of Russ."

"Poor Russ," Alice said.

"He's taking it pretty hard," Brynne admitted. "According to Eli, he feels guilty because Tiffany died before they could get together. He would have helped her."

"Eli gives you inside information?" Alice asked hopefully.

Brynne took a deep breath, released it slowly, reminded herself how much she loved her nosy but well-meaning mother. "No," she said firmly, "he doesn't. That would be unethical, and Eli is all about ethics." A pause. "Like I said, most of this is public knowledge. The rest was probably leaked. You know how things like that work around here."

Both Mike and Alice were silent.

Finally, Alice asked, "Did this Tiffany person have family in Texas? Someone to claim her?"

"No," Brynne answered, more patiently this time. "People pitched in to pay the expenses, and Russ had her buried locally. This whole thing has really thrown him—I guess because Bethanne's almost certainly dead and Tiffany was family, even if she was a stranger."

"He still has Shallie," Mike put in. "From what I've seen, she and Cord have been mighty good to Russ. Helping him get back on his feet and all."

"Yes," Brynne said, feeling a special warmth for her friends. "They've been good to him. They really care, and given some of the stories Shallie's told me about being fostered with the Schafers, that's pretty amazing."

"Well, please remember us to Russ," Alice said. "I trust

you took him a food basket, too—the way you did for the Lansings?"

"I did." Brynne smiled sadly, though no one was there to see her expression. "Let's just say Russ was a bit more appreciative than Fred and Gretchen were. At least, he invited me in and said thank you."

"It's not about being thanked, of course," Alice reminded her daughter, who didn't need reminding. "Poor Gretchen would probably be ashamed to have visitors. I doubt that old house of theirs is in good repair."

"Neither of them will let anybody get within ten feet of the front door, even when they're not pretending to be out," Brynne said. "They turned Freddie's computer over to the sheriff's department, but it's pretty clear that they were just trying to avoid being served with a search warrant."

"What are they looking for?" Mike asked. "Eli and his people, I mean."

"I don't know, Dad," Brynne answered patiently. "Freddie was involved in some fairly extensive criminal activities before any of this stuff happened. They're probably tying up some loose ends. Checking to see if any of the people Freddie ran with had reason to force him into hanging himself."

"Awful," Alice said, with distaste. "This is just *awful*."

Mike had his own theory. "Looks to me as though Freddie struck out with that Tiffany gal. Maybe he did that thing you hear about online—catfishing. She got here, didn't like his looks, and when she rejected him, he killed her. Wouldn't be the first time something like that happened."

Brynne frowned, puzzled. "Catfishing?" she asked.

Mike was obviously pleased to fill his daughter in on modern lingo. "That's when you bait somebody online— use somebody else's photo for your profile, pretend you're a whole different person. That's catfishing. No big surprise that it ends badly most of the time."

Brynne recalled the young man she'd heard in the restaurant one recent morning, referring to Freddie as an *incel*.

An involuntary celibate.

Talk about sad.

She laughed softly, just to soften the mood. "Thanks for that, Dad. I might have gone my whole life thinking catfishing was a means of catching supper."

Mike chuckled. "We'd better get off the phone," he said. "Let you get back to running that restaurant. Your mother and I shouldn't have stuck you with the whole job."

Strangely, Brynne's throat tightened. She *liked* running Bailey's. Even loved it.

"I'm doing fine," she said. "Have you checked the Excel sheets I sent after the New Year's Eve party? We made a fortune."

"*You* made a fortune," Mike corrected her. "After taxes and expenses, Brynne, that money is yours."

"I have all the money I need," Brynne said.

Her mother clearly wasn't listening. "I just realized that there have been two deaths in the community," she said, sounding worried. "There is bound to be a third one, and soon."

"That's superstition, Mom," Brynne told her mother, echoing what Eli had said. "This is a small town and the brain looks for patterns. That's all it is."

Eli would have laughed if he'd overheard that. She'd absconded with his argument, which was priceless, since she didn't quite believe the theory herself.

They'd had it several times, in fact, at her table when they shared a meal—alas, usually breakfast—or snuggled up on

Eli's couch, between movies on Netflix. They'd ended up throwing popcorn at each other, much to Festus's delight, and laughing like a pair of fools.

And afterward?

Well, that was even more fun than throwing popcorn.

"I hope you're being careful," Alice fretted.

Brynne was momentarily startled, thinking her mother was referring to the intimacy she and Eli shared. Fortunately, she realized pretty quickly that Alice was still on the death-comes-in-threes theme.

"Always," Brynne said gently, because she knew she was everything to her parents, even as Freddie Lansing had been everything to his.

Loving another person so completely was a major risk.

After the call, Brynne left the restaurant to Miranda and Frank, since the lunch rush was still about ninety minutes out, climbed into her roadster and headed for the house on Pine Street, the modest split-level ranch she'd grown up in.

Hank, the neighbor her dad hired for occasional mainte-nance and odd jobs, was there, replacing floorboards on the front porch. A kindly man, tall and thin and blessed with a shock of steel-gray hair, stood up to greet her with a broad smile and a fairly loud, "Brynne! Did your dad send you over here to make sure I'm earning my pay?"

Brynne laughed, though she was still dealing with a mild case of shock—not only were her parents coming home early, but they planned on taking over the family business. And, while they hadn't said so outright, it hadn't sounded as if those plans were temporary.

"No." She smiled, shoving her hands into the pocket of her puffy jacket. "I'm pretty sure my dad would trust you with his life. I'm here to get some of my things from the storage shed."

"Need any help?"

Coming to the house had been, for Brynne, that rare impulsive move. She hadn't considered the volume of stuff she wanted to take home in comparison to the minisized car she drove.

Hank had a pickup truck.

"How much to have you deliver a full load of art supplies to the restaurant?"

If she was about to be unemployed, even partially, she wanted to use any extra time to sketch and paint.

"One week of free breakfast specials," Hank said, with a broad grin.

"You've got a deal," Brynne said, trudging on toward the large storage shed in her parents' backyard.

Over the next half hour, she sorted through boxes and bins, deciding which pens and brushes and paints to take and which to leave. She wanted her easels—two freestanding and one designed for a tabletop—her extensive collection of watercolor, acrylic and oil paints, blocks of expensive paper, along with the appropriate brushes, and a stack of gallery-wrapped canvas nearly as tall as she was.

Hank loaded everything into the back of his truck, being very careful about it, and hauled the works over to Bailey's, where he went the second mile by carrying everything up the stairs to Brynne's apartment and into the first spare bedroom.

Brynne helped where she could, but she mainly got in Hank's way.

He was too polite to mention that, of course.

When the job was finished, Brynne handed him a fifty-dollar bill and offered her sincere thanks.

Hank looked confused. "What about breakfast?" he asked.

"This is extra," Brynne said. "How about an early lunch?"

"Mavis packed me a lunch, like she does every morning," Hank said, reluctantly pocketing the fifty dollars. "Is there anything else that needs doing?"

Brynne smiled. "Not today. But you'd better show up for breakfast tomorrow, or I'll come looking for you. And bring Mavis—she eats for free, too."

Hank chuckled and shook his head. "You're just like your dad," he said. "Way too generous. With all the people he and Alice used to feed for free, even in the beginning, when they were trying to make a go of this place, Mavis and I used to wonder how they stayed out of the red."

"I guess the old saying is right," Brynne replied, with a soft smile. "It's more blessed to give than to receive."

"That's in the Good Book," Hank recalled.

"I know," Brynne answered.

Five minutes later, she was in the bedroom she'd reserved for Davey, feeling guilty because her art supplies took up most of the space.

She managed to shift into a better mood by assuring herself that almost three months would pass before Davey and Maddie arrived to spend their spring vacation with her. In the meantime, she would find studio space—somewhere.

For now, she had plenty to keep her busy, between the restaurant, her parents' imminent return and, of course, Eli.

Time with Eli, considering the demands of his job, was a catch-as-catch-can kind of thing, especially now that he was tying up the remaining loose ends related to the deaths of Tiffany Ulbridge and Freddie Lansing.

Judging by the rising noise level from downstairs, the lull was over and the lunch rush was underway.

Brynne put aside all thoughts of the recently, if not dearly, departed, and returned to the restaurant. In the kitchen, she washed her hands thoroughly and tied on a clean apron.

In her head, she heard her father's voice. *Time to hit the ground running, kiddo. We're burnin' daylight!*

She was still smiling when she entered the serving section of the restaurant and came face-to-face with the last person on earth she would have expected to see.

Clay Nicholls sat alone at a table in the center of the room, holding a menu and pretending to be absorbed in the selections.

The lunchtime chatter, so lively only moments before, died away completely when Brynne came in.

She stopped as suddenly as if she'd run smack into an invisible force field, blinked a couple of times, devoutly hoped she was hallucinating.

She wasn't.

Clay was there. Live and in person.

Shit.

There was nothing to do, she decided, but to brazen this thing through. Looking neither to the left nor the right, though she could feel a few dozen pairs of eyes fixed on her every move, Brynne marched over to the table, grabbed the menu out of Clay's hand and slapped it down hard on the tabletop.

"What are you doing here?"

Clay looked up at her calmly. A corner of his mouth quirked in amusement.

Brynne wanted to slap him. She really did.

"Is that how you greet all your customers?"

"No, Clay," Brynne said, her voice taut, "that's how I greet *you*. Unless Davey and Maddie are with you—and obviously they are not—you have no business being here."

"I'm only passing through, Brynne. On my way to a law enforcement seminar in Seattle."

"Sure you are," Brynne retorted, "and Painted Pony Creek, Montana, is part of a direct route between Seattle and Boston."

Miranda appeared at Brynne's side and asked quietly, "Is everything all right here?"

"Yes," Clay said.

"No," Brynne said.

"I just want to talk to you for a little while, Brynne," Clay pressed. "That's all. Make some plans for when the kids come to visit—"

"All of that could have been done by email, or over the phone," Brynne interrupted.

Clay smiled. Once, that smile had been combustible, at least to Brynne.

Now it was simply obnoxious.

"Some things should be done—and said—in person."

"And some things should just be forgotten," Brynne insisted.

"Oh, look," said Miranda, a little too loudly, craning her neck to peer past tables and booths full of paying customers to Bailey's front window. "Here's Eli."

The little bell over the door tinkled, and a rush of cold air swept over Brynne, reviving her, cooling the heat pulsing in her face.

In that moment, Brynne thought she could quite literally have heard a pin drop.

Eli caught her eye as he passed her on his way to his usual stool at the counter, but he didn't speak.

"Excuse me," Brynne told Clay, and then could have kicked herself for being polite to him.

She turned away, slipped behind the counter, grabbed the coffeepot and poured a cup for Eli.

"Is that him?" he asked quietly. Seriously.

Brynne nodded, lips pressed together so tightly that they hurt a little.

"What's he doing here?"

Brynne's eyes filled with tears of frustration and anger. "I'm not sure."

Ignoring his coffee, Eli turned on the stool and looked directly at Clay.

Miranda was still at the table, taking down Clay's order.

When Eli turned back to Brynne, he asked, "Are you all right?"

Brynne shook her head. "I need to get out of here," she whispered, feeling like a foolish child, afraid of the dark.

"Okay," Eli said reasonably. "Get your coat. I'll buy you lunch over at Sully's. About time you sized up the competition."

Brynne bit her lower lip, relaxing a little, now that an escape route had opened.

She fetched the jacket she'd worn earlier from a row of hooks beside Bailey's back door, and returned to the front of the restaurant, where Eli waited.

"I hate this," Brynne said, once she was buckled into the passenger seat of Eli's official SUV. "I feel like such a coward, running away from my own business—"

"Ease up on yourself," Eli said, checking mirrors as he reversed the SUV onto Main Street. "You're probably in shock. It'll wear off if you take time to catch your breath."

"He wasn't supposed to come out here until Davey and Maddie's school lets out for spring vacation."

"I take it he didn't bring them," Eli remarked. His tone was even. Untroubled.

"No," Brynne answered, breathing slowly and deeply. "He claims he's going to Seattle for a conference. *Clearly*, the Creek is a logical stop along the way."

"Take it easy, Brynne. You're not doing yourself any good by getting all stressed out."

"Well, that's easy for you to say!" Brynne accused, without intending to say anything of the kind. "*You* aren't the one he cheated on. *You* aren't the one whose dreams were torn down and then set on fire—"

Her voice fell away, and she sat there, in that rig that smelled pleasantly of leather, dog and Eli Garrett. She would have given anything she owned to take back what she'd just said.

"Maybe you should hear the man out," Eli suggested, very quietly, after a long interval of silence.

They were pulling into the gravel lot at Sully's Bar and Grill by then.

"There is nothing he can say that I want to hear," Brynne said miserably. "Unless it's about the kids."

"They're pretty important to you," Eli said, parking the SUV but making no move to get out. "The kids, I mean."

"*Too* important," Brynne admitted, choking up. She couldn't look at Eli just then, though she couldn't have said why. "I love them too much."

"How is that possible?" Eli asked, very gently. He didn't touch her, which was both a disappointment and a relief. "Kids are like everybody else. They need all the love they can get."

"They're *not mine*," Brynne said. "Why can't I just face that and move on with my life?"

"I don't know, Bailey. I thought you *were* moving on with your life."

Brynne covered her face with both hands, pressed her eyeballs hard with the tips of her fingers.

That hurt, so she stopped.

"I don't love Clay Nicholls," she said, "if that's what you're implying."

"Maybe you don't," Eli agreed, "but it's obvious that you haven't resolved everything where he's concerned. If you had, you wouldn't have flipped out the way you did. You wouldn't have needed to run away."

Brynne dropped her hands to her lap, clenched them into fists, slammed them once against her thighs. At last, she turned to glare at Eli.

"Now you're calling me a *coward?*"

Eli whistled once, in exclamation. It was not a happy tune. "I didn't say that," he pointed out. "You need to work through this whole Clay Nicholls thing, Brynne, with or without professional help. Until you do, or at least start making an effort, you and I will have to cool it."

"I told you, *I don't love Clay!*"

"I believe you, but you need to deal with whatever it is you *do* feel for him. I care for you *a lot*, Brynne. Maybe I even love you. But until you bury a few ghosts, I don't see us—you and me—going anywhere that would be good for us."

This was it, Brynne thought miserably.

She and Eli had barely begun to date.

Now they were breaking up.

Brynne wanted to sob, but she was too proud to do that.

The silence was thick and heavy, weighing on Brynne's spirit, causing her shoulders to droop and her head to bow.

A single tear trickled down her left cheek.

Eli, with the saddest smile Brynne had ever seen, wiped it away with the side of one thumb.

"Don't," he all but whispered, his voice was so low, hardly more than a breath. "Please."

Brynne sniffled, praying that one tear wasn't the harbinger to a torrent of ugly crying. "So, we're back to being just friends?"

"For now," Eli replied, after a long time. "I'm not angry, Brynne. I'm not jealous of that guy you dated before. You loved him. Things turned sour, and that hurt you. I understand, believe me."

"But?"

"But Clay can still rile you up, and that means you're not ready for another relationship. Not a serious one, anyway, and that's the only kind I want. I don't do anything by halves, Brynne. I'm either in, or I'm out. Nothing in between."

He sounded so calm. So sad.

And his mind was made up.

He didn't want her.

All that they'd shared in their short relationship was for nothing. They hadn't *been* in a relationship, not really.

They'd had a fling, and it was over. Just like that.

Festus, who had been sitting in the back seat all along, made his presence known.

He gave a single, despairing whimper, and Brynne's heart fractured like shattered glass.

CHAPTER FOURTEEN

"Are you *insane*?" Sara asked, slamming a cup of hot coffee down in front of Eli so hard that some of the brew spilled onto her kitchen table.

Festus, curled up beside Eli's chair, made a disconsolate whining sound.

Eli opened his mouth, intending to reply that he was probably as sane as he'd ever been, but Sara didn't give him a chance to speak, so he closed it again. Less chance of sticking his foot in it that way, he supposed.

"Brynne's ex-lover shows up, out of nowhere, she *understandably* freaks out and what do *you* do? *You*, in your infinite masculine wisdom, swing right up onto your high horse and *break things off*."

Festus whined again.

Eli sighed. "I didn't exactly 'break things off.' I only told her that she probably wasn't ready for anything serious." He paused, cleared his throat. Suddenly, his previous reasoning didn't seem as solid as it had before. "It's not like I was judging her, Sara."

"Idiot," Sara said, hauling back a chair and falling into it. "Of *course* you were judging her! She got a shock—a pretty nasty one from the sounds of it—and instead of trying to understand that, you decided she was wrong to react the way she did. How *dare* you assume you know what Brynne is or isn't ready for? She's a *grown woman*, Eli, not the teenager you dated in high school!"

Eli sat back in his chair, released a long breath. He was, for the present, at a loss for words.

Sara was on a roll. "You couldn't have just put your arms around her? Held her?"

Eli found his voice. "If Brynne wanted holding, she has an odd way of showing it. She was *furious*."

"*With Clay Nicholls*, you damn fool!" Sara said. "I don't blame her one bit. Imagine, just showing up in somebody's life like that? Clearly, there was no text, no phone call, nothing! Brynne is minding her own business and *wham!*" She slapped her hands together, hard, making both Eli and Festus flinch. "There he is, landing at her feet like a hand grenade with the pin pulled!"

Eli shoved a hand through his hair. "You weren't there," he reminded his sister quietly. "When I said Brynne was furious, I meant *with me*. She got her back up and asked me if I was calling her a coward for running away."

"I know what happened, Eli," Sara said, very slowly, as though speaking to someone born without a brain. "You just told me. You jumped to a lot of conclusions, it seems to me, and I just hope you haven't blown your chances with Brynne. *Again*."

That *again* stung. Sara was referring, of course, to the stupid decision he'd made in high school, dumping Brynne so he could fool around with Reba. Was he *ever* going to get past that ancient tom-fuckery?

It hadn't been anything dramatic; he'd simply stopped calling Brynne, stopped passing her notes, walking her home after class, that kind of thing.

Yeah, he'd been a mega jerk.

He'd also been *seventeen*.

He said as much to Sara, who was not appeased.

"And now you're nearly thirty-five. What's your excuse *this* time?"

"You," Eli said stiffly, "are not being helpful." He pushed back his chair, stood. He had a meeting with Dan Summers in his office in fifteen minutes to go over the information Dan had culled from Freddie Lansing's personal laptop.

"Call Brynne, Eli. Apologize. If she's willing to speak to you again, then *listen* and keep your slapdash psychological insights to yourself."

Eli bent, kissed his sister lightly on the top of her head. "Interesting speech, Sara. Especially coming from a woman so burned-out on men that she won't even have coffee with a guy, let alone risk loving one."

"Get out," Sara said, still testy. "I don't want to talk to you right now, Eli. In fact, I want to do you bodily harm!"

"Since you have access to a Glock, I won't argue."

Festus was already pressing his nose to the back door. Poor critter wasn't used to this much human interaction.

He wanted to escape, and so did Eli.

So he left, feeling more frustrated and more confused than when he'd arrived.

Brynne had fled to her apartment when Eli dropped her off behind the restaurant, without giving him so much as a backward glance.

Upstairs, she'd rushed into her bathroom, splashed her face repeatedly with cold water and combed her hair.

Only then, having gathered her dignity around her like a blanket, did she go downstairs.

Clay was gone.

The lunch rush had slowed to a crawl, and the few customers occupying the tables and booth were late arrivals, having missed the drama.

Miranda sat at the far end of the counter, next to the jukebox, playing one of her endless games of solitaire. Frank, the fry cook, was washing glasses behind the bar.

"He left?" she asked Miranda, in a low voice.

"You mean that handsome fella from Bean Town?" Miranda countered lightly. "Yeah, he's gone. Had to get back to Kalispell and catch a plane."

"That's it?" Brynne almost hissed. "He just drops in here, wrecks everything and then *leaves*?"

"He said he'd call or text later," Miranda said, her tone noncommittal. "*Where* is that damn four of spades?"

"The bastard," Brynne said.

Miranda looked up, smiled. "A bastard he may be, but he's a good-looking one, that's for sure. Doesn't measure up to the sheriff, of course, but he's mighty easy on the eyes, just the same."

"He's a liar and a cheat!" Brynne found a cloth and began scrubbing at a nonexistent spot on the counter.

Miranda sighed heavily. "Unfortunately, that's the way some men are."

Brynne stopped rubbing at the invisible spot and rested her elbows on the counter, covering her face with both hands. "I've ruined everything, Miranda," she said, in despair. "I blew up at Clay, in front of God and everybody, and now Eli thinks I'm still hung up on the guy!"

"Are you?" Miranda asked, very gently.

"No!"

"Then why so much anger? You've always been so cool, calm and collected—like your mother. Today, I saw a whole other side of you, Brynne. A stranger."

"First Eli lectures me, now you. I'm a *human being*, with feelings."

"I'm not lecturing you, honey," Miranda said, resting a hand over Brynne's. "Of course you're human and of course you have feelings. But in all the years I've known you—since you were knee-high to a lawn sprinkler—I've never seen you so upset."

Brynne wanted to cry again, but she managed to stem the flow. After all, she was no weakling, and she was country proud. She raised her face from her hands and looked directly at Miranda.

"What should I do now?" she asked the older woman, in a very small voice.

Miranda smiled, squeezed Brynne's hand again. "*Nothing*," she replied kindly. "Nothing whatsoever. Wait. Think things through. If you keep your head, well, when it's time for the next step, you'll know *exactly* what to do."

Brynne drew a deep, restorative breath, let it out again. "Thanks, Miranda," she said.

"Hey," Miranda replied, still smiling. "I promised your mom I'd look after you while she and your dad were away. I'm a woman of my word."

Brynne leaned across the counter to plant a quick kiss on Miranda's cheek. Then, straightening, she told her friend about the phone call from her parents. Between picking up her art supplies from the shed in their backyard, the unexpected confrontation with Clay and the subsequent disastrous conversation with Eli, she'd forgotten to mention it.

Miranda was clearly pleased that Mike and Alice were coming home early; like pretty much everyone else, she'd missed them and, she'd complained more than once that was tired of the cold weather and wanted to spend a few weeks with her sister, down in San Miguel de Allende. Soak up some sunshine, enjoy some true Mexican cuisine, she'd often said, and stop thinking that two people had died recently, within mere days of each other, and there was bound to be another death to round things out.

"You really believe that?" Brynne asked. "That deaths come in threes?"

"Around here," Miranda said, "they do."

Brynne thought about Eli's theory, but she saw no point in outlining it for Miranda.

Mostly because she didn't want to let Eli occupy any real estate in her head.

She did miss Festus, though.

"I've always thought so, too," she finally confessed. "But it does seem like superstition, doesn't it?"

"Call it what you will," Miranda said, gathering her dog-eared deck of cards and tucking them into an equally battered box. "I've lived in this town all my life, and I've seen it happen over and over again."

"But isn't it possible that, well, our minds just automatically sort deaths into groups of three?"

Miranda sighed, stood up, straightened her apron. Her shift would be over soon, and she'd leave for the little house on Willow Road, where she had lived since birth. When she wasn't at work, or at church, she holed up in the shed behind her house and spun clay into pots and vases, plates and bowls.

She lived alone—had never married—and Brynne wondered if, as busy as she kept herself, she ever got lonely.

From there, it wasn't a big leap to imagining *herself* as an older woman, living in the Pine Street house, like her parents before her, splashing paint onto canvases or watercolor paper.

No husband, no children. Just herself, and maybe a dog, or a few dozen cats, whiling away the sunset years of her life.

Much as she loved painting—not to mention dogs and cats—the image saddened her deeply.

Caught up in that revelry, she still managed to shift her imagination to another scenario entirely—herself, but this time, with Eli. Both of them aging, comfortable with each other. In this version of the future, they had grown children, and grandchildren, too, though Brynne didn't see them in her mind's eye.

She only saw herself, silver-haired, happy, and Eli, also gray, but still as strong and able as ever.

Before she could succumb to another emotional meltdown—was she premenstrual, or what?—Brynne took charge of herself and focused on doing the next right thing, which was to help Frank restock the shelves of liquor behind the bar.

The evening waitresses, Sally and Joan, arrived, and Miranda went home.

Harry replaced Frank in the kitchen and, when necessary, behind the bar.

Brynne retreated to her apartment, fed a loudly meowing Waldo and took a long, hot shower.

Afterward, she dressed in her oldest pair of jeans and a raggedy T-shirt, went into the guest room where her art supplies were stored, found a midsize canvas and propped it up on the giant easel.

It was bad planning, she supposed, to start playing with acrylic paint in such a close space—the easel was wedged in between the bed she'd bought for Davey and a chest of drawers, and the floor was carpeted—but she needed color, and plenty of it.

For as long as she could remember, Brynne had hungered for bright splashes of color, woven them like broad, gleaming ribbons into the very fabric of her soul.

She brushed a magenta stripe across the center of the canvas, then a turquoise one, followed by a splash of vibrant orange.

Soon, she was happily lost, and the only image occupying her mind was the one in front of her.

It took a while to shake off the distractions—seeing Brynne so undone by the presence of a man she'd clearly loved, listening to Sara declare him the official village idiot—but by the time he'd reached the office, sat himself down in the chair behind his desk and gone through a sheaf of messages, Eli was back in work mode.

Dan arrived right on time, bringing coffee from a drive-through joint, and Eli was grateful for the java. It was better than the often-scorched stuff he usually drank on the job. Connie firmly maintained that she'd been hired as a dispatcher and receptionist, not a waitress, and Melba was equally adamant: she wasn't going to brew a single pot of coffee unless the male deputies took their fair turns.

All this distilled down to the unfortunate fact that only Amos Edwards, the lowest man on the totem pole, *ever* attempted to brew the sludge he called coffee.

Everyone else, including Eli, tolerated the stuff.

Thus, he welcomed the brand-name concoction Dan brought in.

The big man took a seat across from Eli, popped the little tab on his own cup and took a cautious sip. Then he made a satisfied sound and grinned.

"Melba hates it when I do that," he said happily.

Eli grinned. "Speaking of your better half, how's the reconciliation coming along? I'd ask her myself, but she hasn't been in the greatest mood since we found Freddie Lansing hanging from a rafter in that old barn."

"Thing like that'll ruin a person's day, all right," Dan observed. He was being cagey; the gleam in his eyes told Eli that much.

"You don't want to talk about it. Fair enough."

"You could always ask Melba."

"Not without getting my lips torn off, I can't."

Dan gave his thunderous laugh. "My woman's got fire in her, and that's the God's truth."

"You love her." It was a statement, not a question.

And Brynne played on the edge of Eli's mind, like a wildcat circling just beyond the reach of the firelight.

"Hell, yes," Dan said. "Worst mistake I ever made was choosing the Bureau over her and our kids. I had my head stuck square up my ass."

"Why *did* you choose the Bureau?" Eli pressed, knowing he was on private ground, but wanting to know badly enough to risk it.

"I was stupid, that's why," Dan told him. There was no trace of his usual humor in his eyes or his facial expression. "Thought I was a hotshot. I was going to prove I could make a real difference. Run with the big dogs, and take down my share of the sons of bitches who think it's their God-given right to trample anybody who gets in their way. Kidnappers. I had a *real* justice boner for them—the ones that stole children and did the rotten things they do to them. I wanted to be their own *special* boogeyman."

He felt silent. Looked away for a long moment.

Then he said. "I still feel that way. I've got two daughters, Eli, and if anybody tried to hurt either of them—"

"I know," Eli said quietly. "What changed your mind, made you take up private security?"

"Turns out, the Bureau was all stocked up on superheroes. They wanted paper pushers, mostly. Computer guys. It wasn't one damn bit exciting—in fact, all it did was make me regret leaving Melba and our kids even more than I already did."

"So now you hack your way through jungles and tangle with drug cartels? For the excitement?"

"*Hell*, no," Dan answered. "I did it for the money. Now I've got enough put aside to give my lady and the girls everything they could possibly want. I'm ready to retire—at least from the kind of work I've been doing for the last few years. Ready to get married to Melba again, maybe father a couple more kids."

"Melba isn't buying that scenario?"

Dan sighed. "She told me what I could do with my 'blood' money," he said. "She doesn't want to get pregnant, either." He leaned forward, his face earnest. "Just tell me one thing, Bro. What the devil do women *want*?"

Eli laughed. It was a raw sound, revealing more than he would have liked. "Whatever we don't happen to be offering at the time, I guess," he said. A long pause followed, then Eli tapped his fingers on the surface of his cluttered desk. "Tell me what Freddie Lansing's been up to out there in cyberspace."

Dan took a fairly thick sheaf of papers from his briefcase and pushed them across the desk to Eli.

"Read. We'll talk when you're done," he said.

Eli took a bracing sip of coffee and read.

As he scanned out the printouts of Freddie's emails and random posts on various websites, he felt a combination of pity, disgust and horror.

Freddie hadn't been just bad, he'd been downright *evil*.

Like most incels—or "nice guys" as many social misfits called themselves—Freddie had had no interpersonal skills whatsoever.

He'd pursued random women—and sometimes girls—all over the web. He'd invited complete strangers to move in with him, to live in his boyhood room, going so far as to list extensive requirements: virgins only, no vegans, no religious or political types, no one taller than five-five or weighing more than a hundred and thirty pounds.

And those were only the beginning of his delusional demands.

He would accept certain races—how noble of him—but absolutely refused others. His prospective wife/woman would cook him three meals a day, keep his clothes clean, know how to cut his hair and follow his orders without question.

Eli's stomach turned; he took a chance and swallowed more coffee in hopes of keeping his vending-machine lunch down.

Dan must have read the revulsion in his face. "Wait till you see his profile pictures," he said. "You're not going to be happy."

Eli flipped through the pages and found the photos Freddie had used as bait.

He was stunned to see his own much-younger face looking back at him.

He spat a raspy curse.

Then he sat back in his chair and closed his eyes, fighting down a rage the likes of which he'd never experienced before.

That monster had used his face—*his face*—to troll social media for victims, some of them mere children.

"I took them all down, Eli," Dan said, his voice a low rumble, like thunder rolling in over the plains. "The pictures, I mean. And from what I could figure out, nobody took the bait—except Tiffany Ulbridge."

Eli murmured a word he wouldn't have said aloud.

"It's all there, in those printouts," Dan went on. "When Tiffany got here and met up with Freddie—the real Freddie—she was thoroughly pissed off. She'd been catfished, come a very long way to hook up with you in your early twenties. My guess is, she told him off, and he, being your typical nice-guy, wasn't *about* to finish last—so he shot her."

Eli nodded, turned the pages of profile photos facedown on the desktop and finished reading Freddie's posts.

He'd gone into the blackest fury imaginable, splattered the dark web with vile insults directed at Tiffany but striking, like shrapnel, at all women.

No, he hadn't confessed to killing her.

But he *had* wished her dead, her and every other woman who had ever rejected him.

There must have been hundreds of them.

"So you definitely think Freddie murdered Tiffany Ulbridge?" Eli asked, weary to the marrow of his bones.

It was at times like this that he wished he'd chosen another line of work, one that didn't involve battling the absolute scum of the earth. He'd have made a good carpenter, for instance. He was halfway decent at training horses, though he lacked

Cord's almost supernatural talent. Hell, at the moment, he would have gladly flipped burgers or tended bar.

Trouble with that reasoning was, *somebody* had to stand in the breach and block the flow of darkness as best they could. As controversial as being an officer of the peace was in this notch of history, as ineffectual as Eli and many other cops felt sometimes, what would the world be like without good cops—and the vast majority of them *were* good—always ready and willing to fight the common and uncommon evils that would otherwise creep over the whole human race like black mold.

The objective, Eli knew, was overwhelming. Even impossible: a fool's quest. Don Quixote in an SUV with a badge painted on the side.

And yet, like that crazy knight of old, Eli had to keep tilting at windmills, if only because occasionally—*just* occasionally—his lance happened to strike down a monster instead.

Whether he liked it or not, that was his calling.

He had no choice but to live it.

"Some of the reports are back from the lab in Kalispell," Eli said, rallying himself from the mental mire he'd stumbled into, reading Freddie's ravings and considering the futility of confronting yet more evil.

"Fill me in," Dan said.

"The gun—the one we found in the barn, on that cot—was definitely used to kill Ms. Ulbridge. Ballistics matched."

"Okay," Dan replied. "What about prints?"

"No prints. Freddie must have wiped the thing down."

"Any gunpowder residue on his hands or clothes?"

Eli shook his head. "According to Sam Wu, over at Alec's office, before he hanged himself, Freddie took a shower. Dressed himself in clean clothes."

"Fairly typical for suicides," Dan affirmed.

"Yeah," Eli said thoughtfully. "But something about this bothers me, Dan," he confided. "It's almost *too* clear-cut. Last week, when I went to tell Fred, Sr., and Gretchen that their boy was dead, I had this odd sense that I was missing something. And I'm not over that."

"You going to Freddie's funeral?"

"Yes," Eli replied. "But not as a mourner. The Lansings would probably lose it if I showed up for the ceremony, so I'll be watching from the director's office, via the security cameras."

"Any chance I could join you? A second pair of eyes can't hurt."

"I would be grateful if you did," Eli answered.

Dan raised his bulky, muscular self to his feet. "I'll be there," he said.

"I'll be in touch with the details," said Eli. "We have to use the back way. Like I said, Fred, Sr., and Gretchen would not be pleased to see us there. In their minds, I'm the cause of all Freddie's problems. If I'd just let him alone, etc., etc."

Dan's nod was solemn and sympathetic. "I'll be waiting," he said. Then he smiled sadly. "It'll be good to get out of the house for a while—even if it's for a funeral."

"Melba giving you that hard a time?"

Dan rolled his eyes. "She's being *nice* to me, at least when the girls are around. I told her she's not fooling them—they're smart kids—but she pours it on anyway. When they're at school, she's at work, but if we happen to find ourselves in the same room at the same time—and she does her best to avoid that—she treats me like something stuck to the bottom of her shoe."

Eli sighed, stood up to walk Dan to the outside door.

"This is a standoff," he said. "Two stubborn people, nose to nose, each of them refusing to give an inch of ground."

Dan gave him a challenging look. "From what I hear, you speak from experience, my friend."

Eli shoved a hand through his hair, frustrated. "Exactly what did you hear?"

"That Brynne's former squeeze turned up at Bailey's and she had a meltdown. Given your current low mood, I'd say you won't be winning any prizes for diplomacy in the near future."

"Holy crap," Eli breathed. "Is this whole damn *town* wired for sound?"

Dan laughed. "Yeah," he said. "The drums started beating when you and Brynne left the restaurant together and she came back alone."

"Sometimes I feel like I'm walking around with one of those cartoon thought bubbles over my head. Today, it says, 'Yep, good ole Eli Garrett screwed up again.'"

As they passed the reception desk, Connie made a point of pretending not to listen. She stared at her computer screen, fingers thumping busily on the keyboard.

Eli respected Connie; she was a valuable employee, always cool in the face of an emergency. He was pretty sure she was also an inveterate gossip, though he couldn't prove it.

Gossip or not, Connie was a professional, and any news she leaked would be carefully vetted first, lest an investigation or a case be compromised.

Still, Eli regretted the thought-bubble remark because she'd definitely heard it.

Hell, she probably knew more about his life than he did.

Dan said his goodbyes and left. Eli went to the community coffeepot, saw the black dregs of the last brewing and sighed.

He changed out the basket, replacing the used grounds with fresh.

Then he rinsed and filled the pot and started a new batch.

Connie was grinning when he turned around to face her.

"You're learning, Sheriff. I'm proud of you."

"That makes one person in the universe," Eli replied, weary again. He really needed more coffee, having finished the cup Dan brought while exploring the horrors of Freddie Lansing's mind.

"You need a vacation," Connie announced. "Or maybe a honeymoon?"

"Not you, too," Eli lamented.

"That thought bubble you were talking about? It usually reads, 'I'm so in love with Brynne Bailey, I can't see straight.'"

"Off-limits, Connie. I'm not discussing Brynne with you."

"Fine," Connie said sweetly. "I don't mind telling you that I'm dating somebody new."

That caught Eli's attention. Connie had been divorced for five years, and she was married to her job. Said so herself, constantly.

"That's the first good news I've heard all day," Eli said. "Who's the lucky man?"

"You'll be surprised."

"I've been surprised a lot lately. Go ahead, spring it on me."

"Russ Schafer."

Eli *was* surprised. He'd had Russ pegged as something of a nice-guy, without all the creepy stuff. Or the aversion to taking showers.

"Don't judge me," Connie warned. "Or Russ."

"I'm not," Eli replied, raising one hand, as if to swear an oath.

"He's really smart, you know. He's designed an app that would blow your mind, and he's negotiating a deal to sell it."

He had all that fancy equipment, and he'd mentioned coding.

No word of a girlfriend, though.

"So you're after his money?" Eli teased.

"We've been seeing each other for weeks," Connie said. "I fell for Russ *before* he told me about the app."

"It must have been hard for you when we were questioning him about Tiffany Ulbridge," he ventured.

"It was," she admitted. "But I knew he was innocent. Russ has been depressed for years—who wouldn't be, with the up-bringing he had?—but he'd never murder anyone. Especially not a blood relative."

"I'm happy for you, Connie," Eli said. "I really am."

"I know. And I'd like to be happy for you, but you seem to have your head up your butt where a certain woman is concerned."

Eli raised both hands. "I meant it when I said I wasn't going to talk about Brynne. It's personal."

Connie smiled. "No problem. I'll just keep an eye on the old thought bubble, see if you come to your senses."

"Why is it," Eli asked pointedly, "that everybody in this town seems to think my love life is in the public domain?"

"So you *do* have a love life. Hallelujah!"

"Connie."

"All right, all right. I get it. You're the strong, silent type, keeping your own counsel."

"My business is just that—*my business*. Not yours. Not the town's."

"Got it," Connie said, sounding just a touch too perky for Eli's taste.

Behind him, the coffee machine chortled, releasing a delicious fragrance.

Eli said no more. He retreated to his office and closed the door.

Spent the next twenty minutes rereading the printouts, scouring every email, every post.

Something nibbled at the edge of his mind, just out of reach.

What was it?

What was he missing?

He finally gave up, went back to the front office, poured himself a cup of coffee.

"Why the frown?" Connie asked.

He told her.

There was something there, in the Freddie-Tiffany situation, that he couldn't get hold of.

"Relax," Connie said. "Let it come to you."

That was good advice, Eli supposed.

If only he could follow it.

CHAPTER FIFTEEN

The art frenzy lasted until after dark, when Waldo eased through the partially open bedroom door and, purring, curled himself around Brynne's ankles as if peeling an orange in reverse. His whiskers tickled her bare feet.

He was definitely hungry.

Brynne glanced at her phone, propped on the dresser top, and realized two things—time had definitely gotten away from her, and several texts had come in while she was working.

Quitting time.

She dropped her brushes into a plastic coffee container filled with water and reserved for the purpose, letting them soak until she could clean them properly. Unlike watercolors, acrylic paints couldn't be washed away in the sink without catastrophic damage to the plumbing.

Making her way toward the kitchen, careful not to trip over a still-winding cat, Brynne cleaned her hands with disposable wipes, then washed them under running water.

She fed Waldo and refilled his water bowl, then returned to her improvised studio to reclaim her phone with clean hands.

While deciding what she wanted for dinner, she thumbed open the texts and read them in order.

From Clay: Brynne, I'm sorry for dropping in unexpectedly the way I did. I just wanted to see for myself if you were open to giving things a second try. Clearly, you aren't, and I'll respect your wishes. Again, I apologize for intruding in your life.

From Sara: If you need to talk, I'm here.

From Davey: Dad says he came to visit you and you weren't happy to see him so he's going to leave you alone from here on out. Will you still be happy to see Maddie and me, if we come to spend part of spring vacation with you?

Finally, from Eli: I was wrong, and I'm sorry.

Tears burned behind Brynne's eyes, and she pressed her lips together to keep from breaking down again.

She brewed a cup of tea, plunked herself down at the table, and pressed the buttons that would connect her with Clay.

He sounded confused when he answered, "Brynne?"

"You're right," she said, not unkindly. "It's over between us. I appreciate your apology, but I think I need to say sorry, too. You caught me off guard, and I reacted like a crazy person."

Clay was quiet for a long time. "The kids are worried that you'll uninvite them, come spring."

"I know," Brynne said. "I'm calling them next. They are definitely still welcome here. In fact, I can barely wait to pick them up at the airport."

Clay expelled a long, relieved breath. "Their aunt Elle—Heather's sister—is a flight attendant. She'll arrange to escort them as far as Kalispell. That way, you won't have to deal with their fool of a father."

"You've made mistakes. So have I. Let's agree to wish each other well and move on with our lives."

You talk a good game, Brynne Bailey, scoffed a voice in her mind, *but can you go after what you really want, or are you going to keep on camping out in the past like you've been doing since you left Boston?*

Do you even know *what you want?*

Brynne sighed, looked down at her clothes and smiled. She looked as though she'd covered the studio/guest room floor in gallons of paint, then rolled in it.

Yeah, she knew what—and whom—she wanted.

But did she have the courage to move beyond her fears and doubts and go for it?

Fortunately, she didn't have to decide tonight. Or tomorrow. Or next week.

There was no rush.

"Thanks, Brynne. For getting back to me, I mean. I've been kicking myself ever since I left Painted Pony Creek." Clay paused, cleared his throat. "It's a beautiful place, by the way."

"It is," Brynne said. For the first time since her return, she felt truly at home.

She *belonged* right here, in this place, with these people, and knowing that for certain was a powerful blessing. Now she could plant her feet, square her shoulders and go forward into all that awaited her.

There would be joy, and sorrow.

Wins and losses.

All the polarities that make up a human life, fully lived.
And she was ready.

Or, at least, she *thought* she was.

After speaking with Clay, she put through a call to Davey
and Maddie, told them the visit was very much on. Mentally,
she bedecked every limb of every maple and oak tree along
Main Street in bright yellow ribbons, just for them.

Sara received a text. I'm okay. Honestly. We'll get together
soon.

By then, she'd dealt with everyone in her text list except
Eli.

And she didn't know quite what to say to him.

She couldn't help wondering if he'd been projecting when
he'd told her she wasn't ready for a relationship. Maybe *he*
wasn't ready, and hadn't realized it yet.

Furthermore, as sheriff of Wild Horse County, with two
recent deaths on the books, technically unresolved, he was
understandably distracted.

On the other hand, he *had* apologized, and she didn't want
to leave him hanging, if only because she'd been wrong, as
well. She'd seen Clay sitting at a table in her restaurant, gone
from zero to a hundred in about two seconds and behaved
like a hormonal teenager.

So she opened Eli's text and replied. I'm sorry, too. Let's step
back for a few days—at least until after the Lansing funeral—
and then take another run at acting like grown-ups.

Immediately, the small, flickering dots appeared, indicat-
ing an imminent response.

Brynne waited.

A smile curved her mouth when his answer came through.

I'm all for acting like grown-ups. Together. But I'll settle for a fighting chance to get back in your good graces. Text me when I can grovel properly.

Her reply was a single emoji: thumbs-up.

Eli and Dan watched the proceedings from the spacious office Alec and Sam shared with Pete Gilford, the funeral director and, conveniently, only son of the local florist. The surveillance cameras were state-of-the-art, taking in the corridors, lab and autopsy room.

These days, of course, there were cameras everywhere, which was mainly a good thing, in most cases. Here, it fell on the side of creepy.

Too bad there were no lenses trained on that vacant lot behind Russ's motel, where Tiffany Ulbridge had died brutally and far ahead of her time, or the inside of that abandoned barn, where they'd found Freddie Lansing dangling from a rafter.

The shots Dan had found online of that place were all stills—the backpack, the cot, the chinks of sunlight showing through the plank walls.

Eli sighed, realizing he was about to chase yet another white rabbit down yet another hole, and returned his attention to the monitor, and the separate panel—one of several—showing the chapel.

Doris's tasteful arrangements occupied every tabletop there and in the viewing room, and covered Freddie's gleaming fiberglass coffin like a blanket of snow.

Most of the folding chairs were filled, though there was a barrier of empty space beside and behind Fred, Sr., and the Mrs.

Eli studied their grieving faces closely, bothered again, as he had been the night he'd gone out to their place and told them what had happened to their only son.

He'd taken Connie's advice, tried to quit digging and think of other things, but it hadn't helped. Whatever he was looking for, it was so subtle as to elude the senses, quite possibly a faint impression or subliminal insight.

The community of Painted Pony Creek had really come through for Fred, Sr., and Gretchen, leaving food on their porch, collecting donations for the coffin and burial plot in the town cemetery, showing up for the service.

He spotted Sara, sitting with Eric, Shallie, Cord and J.P.

Brynne came down the aisle, wearing a soft-looking navy blue dress and a white straw hat with a matching band. Fred, Sr., turned in his seat to glare at her, and she nodded politely, taking a seat beside Eric.

Other locals trailed in—Miranda, a longtime fixture at Bailey's and in the town in general. Deputy Amos Edwards and his wife, Alec and Sam Wu and Alec's physician daughter, Marisol.

Ranchers and farmers came, along with a contingent from Sully's Bar and Grill and even a half dozen of the thugs Freddie had hung out with at the pinnacle of his criminal career, such as it was.

Most of these people were there out of simple kindness, not affection for Freddie, his memory or his parents. At least a few had come for a whole different reason—to see for themselves that young Mr. Lansing was in the box.

Not that the casket was open. Freddie wasn't looking his best these days; the flowers, in Eli's opinion, might well be there to hold the lid down.

Once again, he returned his attention to Fred, Sr., and Gretchen.

They looked sad, no doubt about that.

They also looked angry.

Fury buzzed around them, a discernible vibration, nearly audible.

Mr. Lansing's face was ravaged with grief, wet with tears he probably wasn't aware of shedding, but he *exuded* hatred. Gretchen looked even angrier, but her eyes were dry, focused like lasers on her son's casket.

Maybe she'd already cried all the tears she had inside her.

Whatever state she was in, Eli wouldn't have been surprised if she leaped to her feet, whirled on the gathering of dutifully sympathetic folks and screeched at them like a banshee. She must have known, after all, that they weren't there because they missed Freddie; they'd come because it was the right thing, the kind thing, to do.

Given the boy's track record, it was hard to imagine how Gretchen—or her husband—could expect anything more.

And there he went again, expecting folks like them to be reasonable.

Never gonna happen.

"I'm going to be real glad when this is over," Dan said, without looking away from the monitor. His eyes moved constantly from one panel to another. "Those are two of the worst people I've ever run across—and *that*, my friend, is saying something—but damned if I don't feel sorry as hell for them."

"I know what you mean," Eli agreed. His gaze had strayed back to Brynne; she was stunningly beautiful, even in the gloomy light of a funeral home chapel, and the sight of her was soothing. Just by being there, she tamed something wild inside him, something reckless and primitive.

Dan wasn't done talking. "I almost wish I'd stayed with the kids. This is your case, after all, not mine."

Eli knew Melba was on duty, so her mother must be looking after the children, and probably Hayley, too.

"You've been a lot of help," Eli assured Dan. "Write up an invoice and I'll put in a requisition with the county auditor, so you can get paid."

Dan waved a hand the size of a bear claw and said dismissively, "This one's on me. You want to pay me back, put in a good word for me with Melba. That woman is out-and-out cussed. The more I try to convince her I've mended my ways, the more she gives me the stink eye and tells me to back off."

Eli allowed himself the brief semblance of a grin. "Remind me never to piss that woman off."

His gaze kept straying back to Brynne, and she must have felt it, because she turned her head and looked directly into one of the cameras. Her eyes were clear and still.

As if he'd actually been caught staring, Eli steered his attention back to the Lansings, then the little cluster of juvenile delinquents sitting in the last row of folding chairs. They wore worn leather jackets, dirty jeans, dark hoodies and smug-ass attitudes.

They'd run with Freddie, but the closest they'd probably come to mourning a supposed friend was being glad he was in the coffin, instead of one of them.

Eli decided to keep an eye on that motley crew, not because he thought they'd been involved in either Tiffany's death or Freddie's, but because of the attitudes. If they planned on disrupting the service in any way, he'd shut that shit down in a heartbeat.

The funeral director's wife, Marion, took her place at the organ.

Her husband went to stand behind the podium. He adjusted the mic, and it emitted a shrill squeal.

The mourners sat up straighter in their folding chairs, hands resting in their laps.

Fred, Sr., and Gretchen stared stonily at the plain wooden cross behind the long table that resembled an altar, but wasn't.

There were seven churches in Painted Pony Creek, but the Lansings weren't members of any of them.

Eli decided he was being unnecessarily judgmental, since he hadn't signed up, either. It wasn't that he didn't believe in God—in his estimation, there *had* to be some kind of benevolent force in the world, if only to counterbalance the obvious evil.

Sara was a semi-regular churchgoer, and she'd brought Eric and Hayley up to attend Sunday school and join in various youth-group activities. The folks had said they had to learn the basics but when they were old enough to make up their own minds, they would be free to stay or go.

Sara had stayed, Eli had gone, not out of rebellion, but because he'd preferred the seat of a saddle to the hard pews at the Creek's staid Presbyterian church. He'd ridden or gone fishing or skied, depending on the season and, being out in the open, alone or with J.P. and Cord, had seemed like a form of worship in its own right.

Pete Gilford didn't preach a sermon, and when it came time to extol the virtues of the deceased, he came up dry. He cleared his throat a lot, and shifted his weight from one foot to the other, landing his gaze purposefully on the Lansings several times, only to have it bounce away again.

He was an old hand at conducting funerals, of course, and his performance was usually fairly smooth. Today, though, he couldn't seem to get it right, no matter how hard he tried.

He had no choice but to stumble his way through, and

Eli felt almost as sorry for him as he did for Fred, Sr., and Gretchen.

Pete invited anyone who wished to speak to come to the podium.

No one stepped up.

Eli watched his nephew fidget beside Sara, then lower his head.

The boys in the back nudged each other and smirked, but none of them chose to approach the podium, which was probably a very good thing.

Embarrassed by the lack of response, Gilford swallowed a couple of times and then began his wrap-up. He unfolded a sheet of plain notebook paper, adjusted his glasses, cleared his throat again.

He read a prayer, perhaps provided by the Lansings, though they most likely weren't the praying kind. By the way Gretchen glared at that wooden cross behind the director, she was no fonder of God than she was of anybody else.

The organist played a recessional.

Fred, Sr., and Gretchen rose and stalked down the aisle, grudgingly taking up their position beside the door.

People rose, shuffled out, shaking their hands, saying they were sorry for their loss, the usual stuff that has to be done at a funeral, even if it doesn't lessen anyone's grief.

Dan sighed, pushed back his chair and stood. "Well, I just learned a whole lot of nothing," he declared.

"Me, too," Eli agreed glumly.

With that, they left the funeral home the way they'd come in—through the back door.

The hearse was waiting in the broad alley, hatch raised. The ground was hard with frost, but evidently a hole awaited out there in the graveyard.

Eli shivered, raised the collar of his coat, and wondered how long it would be before Brynne texted him to let the groveling begin.

Strange how much he was looking forward to that.

Three days after Freddie Lansing's funeral, Brynne's mom and dad arrived, tooting the horn in their giant RV to announce their return to all and sundry.

Standing at the front window in the restaurant, between two booths, she watched as her dad parked the rig on a side street. He maneuvered that RV as easily as Brynne did her roadster, and she felt a little swell of pride in the old man.

She'd been in a low mood since the fight with Eli, even though they'd tentatively reconciled, and even her painting hadn't brought her out of the doldrums.

Now, seeing her parents alight from the rig, wearing jeans, boots and matching red puffy coats, her spirits lifted significantly.

Miranda nudged Brynne with one elbow, smiling, and handed over her coat.

"Go on," she urged, in a happy whisper.

Brynne pulled on the coat and hurried outside. The sidewalk had been salted, but there were still icy patches, so she was careful.

Mike and Alice Bailey crossed the street, holding hands, and for a moment, Brynne's eyes scalded and her vision blurred.

God knew her parents drove her crazy sometimes—her mother's penchant for planning weddings at the first sign of a man in her daughter's orbit would only increase now, of course—but they were wonderful people, and she loved them very much.

She'd missed them far more than she'd realized, too.

As she embraced them, first her mother, then her dad, she felt overly emotional, and very grateful that they were her parents. She could just as easily have been born to very different people—like the Lansings.

There was a great deal of laughter, and then the three of them went inside the restaurant, where the air was steamy and fragrant and warm.

Miranda took her turn at hugging the new arrivals, and Frank came out of the kitchen, wiping his hands on his cobbler's apron, to shake hands with Mike and nod a shy greeting to Alice.

The whole scene was festive, even though all the holiday decorations had been removed days before.

Mike refused politely when Brynne offered to prepare a late breakfast or an early lunch, whichever they preferred.

"We need to head on over to the house and start settling in," he said.

"And the dogs have been cooped up since we left Wyoming," Alice added.

The Baileys frequented a network of campgrounds all over the Western United States and parts of Canada, which usually made it easy for Brynne to keep track of their approximate whereabouts at any given time.

In this case, they'd caught her by surprise.

"We stopped at the supermarket to pick up a few necessities," Alice continued. "Gretchen Lansing was there, working away. We offered our condolences, your dad and I, but she wasn't very receptive."

"No," Brynne replied, remembering the death-glares she'd received from both the Lansings on the day of their son's funeral. "It must be awful to be so angry and so bitter."

"She's lost her boy," Alice reminded her daughter, her voice softening with sadness. "I can't even imagine what I'd do if anything happened to you."

Brynne's eyes burned again. "I'm fine, Mom," she said.

Alice hugged her tightly. "Thank the good Lord," she replied.

"I think I hear those pups barking," Mike teased, already edging toward the door. The Baileys had always had dogs; the current pair were rescued Yorkies, and Alice babied them shamelessly. "We'd better get going."

"You're always 'going,'" Miranda put in. She'd been hovering at the edge of things, which was fine, since she was considered part of the family. "About time you settled down in one place for a while."

"We plan to do that right here in Painted Pony Creek," Alice responded. "Our gypsy days are over. Come spring, we plan to sell the RV and use the money to build onto the house and maybe update this place, too." She looked around, assessing the admittedly dated interior, worn vinyl chairs, Formica tabletops and linoleum floors.

Although Brynne was very glad her parents were staying in town indefinitely, she felt a little like a third wheel, where the restaurant was concerned. She wasn't sure there would be room for her, once Mike and Alice returned to work.

Her misgivings must have shown in her face, because her dad gave her a one-armed hug and reassured her. "Don't go worrying that we'll take over completely," he told her. "Your mom and I aren't here to edge you out of the business. You're still the manager, and we'll follow your instructions."

Fat chance, Brynne thought, biting back a laugh.

"*Or*," interjected Alice, with a mischievous glint in her eyes, "you'll *finally* get married and give us some grandchildren."

That time, Brynne *did* laugh. "Don't jump the gun, Mom. Whatever you might have heard to the contrary—" here, she turned a glance Miranda's way "—there's no wedding on the horizon, and there are certainly no babies."

Clearly, Alice wasn't convinced, but she did back off slightly, probably because Mike gave her a meaningful look. "Well, anyway," she chimed, "we'll be off now. I'm dying for a long soak in my own bathtub."

With that, the hustle and bustle of leaving began.

Soon, her folks were back in their RV and headed for the house on Pine Street.

And Brynne returned to her work, waiting tables, consulting with Frank in the kitchen, and feeling unaccountably lonely.

Maybe it was time to text Eli.

One of the things Eli disliked about winter was that it got dark so early.

He left the office in the thick of twilight, consulting his fancy electronic watch as he approached his truck: 4:37.

That day, he'd left Festus at home since he'd been in various meetings and, in between, he'd scoured the regular web for any trace of Freddie's interactions with Tiffany Ulbridge.

He'd come up dry, which was frustrating, but he knew there had to be *something*, some thread of connection. Freddie had navigated the dark web like a pro, but there had been no indication that Tiffany had.

Obviously, Freddie had used a false name, just as he'd used Eli's pictures in several different profiles. He'd followed up on the alternate identities and, again, found nothing.

The state was satisfied that Freddie had been Tiffany's killer, and they were ready to sign off and let the whole incident fade away into history.

From Eli's point of view, they were probably right.

Probably.

Freddie had clearly catfished Tiffany, baited her, possibly for months, and when she'd spurned him, he'd murdered her out of frustration and rage. He wouldn't be the first loser with an if-I-can't-have-you-nobody-can mindset and, sadly, he wouldn't be the last.

Screwed up as that motive was, it made sense, coming from a lowlife like Freddie.

And yet——

It was too easy. If Lansing had developed feelings for Tiffany through their virtual "dates"—virtual dating being a concept Eli found utterly foreign—he would have been hurt by her rejection, but *killing her*?

Every hour of every day, people of all kinds loved and lost. They betrayed, or were betrayed. But was it really that easy, when you loved someone, to shut everything down?

Sure it was, for some people.

But had Freddie been one of those people?

Granted, he'd certainly been no saint, and he'd sported one of the worst attitudes Eli had ever come across, but up until a couple of years ago, he'd been a non-entity, for the most part, like his mother.

Then again, Freddie had planned on doing real harm to Eric, and others. That meant he'd been capable of violence.

It had certainly seemed that way when Eli visited the Lansings on New Year's Eve.

No closer to an answer than before, Eli drove home through the thickening darkness, feeling the chill in the air even though he had the truck's heater going full blast.

He missed Brynne.

He missed his dog.

He wanted to be inside his house, with a fire going and something savory warming up in the microwave.

For all those reasons, he was distracted.

He parked the truck in the garage, whistled for Festus, who usually greeted him in the backyard, barking for joy.

Eli frowned, listening. The dog *was* barking—frantically—but the sound was muffled. Then he heard the thumping, realized that Festus was hurling his agile little body against the back door, or maybe even the wall.

What was up with that?

He hurried through the gate, saw no one in the glare of the motion-sensor lights.

Scanning the back porch, he noticed that the small wooden door that covered Festus's private exit when it wasn't in use had been closed and bolted.

That was his last conscious thought before something hard struck him in the back of the head.

The pain followed him into oblivion, throbbed there, his only link to the world outside his brain and the rest of his body.

Presently, he surfaced, only to find himself lying facedown in hard-crusted Montana snow. Crimson blood poured down the sides of his face and his neck and pooled around his head like a gruesome halo.

Festus was still barking, still slamming himself against the barriers keeping him inside.

"Easy boy," he whispered. It was a reflex.

Someone was crouching beside him now; he saw small booted feet, worn jeans, a man's heavy coat.

"You love your dog," said Gretchen Lansing, in a strange

singsong voice. "Freddie loved his dogs, too. It's a good thing
he died before you had them taken away, *Sheriff Know-it-all*,
because losing them would have killed him as sure as that
noose when it tightened around his neck." She paused. "Once
I'm sure you're done for, I'll dispose of the dog."

Eli scoured the depths of his brain and brought up a question. "Did you kill your son, Gretchen?"

She gave an ugly laugh. "Freddie hasn't done nothin' I
told him to do since he was a babe in arms. He hung himself because...well, things just got too hard for him, after
that internet slut called him a lying creep and turned her
back on him."

Eli remembered his Dick Tracy watch and moved his hands,
which were alongside his broken head, to press the SOS button.

He managed that, but not before Gretchen stood up and
kicked him hard in the side.

The blow cracked a few ribs, and he suppressed a groan.
"You won't get away with this, Gretchen," he said reasonably. Thickly. "The place is wired. There are cameras, and
even if you find them, you'll be arrested, because everything
is being logged, back at my office."

For God's sake, Connie, notice the blip and tune in.

"I don't care if I go to jail," Gretchen informed him. "I've
got nothing left, now that Freddie's gone. Nothing."

"What about Fred, Sr.?"

"He's a bastard. I hope he rots in hell."

"Did you kill Tiffany Ulbridge?" Eli spoke very slowly,
very deliberately, hoping he'd asked the question aloud, instead of just thinking it. He was fading again, being sucked
down into some yawning abyss.

"Yes," Gretchen replied, a note of pride mixed in with all

that crazy. "She was a stuck-up little bitch. Thought she was too good for my Freddie. I wasn't going to let her get away with what she did to my boy, any more than I'll give *you* a pass, after all you did to mess up my son's life!"

Out of the corner of his eye, Eli saw, through the pain and the blood and the gathering darkness, that Gretchen was holding the snow shovel he kept on the back porch.

It dripped red.

He heard the dog, whimpering now. Defeated.

He heard a siren, distant, then closer, and closer still.

The squeal of brakes followed, lights blared.

"Police!" yelled a familiar female voice. "Drop your weapon or *I will shoot!*"

Melba. Eli would have smiled, if he hadn't been losing consciousness.

He sensed, rather than saw, Gretchen raising the shovel for a hard swing.

There was a single shot.

And then Eli fell end over end into the darkest of darkness.

As he tumbled, one persistent glimmer shone in all that gloom; oddly, it was not an image, but a name.

Brynne.

CHAPTER SIXTEEN

He was alive.

At first, Eli thought he was still in his backyard, face down in frost-hardened snow, bleeding like the proverbial stuck pig, but then he flash-focused on the ceiling tiles and realized two things: he was lying on his back and he was inside.

Make that *three* things: he had a headache and it was epic.

His vision blurred again, and he groaned.

The *beep-beep-beep* sound of medical equipment finally brought it all together in his beleaguered brain: he was in the county's one and only hospital.

He felt a smaller, smoother hand curl around his, pressing something cylinder shaped into his palm.

"Push this button when the pain gets bad." The voice was Sara's.

He thumbed the button and, sure enough, after a few seconds, his head hurt marginally less than it had before.

"What—?" That single word was all he could manage, and it came out as a ragged croak.

"Gretchen Lansing clocked you with a snow shovel," Sara replied, guessing the rest of the question he hadn't managed to complete. Her voice quivered with tears she was probably too proud to shed. "She would have killed you, if it hadn't been for Melba."

Flashes of the attack flickered colorfully on the inside of his forehead. "Festus," he said, trusting his sister to fill in the blanks.

She laughed softly, sniffled. "He's fine. Melba brought him to us as soon as you'd been loaded into the ambulance."

He was silent for a long time, trying to scrape up the energy to ask for more information. The effort exhausted him.

"Brynne is here. So are Cord and J.P. Marisol issued an edict—one visitor at a time. Right now, I'm it."

"Melba?"

"She's here, too."

"Am I—?"

"No, you're not going to die. One of Marisol's colleagues flew in from Missoula to drill a hole in that hard skull of yours, though. Landed on the hospital roof in a helicopter. Your brain was swelling, so they had to relieve the pressure."

"Ouch," Eli whispered.

Sara chuckled and kissed his forehead. "My turn to sit with you is just about over. Are you up to a visit from Brynne?"

He thought, semi-coherently, of Brynne's policy of not dating cops and the reasoning behind it. If she'd relaxed her defenses a little, early on, she must have raised them again by now.

An invisible elephant lumbered up to his bedside, raised one enormous foot, and smashed it down on his head. "How—how is she—taking this?"

"How do you *think* she's taking this, Eli? She's terrified, like all the rest of us."

He didn't have the wherewithal to argue, especially not with his stubborn sister. "Melba first," he murmured, pressing the button again, this time in vain.

"The meds are on timed release," Sara informed him. "You'll have to wait another half hour before you can get a small shot of joy juice." She kissed his forehead again, squeezed his hand. "Hang in there, tough guy. Marisol says the pain will let up considerably now that that big fat brain of yours is deflating like a beach ball."

Eli chuckled at the image, then groaned. Turned out, it hurt to laugh.

He felt Sara's smile, rather than saw it.

Several minutes later, when Eli's vision had steadied itself a little, Melba appeared beside his bed.

She was ashen.

"You look—terrible," Eli said.

"Look who's talking," Melba retorted, with shiny eyes and a flimsy smile.

Eli had to blink a lot to keep her face in focus. "Gretchen?"

"I shot her," Melba said. "She's alive, though. The bullet went through her upper arm. She's had surgery, and she'll recover."

Eli lifted a corner of his mouth, very slightly and with a great deal of effort. "You missed?"

Melba pretended to take offense. "The hell I did," she replied. "I'm a better shot than you are, and we both know it. I know the rule book says if you're going to shoot, go for central body mass. I winged her, so she'd drop that damn shovel."

That was probably true that Melba was a better shot, since she spent way more time at the range than he did, but he

didn't have to admit it. Being whacked in the head with a
snow shovel ought to give him a pass on *something*.

"Thank you," he said.

"Anytime," Melba answered, as lightly as if she saved fel-
low officers from being beaten to a bloody pulp by a crazy
woman every day of her life.

"You got there fast." There were long gaps between the
words; he could barely stay awake.

"Lucky for you, I did," Melba agreed. "I was about a mile
behind you, on the highway. When I stopped by the office
earlier, Connie said you forgot your briefcase, so I was bringing it to you."

"Sara tells me I have a hole in my head," he told his best
deputy.

"Well, homey," Melba replied, borrowing a term from
Dan, "that's not exactly breaking news."

He laughed. And *damn*, it hurt. The pain was vast, echoing.

Surprisingly, Melba rested a hand on his shoulder. "Take
it easy, okay?"

He had more to say, though the effort was monumental.
"How long am I going to be out of commission?"

"You'll have to ask Marisol Storm about that. My guess
would be, around six weeks."

"Six weeks," Eli repeated, feeling glum.

"I guess you'll need to appoint an acting sheriff," Melba
ventured, unusually cautious. She was rarely subtle—or diplomatic. "Cut to the chase," that was Melba's motto.

Eli's voice felt like gravel in his throat. "Guess so, Deputy.
Tag, you're it."

"Really?"

"Yeah, really. You're the best officer on my team."

"Geez. Thanks."

"Just don't forget—I have two years left in my current term. This is *temporary*, Summers, so don't be plotting to overthrow me, okay?"

"I won't be doing that," Melba said, unable to hide that she was happy about the appointment, temporary or not. She paused, turned solemn again. "Actually, I've got some news on the job front, but it'll keep."

"Tell me." It was an order, not a request.

"Chief Porter is retiring on the first of May," she answered, with some reluctance and a hint of pride. "I've been offered his job. Melba Summers, chief of police, Painted Pony Creek, Montana."

Eli smiled, though his feelings were mixed.

Losing Melba to the local police department was a blow—she was one of the best cops he'd worked with in his entire career—but he was glad for her, too. She'd earned this opportunity, and she more than deserved a chance to flex her leadership muscles.

"I'm proud of you," he said.

She squeezed his hand, and he saw that her eyes were glistening again.

"Brynne's turn," she said, after a few moments of silence. Except, of course, for the beeping of that infernal machine.

Brynne paused in the doorway of Eli's room in the ICU, taking in his prone form, the bandage wrapped around his head, the IV needle and the monitors. She was deciding whether to cross the threshold or turn on one heel and run.

Run and run and run.

Then Eli turned his head, and she saw that his eyes—his beautiful, expressive eyes—were nearly swollen shut. His face was a mottled mix of purple, a weird shade of yellow and pale green.

He actually smiled.

"You should see the other guy," he said.

Brynne realized her face was wet with tears; she made a snuffling sound, still paralyzed.

He stretched out his free arm. "Come here," he murmured. "Please."

Brynne felt herself moving toward him, though it seemed she'd had nothing to do with the motion. She hurried the last few steps, sobbing inelegantly, and took his outstretched hand.

Her fingers interlaced with his, she sank into the chair beside his bed and pressed his hand to her face.

"It's okay, Brynne," he told her, his voice both gruff and gentle, and so low she had to strain to hear him. "*I'm* okay."

"You nearly died!"

"A miss is as good as a mile," he pointed out.

"What if that awful woman had *killed* you, Eli?"

"She didn't. Look at me. I'm none too pretty, but I'm alive."

"They had to drill a hole in your *head*!"

He smiled. "So I'm told."

She leaned forward, rested her forehead on his right shoulder, still clutching his hand. "Of all the jobs you could have had, Eli Garrett, *why* did you have to be a *cop*?"

"I tried flipping burgers at Sully's. They kept falling on the floor."

"That isn't funny."

Eli arched one eyebrow, then winced. "I think it is," he said.

"Then you're crazy."

"Maybe you had to be there."

She made a scoffing sound.

He went right on talking when he should have been, well, *healing*. "Do I have stitches in the back of my head? Feels like it."

"*Staples*," Brynne wailed, partly in horror and partly in frustration.

"For a small woman, Gretchen packs a wallop."

Brynne felt her mouth twitch. "Stop it!"

"Stop what?"

"Stop trying to make me laugh! This is serious!"

"Is it? People get hurt every day, Brynne, all over the world. And it's often a lot worse than this."

"*Cops* get hurt every day," she argued stubbornly.

"I can't quit," Eli said.

She knew that. And she wouldn't ask him to turn in his badge.

To Eli, law enforcement wasn't just a job, or even a career. It was a *calling*, as surely as if he'd been a minister or a priest.

But could she live with that?

He turned his hand, cupped her chin in his palm, caressed her cheeks lightly with his rough fingertips. "I love you, Brynne," he said, softly. "I have since we were kids—I was just too clueless to realize it." A brief pause; she watched him summon the last of his energy. "You don't have to respond to that. I just want you to know how I feel."

Brynne's eyes stung fiercely, and she had to tuck her lips in and press them together hard just to keep from sobbing again. Eli was badly hurt, and he'd regained consciousness less than half an hour ago.

He did not need to deal with a hysterical woman.

"I love you, too," she said. "So much." Then she gave a teary little burst of laughter. "Here we are in a hospital room, declaring our feelings for each other. No candlelit dinner or romantic sleigh ride for us."

Eli smiled, squeezed her chin softly, dropped his hand. "Is this the part where I grovel?"

Brynne swiped at her eyes with the sleeve of the tatty old sweatshirt she'd put on to paint after her mom and dad left Bailey's for their house.

"Absolutely not. Groveling can definitely wait."

A crooked grin. "Good."

She was serious again. "I love you," she repeated. "But I'm honestly not sure I have what it takes to withstand the day-to-day realities of your job, Sheriff Garrett."

He was quiet for a long moment—so long, in fact, that Brynne thought he'd dropped off to sleep. Clearly, that would be the best thing for him, given the beating he'd taken from Gretchen Lansing; his poor, battered body needed all the rest it could get.

But then he asked another question, one that surprised her a little.

"Would you really want to live in a world without cops, Brynne?"

"No," she replied, after taking a few seconds to ponder her reply. "But I'd love to live in a world that didn't *need* cops."

Eli closed his eyes.

Another brief silence fell.

He ended it with a wistful, "Wouldn't we all?"

With that, he slept.

Brynne sat there, watching him, for several long minutes. Then, weak-kneed with shock and weariness, she got to her feet and shambled out into the corridor, past the nurses' station and into the waiting room.

Cord and J.P. were pacing, moving in opposite directions,

passing each other without making eye contact. Neither one of them had said more than two words since they'd arrived; the constant walking was their vigil.

Sara sat huddled in one of the hard plastic chairs, talking on her phone.

Melba was absent; she'd probably gone home. Brynne certainly hoped so, because she'd been through a lot that day.

"He's sleeping," Brynne said, to everyone in general.

Dr. Marisol Storm, the coroner's daughter and a staff member at Painted Pony Creek County Hospital, appeared in the wide doorway of the waiting room, holding an electronic tablet in one hand and a stylus in the other.

She was in her midthirties, a strikingly beautiful woman with raven-black hair and large, thick-lashed amber eyes. Her mother, Alec Storm's ex-wife, was Hispanic, and Marisol had divided her growing-up years between the Creek and Mexico City.

Knowing she was Eli's attending physician, everyone went still, their attention turned to her.

She smiled, and the effect was breathtaking, even under those circumstances.

Brynne slanted a glance in J.P.'s direction, realizing only after the fact that she was checking his reaction. Unlike Cord, J.P. was still single, and he and Marisol had dated for the first year after he was discharged from the armed forces.

Injured in combat, J.P. had been at Walter Reed for six weeks, then returned to the Creek, with Trooper, his service dog, a constant companion.

"We can all be grateful," Marisol said, "that Eli Garrett has one of the hardest heads in the state of Montana. His skull is fractured, but we think it will mend, given time. The swelling in his brain is definitely going down." She paused, consulted the tablet she carried, went on. "He'll have to stay with us for a week or so, but unless he has a setback, we'll be moving him out of the ICU tomorrow or the next day and into a regular room."

Sara, who had been a bulwark of strength since she'd arrived at the hospital, shortly after Eli was brought in, crumpled with relief and began to cry.

Brynne crossed the room, sat down beside her friend and took her into her arms.

Sara pressed her face into Brynne's shoulder and wept without shame.

Neither Cord nor J.P. spoke, though they looked almost as worn-out as Eli had when Brynne kissed him goodbye and left his room.

Marisol swept them all up in her golden gaze. "I think you should all go home and get some rest," she said. "Especially you, Sara. Eli will almost certainly be his old self in six to eight weeks, but it's going to be a long, difficult haul in the meantime, and he'll need his family and friends to be in tip-top shape."

"What about Gretchen Lansing?" J.P. asked, and his tone indicated that he wasn't inquiring about her prognosis for a full recovery. "Is she ambulatory? How do we know she won't find Eli's room somehow and finish the job?"

Brynne felt Sara stiffen in her arms, then straighten and pull away.

She stared at Marisol, waiting for an answer.

Marisol gave J.P. a look that might have been described as wry, in another context. "Mrs. Lansing is recovering on another floor, and there's a security guard outside her door at all times. *And she's* handcuffed to the rail of her bed, so it's safe to say she won't be going anywhere until it's decided whether or not she's fit to stand trial."

"*Fit to stand trial?*" The question came from Cord, but any one of them would have responded the same way, if he hadn't asked first. "Are you saying that woman might *get away with this?*"

"Cord," Marisol pointed out, gently but firmly. "I'm a doctor, not a judge or a member of the grand jury. I don't decide these things."

Cord subsided. Shoved a hand through his dark hair in frustration.

"I *can* assure all of you that Sheriff Garrett is completely safe here," Marisol added.

Brynne spoke up, at last. "What about her husband? What's being done to protect Eli from *him*?"

If she received an answer she didn't like, she would park herself in Eli's room and protect him *herself*.

"Mr. Lansing has not been charged with a crime. That said, he is permitted to sit with Mrs. Lansing. I've spoken with Mr. Lansing, and he is quite undone by what's happened, especially so soon after their son's death."

"That isn't good enough," Sara protested. "Fred Lansing is a horrible man, and he probably sees Gretchen as the *victim* here, not the perpetrator."

"Sara's right," J.P. interjected. "He's as crazy as his wife. Suppose he decides to carry out his idea of justice?"

"Security has been alerted that Mr. Lansing is not allowed to set foot on this floor," Marisol said.

J.P. shook his head, turned to Cord. "Who's standing the first watch? You or me?"

"Since we're liable to butt heads over this," Cord reasoned

quietly, "with both of us wanting to stay, we'd better flip a coin."

Sara watched the two men with obvious relief. She had been at the hospital almost as long as Eli had, the attack having occurred around four in the afternoon.

It was past midnight now.

Strange, Brynne reflected. She hadn't given a single thought to the time of day until that moment; she'd rushed to the hospital as soon as Sara called, a little after five.

Now Marisol crossed the room and spoke quietly to Sara, assuring her that her brother would be well looked after and urging her to go home and rest.

Sara *did* have dark circles under her eyes. She was pale, too, and though Brynne had tried to convince her to go downstairs to the cafeteria and grab something to eat, she hadn't been willing to leave the ICU.

"Think about the kids," Brynne prodded. "They're worried, too. They'll need you, Sara."

For a moment, Sara looked fierce, but her expression softened. "You're right," she said. "I should go home. But so should you, Brynne."

Brynne thought of her poor, concerned parents, probably wide-awake, despite the late hour, and waiting for news. She'd phoned them in a panic when she'd gotten word that Eli had been rushed to the hospital and taken in for surgery, before hurrying there herself. She'd ignored their texts and voice mails since then, focused on Eli, too agitated to concentrate on the simplest thing that didn't concern his well-being.

She turned her head to look at J.P. and Cord.

"I won the toss," Cord said, looking back at her and Sara. "Both of you go home. I'll be sitting within six feet of Eli's bed until morning and, believe me, *nobody* is going to get close to him except Marisol and the nurses."

J.P. slapped Cord lightly on the back, though his gaze rested on Sara. "I'll be back to relieve my buddy here at 7 a.m. sharp, and I can make the same promise."

Sara nodded wearily, and a tear slipped down her right cheek. "Thanks," she said, almost in a whisper.

Brynne added her thanks; Cord and J.P. were Eli's closest friends, and they were strong men, country tough.

She and Sara collected their coats from the rack provided by the hospital, and left the waiting room, headed toward the bank of elevators. J.P. followed behind them, saying nothing.

He was quite literally, Brynne reflected, a man of few words.

Downstairs, in the main lobby, they encountered Dan Summers, who was just coming through the front doors and into the lobby.

His expression was grim.

"How is he?" he asked.

J.P. stopped to give an update, while Sara and Brynne, barely functional now that they could relax a little, greeted the newcomer distractedly and went on.

They were barely outside when J.P. caught up to them.

"It's dark," he said. "I'm walking you to your cars, and I don't want any arguments."

Brynne said nothing.

Sara gave an exhausted snicker.

What, Brynne wondered, was *that* about? She was too tired to pursue the issue, though. She just wanted to go back to her apartment, feed her cat, make a brief call to her parents and fall into bed.

A shower could wait until morning. She might not even undress.

The trio reached her roadster first.

She unlocked it with a key fob, and J.P. and Sara waited, side by side, until she was behind the wheel with the headlights on and the doors secure again.

As she drove away, she caught a glimpse of Sara and J.P. in her rearview mirror, and something about the way they walked, a little apart, heads lowered, hurt her heart.

Again, she wondered.

Again, she was too tired to frame a question, even in her own mind.

When she arrived at Bailey's, her parents' car, a modest sedan, was parked in back, leaving just enough room for her roadster.

Her dad was standing on the back porch when she got out of the roadster.

"You should be at home, sleeping," she told her dad, in mild reprimand. "It's late."

"How are we supposed to sleep when our daughter's young man is undergoing brain surgery?" Mike Bailey countered, though gently.

Brynne made her way toward him, her hands shoved into the pockets of her warmest coat. "It wasn't exactly brain surgery," she said. "They had to drill a hole in Eli's skull because his brain was swollen."

Mike winced. "Yikes," he said.

That was as close as Mike Bailey ever got to swearing.

"Is Mom here, too?" Brynne asked, reaching the steps.

Her dad stepped aside, holding the back door open for her. "Of course she is," he replied. "We've been calling and texting all night, and getting no response whatsoever. We were really worried, Brynne."

"I'm sorry," Brynne replied, going inside and starting up the back stairway. Light spilled from the landing above, which meant the apartment door was standing open, probably with Alice Bailey framed within it. "I was pretty distracted."

She could have said the Wi-Fi connection wasn't very good at the hospital, since that was so often true in other places, but the Creek's medical facility was relatively new, and most electronic messages came and went with little or no problem.

Alice was indeed waiting in the apartment doorway, holding a clearly cranky Waldo in her arms. He was squirming to be put down, but Brynne knew her mom thought she was comforting the poor creature, and she didn't have the heart to correct her.

She smiled at her mother—and by extension her cat—and stepped into the apartment.

Every light was on.

There was freshly brewed coffee.

The minor irritation Brynne had felt from the time she'd spotted her parents' car subsided, replaced by a quiet sense of gratitude.

It was nice not to be alone, especially tonight.

Or this morning.

Whichever.

Brynne kissed her mother's cheek, then slipped off her coat and hung it in the tiny closet beside the door.

Waldo wriggled free of Alice's embrace and leaped to the floor, still complaining. He did not countenance being manhandled, even by a woman.

Brynne had fed the contentious little animal earlier, but

now she bribed him into silence with a few flakes of tuna from the container in the fridge.

"That cat is spoiled," Alice said fondly.

"So true," Brynne replied, with a tired smile.

"Darling, you look utterly *exhausted*," her mother observed. "Why don't you shower and put on some snuggly pajamas? While you're doing those things, your dad and I will fix you an early breakfast."

"I'm not hungry," Brynne said, grateful for the thought. "And I'm not sure I have the stamina for a shower. I was planning on giving Waldo the required ration of canned fish and flopping facedown on my bed."

"You may *think* you're not hungry," Alice pointed out reasonably, "but that doesn't mean your body isn't in need of sustenance. You've been through something traumatic."

There had been times in Brynne's life when her mother's persistence, however well-intentioned, would have gotten on her last nerve, but tonight was different. She *wanted* to be taken care of, told what to do, if only until she'd regained her composure.

Eli would recover, but none of them had known that until he'd been out of surgery for hours, and moved from the ICU recovery room to the bed he was, hopefully, resting in now. Before Marisol's first update, delivered at 10:42 p.m., his condition had been classified as critical; Eli had, in truth, come *very* close to dying.

So Brynne replied with a meek "Okay," and went off to take a quick shower. She emerged from her room nearly half an hour later, clad in her warmest—and silliest—pair of pajamas, bright yellow, fluffy ones that made her look—and feel—like Big Bird.

Miranda had given them to her at Christmas, as a joke.

They were warm, though, and they were soft, and because they reminded her of Miranda, a dear friend, they felt like a hug.

That night, Brynne needed all the hugs she could get.

She broke down and cried when her dad pulled back a chair for her and her mom set a plate of steaming waffles, swimming in butter and syrup, at her place. There were eggs, too, and four crisp slices of bacon.

Everything exactly the way Brynne liked it.

"I feel like such a baby," she wept.

Her dad handed her a clean, folded handkerchief, plucked from his shirt pocket. Who but Mike Bailey still carried a handkerchief, and who but *Alice* Bailey still pressed them after every washing.

"Eat," Alice said, helping herself to coffee and sitting down at the table.

Mike sat down, too. "We had to dig around downstairs for the waffle iron," he said, probably trying to distract Brynne from her teary mood. "You ought to get one for the apartment."

"I'll put that on my to-do list, Dad," Brynne said, after drying her eyes and dabbing at her nose. "number seventy-two, right after nominating myself for an alien abduction."

Mike laughed. "That's my girl," he said.

Alice, who was sipping coffee, looked very serious all of a sudden. "Why didn't you tell us you were dating Eli Garrett?" she asked.

Brynne noticed, for the first time, that neither of her parents had plates in front of them. "Aren't you two eating?"

"We ate earlier while we were waiting to hear back from you," Alice said.

"Right," Brynne replied, resigned.

The waffles were heavenly.

"Weren't you going to tell us about Eli?" Alice persisted. She was an old pro; it took more than deflection to throw her off the trail.

"Of course I was going to tell you," Brynne answered, between bites. "When I was sure there was something to tell."

"Isn't there?" Alice asked.

"I'm in love with him," Brynne admitted, albeit cautiously.

"But?" Mike put in.

Brynne laid down her knife and fork. "But he's a cop."

"And that means he's like Clay Nicholls? It means he'll cheat?" Alice wanted to know.

"It means that he could be *killed* in the course of an ordinary day," Brynne replied. "It means that some madwoman might be lying in wait to bash his head in with a snow shovel!"

"Sweetheart," Mike said, gruff in his gentleness. "*Anyone* can be 'killed in the course of an ordinary day.' Or at any other time."

"Yes," Brynne agreed tersely, "but let's face it, cops are in a *lot* more danger than the rest of us, 24/7, 365 days a year!"

Alice blew out a breath, and it struck Brynne that her mother was still ravishingly beautiful, despite her advancing age.

Which was beside the point.

"Are you saying that you're *afraid* to build a life with a man you admittedly love because he might be killed in the line of duty?" Mike asked.

Brynne's parents exchanged an eloquent glance.

"I didn't realize we'd raised a coward," Alice told her husband.

"You're just saying that because you want to plan a wedding!" Brynne accused, stabbing at another hunk of waffle and pushing it into her mouth.

"I won't dignify that remark with an answer," Alice sniffed.

"Good," Brynne shot back.

"Seems to me," Mike said, used to being caught in the cross fire and therefore unfazed, "that you have some thinking to do, daughter-of-mine. Maybe it's time you decided whether you want to hide out and play it safe, or join the game and give it the best you've got. I can tell you from experience that, win, lose or draw, grabbing life and running with it is your best option."

Brynne was quiet. "It's risky," she reminded her mom and dad, in a small voice.

"You bet it is," Alice replied. "You'll get some bumps and bruises—you already know that, from being with Clay—but look what you would have missed, if you hadn't loved him. Yes, you'd have skipped getting your heart broken, but what about Davey and Maddie? If you could go back to the beginning and make a different choice, knowing what you do now, would you do it?"

Brynne shook her head.

"Now you're in that place with another, better man. You can save yourself—avoid the risks of loving a man who enforces the law—but what *else* will you be avoiding, Brynne? *What else?*"

There were a thousand answers to that question, starting with children.

But there were other joys, things meant to be shared with another person, that one very *special* person.

Sure, the worst could happen. It almost had, that very day.

She would have grieved terribly if she'd lost Eli, there was no denying that.

And yet she would have had memories, as short as their time together had been, to treasure forever: resting her cheek between his shoulder blades as they sped over fields of glistening white on his snowmobile, watching movies on his couch and winding up on the floor, making love. That spectacular kiss on New Year's Eve. Even the dreams she'd never have dreamed without Eli.

Now she had a choice to make.

She could garner more treasures, more memories, to store safely in the warmest part of her heart, or she could chicken out on it all, squawking and flapping her wings and declaring to everyone who would listen that the sky was falling.

Well, she knew what her answer would be, what it *had* to be.

She would stop fretting and throw herself into the game.

Winner take all.

CHAPTER SEVENTEEN

After three full weeks in the hospital, Eli was more than ready to leave.

When Sara pulled into his driveway, Brynne was waiting in the backyard, barely restraining Festus, who clearly wanted to break free, leap the fence and tackle Eli the second he got out of his sister's car.

"Let him go," he told Brynne, with a smile, because *damn* he'd missed that dog.

Brynne looked doubtful—and beautiful, standing there in jeans and a sweater that must have been left over from Christmas, given the appliqued reindeer on the front. A powdery snow had fallen the night before, turning the surrounding landscape pristinely white, and the combination made Eli think of one of those glass balls with small, festive figures inside.

He caught his breath, suspended in the moment.

Then, reluctantly, Brynne released the dog.

Festus sailed over the back fence and leaped into Eli's arms, knocking him backward, laughing, into the soft snow edging the driveway.

They wrestled joyously, man and dog, while Sara fretted and Brynne hovered, nervous but smiling.

For Eli, that canine greeting was the perfect counterbalance to the *last* time he'd fallen onto snowy ground, and it took the sting out of the memory.

"For heaven's sake, Eli," Sara fussed, "get up! Do you *want* to be back in the hospital?"

Brynne said nothing, but she did lean over and offer Eli a hand.

He took it and rose awkwardly to his feet.

Festus pranced around them, tail wagging, grinning in that way dogs do.

Canine contingent, present and accounted for.

"Eli Garrett, you'll be the death of me," Sara complained but, like Brynne, she was smiling. Instead of heading for the house, she opened her car door to get back in. Most likely, she'd left poor, fictional Elliott Starr dangling from the lip of a cliff by his fingertips or fending off an army of bad guys, and needed to get back to her computer.

Brynne looped her arm through Eli's and tugged him toward the backyard gate, which stood open. "Don't worry, I'll keep him nice and quiet," she promised Sara.

"Nice and quiet isn't exactly what I had in mind," Eli said, for Brynne's ears only. "In case you've forgotten, I've been held prisoner in a hospital for three weeks."

She flushed slightly, but ignored him.

Sara settled into the driver's seat, started the ignition, shut her car door and rolled down the window to reply. "If my brother misbehaves," she called to Brynne, "and you're forced to shoot him, I'll understand."

"I'm a dead man," Eli murmured. "Because I definitely intend to misbehave."

"Stop it," Brynne whispered, smiling and waving as Sara buzzed the car window up again, backed up a little way and turned around.

"Not a chance," he replied.

They went inside, man, woman and critter, and Festus, evidently exhausted by his duties as a one-dog welcoming committee, promptly made his way to his fleece-lined bed near the woodstove in the living room.

Brynne had built a fire earlier, and something savory was bubbling away in a crockpot on the kitchen counter. The mingled scents of woodsmoke and—was it chili?—were almost as tantalizing as the woman facing Eli now, with her arms around his waist.

He felt a rush of emotion, standing there like that, with Brynne holding him and being so obviously careful not to hurt him.

In that moment, Eli knew he had everything a man could reasonably want: a beautiful woman to love and be loved by in return, loyal friends and an extended family, a job he could hardly wait to get back to, a sturdy house to call his own and a damn fine dog.

The gratitude he felt was nearly overwhelming. It scalded the backs of his eyes and choked him up considerably.

"Could we just stand here like this until I can convince myself I'm not still back there in my hospital bed, dreaming I'm with you?" he asked, his voice hoarse.

"You're home," Brynne assured him gently, rising onto the balls of her feet to plant a light kiss on his mouth.

He let his forehead rest against hers. "I'm *with you*. That's what *home* means to me now, Brynne."

"Funny," she whispered, her amazing navy blue eyes misting over as she spoke, "but I feel the same way about you, Sheriff Garrett."

He touched his mouth to hers, breathing his answer more than speaking it. "Hell of a coincidence, Bailey."

She laughed, and the sound was the audible version of lying on his back on a Montana mountaintop, watching the northern lights fold and flex against a dark, star-strewn sky.

"I love you," he said, and before she could answer, he kissed her.

It was their first *real* kiss in a long time, and it left them both dazed.

Another kiss followed, even more heated than the last, and Eli finally eased Brynne's arms from around his middle, took her hand and led her to his bed.

Their lovemaking was passionate, since they were starved for each other, but it was profoundly tender, too. Sweet beyond anything Eli had imagined—and he'd imagined plenty—while he was recovering from his injuries.

After every pinnacle came a slow, delicious descent into drowsy contentment, soon followed by another climb.

At some point, Eli must have fallen asleep, and he awakened with a start, ribs aching a little, thinking he was back in the hospital.

Brynne stood beside the bed, wearing one of his T-shirts and nothing else. She switched on the lights and set a steaming bowl of chili on the nightstand, along with a plate with two thick slices of cornbread piled on it.

He was ravenous.

"Sit up," Brynne told him, "and eat your supper."

"Is there dessert?" he asked.

Brynne made a face, fluffed the pillows behind him when

he did as he'd been told and sat up. "You've already had that," she said, with mock primness. From her tone, never mind her angelic appearance, nobody would have known what a tigress this woman could be, under the right circumstances.

Under *him*.

"I'm a hungry man," Eli drawled. "A *very* hungry man."

"Behave or I'll call your sister." She sat down on the edge of the mattress. "Or Marisol."

He laughed, took the bowl of chili in one hand and held the spoon with the other.

The stuff was delicious.

"What do you want to drink?" she asked.

Eli jabbed a chunk of cornbread into the chili and filled his mouth, rendering himself unable to answer, a man enjoying the first decent food he'd had in weeks.

"Milk's good with chili," Brynne suggested.

"Beer," Eli managed.

"Scoundrel," Brynne said, but she left the room, returning a couple of minutes later with an ice-cold can of brew.

Cord, J.P. and Dan had smuggled various emergency supplies into his hospital room, but the beer had been warm and the pizza cold.

Brynne joined him on the bed, leaning against the headboard, watching him eat and drink.

"I am a contented man," he said.

"I suspected as much," Brynne teased.

"Aren't you going to eat?"

She shook her head. "Festus and I had our suppers two hours ago."

He was surprised. "I've been asleep that long?"

"Contentment will do that to a man," she observed, with

a nod. "Also, getting smacked on the head with the flat part of a snow shovel."

Eli winced, but he didn't slow down on the chili—or the beer. The stuff was ambrosia, and Brynne was even better.

"I guess you know Gretchen Lansing is still in the psych ward, undergoing evaluation," he ventured, between bites and gulps. "As I understand it, she's been in a catatonic state from the first."

Another nod. "Do you think they'll find her fit to stand trial?" Brynne asked, straightening her long, beautiful legs. The sweatshirt barely reached the tops of her thighs, and Eli found himself pondering dessert again.

"Your guess is as good as mine," he answered, setting his empty bowl aside, along with the spoon. All that remained of the cornbread were a few crumbs and a butter-slick. "It's probably safe to assume she's full-out crazy."

"Fred, Sr., has been by her side from the beginning, according to Marisol," Brynne said. "He must love her, in his own strange way."

"First decent thing I've ever known that man to do," Eli remarked.

"No more beer tonight," Brynne said, before he had a chance to ask for seconds. "It's time for your meds."

"Okay," he conceded, because there was no arguing with this woman when she was right and she knew it.

Brynne fetched the pills and a cup of water.

Festus was with her when she came back to the bedroom.

Eli took the pills. He'd be glad when the prescriptions ran out, because he'd had about all the pharmaceuticals he could handle in the hospital, but he had to do what he had to do.

If he wanted to go back to work, he had to pass muster with Marisol.

And then there was the thing he wanted more: to ask Brynne to marry him.

He couldn't do that when he was a semi-invalid. His pride wouldn't allow it.

"I've been looking at properties," Brynne informed him, out of nowhere.

That caught his attention. "Why?"

She drew a deep breath, let it out slowly and smiled. "Running Bailey's isn't the same, now that Mom and Dad are home to stay."

Eli was careful, weighing the implications of Brynne's sudden interest in real estate. He'd hoped to build on to *this* house, when and if she agreed to marry him, put up a barn and some fences and buy a few horses.

He'd thought they were on the same page, that they'd be together for the long haul. But maybe he'd been wrong, if she was looking at places to buy.

He frowned, pensive.

"What?" Brynne prompted, snuggling closer.

"You're buying a house?"

She laughed. "No," she replied. "Just a *building*. I need something to *do*, now that my career in the restaurant biz is winding down."

"Like what?"

"Like creating a studio space, where I can paint, with room for a gallery." She paused. "I want to offer art classes, too—workshops, retreats, things like that. I'm even thinking of adding a wedding venue."

"Are you planning to live in this place, too?" He probably sounded a little testy, though he was actually worried instead.

"Not unless the man I'm crazy about fails to propose to me in the near future," she replied.

"Well, I can tell you this—the man who's crazy about *you* is definitely going to propose very soon."

She beamed. "Good," she said. "How soon?"

"Soon."

Brynne sighed heavily, but it was an act.

After a few more moments, she shifted to her knees, straddling Eli's thighs, took his face in her hands and kissed him, softly at first, then with more intensity.

He figured another round of lovemaking might just kill him.

But what a way to go.

"Oops," Eli murmured, an hour later, when he lay spooning with Brynne, both of them spent.

She tensed in his arms. "What do you mean, 'oops'?"

"I forgot something."

"What?"

"A condom."

She turned, warm and fragrant, and nestled closer still. "Yikes," she said.

It was his turn. "What?"

"I forgot something, too. I mean, we weren't making love, since you were in the hospital and everything, and I—well—I forgot to take the pill a few times."

He slid down a little, nibbled at the side of her neck. "Uh-oh," he murmured.

"Eli," Brynne protested, fitful now, but putting up no resistance whatsoever to the nibbling. "This is serious. Suppose I'm pregnant!"

"Nothing would make me happier."

She turned to look into his face, hopeful and scared. "Really?"

"Really. We both want kids—we've agreed on that already."

"But—"

"But what?"

She sniffled. "Call me old-fashioned," she replied, "but shouldn't we be married first?"

"Probably," Eli said, kissing the tip of her perfect nose. "But if there's one thing I've learned in the past few weeks, it's that life plays by its own rules, on its own timetable. There's what *should* happen and what *does* happen."

Brynne sighed, wriggled closer still. Yawned.

"Hmmmm," she said, and immediately drifted off to sleep.

She woke to dazzling sunlight and the sound of Eli's shower running.

Briefly, she considered joining him, but Festus ambled into the bedroom, gave her a pleading look and whimpered.

With a laugh, Brynne got out of bed, shivered in the cold and pulled Eli's T-shirt, discarded the night before, back on over her head. For good measure, she put on her jeans, too, not bothering with underwear.

"Relax, doggo," she told Festus. "Your breakfast is coming right up."

They were in the kitchen when Eli came in, looking scrubbed and very glad to see her. He was barefoot, wearing black sweatpants that had seen better days and no shirt.

Brynne smiled and saluted him with her mug. "You made coffee. Extra points for that, mister."

Eli grinned, crossed the room and kissed her lightly. "Where you're concerned," he said, "I'm a point-gathering fool. If they're good for what I think they are, that is."

"You're insatiable."

Eli poured coffee for himself. "When it comes to you, Bailey, yeah. I am."

"I love you," she told him.

"I bet you say that to every sheriff you meet, provided they have staple scars under their hair and a hole in their skull."

"Every single one," Brynne replied.

He kissed her again, and this time, he lingered a little longer.

Finally, she laughed and shook her head. "Oh, no, you don't," she said, laying her hands on his chest, feeling his heartbeat under her palm, strong and steady. "We are *not* going back to bed. Not yet, anyway."

"Why not?"

"Because I want to show you a building I like. Get your opinion."

"Here's my opinion—as long as it's not a cottage meant for one, I'm good."

"It's a barn, actually," Brynne said. "Or it was."

He frowned. "Don't tell me you're talking about the one on the McCall place," he said, clearly worried. That, of course, was where he and Melba had found Freddie Lansing's body.

"I won't, because it isn't. J.P. wouldn't sell that monstrosity anyway, since it's smack in the middle of his ranch."

"He ought to burn it down," Eli said.

Brynne pretended frustration. "Stop talking about J.P.'s barn. I'm *trying* to tell you that the property I have in mind is the Anderson farm."

Eli looked nonplussed. "The barn on that place is probably going to collapse under the next heavy snow, if it hasn't already."

He wasn't wrong. The farm had been abandoned for many years, and its owners, living on the East Coast, ignored it, keeping the taxes up but doing nothing in the way of maintenance.

"I know," she admitted wistfully, "but it's a beautiful old place with a romantic history."

"It's a teardown," Eli insisted.

"Don't be stubborn, Sheriff. Of *course* it's a teardown." She paused, remembering her sketchbook, and went to find her purse and retrieve the book.

Inside, she'd sketched the buildings she'd already erected in her imagination: a large, lodge-like space with many windows and long balconies, surrounded by several rustic cabins. The finishing touch was a gazebo made, like the cabins and the main building, of logs.

Eli studied the drawings carefully, let out a low whistle of exclamation. "I'd forgotten just how talented an artist you are, Bailey."

"What do you think?" Brynne prompted, unable to contain her eagerness. "Of the *idea*, I mean. Not my art skills."

"It's not bad," Eli mused aloud. "Not bad at all."

Brynne pretended to whack him in the chest. His bare, muscular and extremely masculine chest.

"'Not bad'? That's all you have to say?"

He looked up from the sketchbook, met her gaze. Smiled. "The Creek could use something like this," he said. "It's great."

"That's better," Brynne said.

Eli returned his attention to the sketchbook. "All right if I look through this?"

She hadn't expected that. "I guess," she answered tentatively.

He flipped past the half dozen drawings of plans for the

Anderson farm and stopped at a sketch of Festus, airborne, about to catch a Frisbee.

"Wow," he said.

There were more pictures: Sara, wearing an apron and holding a mixing bowl in the curve of one arm, a spoon in her opposite hand; Miranda, in her dated but always immaculate waitress uniform; Cord, J.P. and Eli seated around a table at Bailey's, deep in conversation; various Painted Pony Creek landmarks, like the courthouse and the library and the peaceful old cemetery on the edge of town.

Bailey's, à la Edward Hopper, with recognizable faces at the tables, in the booth, perusing the jukebox.

Eli studied that one with something resembling fascination, then looked up and grinned. "Elvis pigging out on a hamburger. Sorry I missed *that* visit."

"It isn't a hamburger," Brynne said, pleased. "It's a fried peanut butter and banana sandwich. Don't you know *anything* about the boy from Tennessee?"

He held the sketch closer to his face and squinted. "Is that the Man in Black, juggling bottles behind the bar?"

"The very same."

"Damn, Brynne. This is *amazing*." He met her eyes again, grinned mischievously. "Think you could re-create this on black velvet? We could make it the focal point of the living room."

"Not in this lifetime," Brynne said, feigning indignation. When it came to art, she had to admit, if only to herself, she was something of a snob. To her, paintings on velvet were akin to paint-by-number pieces.

Just no.

Eli laughed again, and Brynne was hoping he would forget about the sketchbook and its contents and hand it back.

He didn't. He turned more pages.

Saw the first image of himself, lying broken in a hospital bed.

In the next, he was standing beside his official SUV, microphone in hand, issuing a report or calling in a report of some kind.

Finally, there he was in a tux, slightly awkward, but smiling.

Beside him stood Brynne herself, clad in an exquisite wedding gown. She was beaming, about to throw her bouquet into the waiting crowd.

Eli examined that drawing for a very long time.

When he looked up again, Brynne was blushing. He seemed wonderstruck.

"It's only a drawing," she said, mildly anxious. She definitely didn't want Eli to feel cornered. Rushed.

"It's the future," he said quietly.

Brynne's throat constricted and her eyes burned again. "I hope so," she replied.

Finally, Eli set the sketchbook aside, laying it carefully on the tabletop. Then he took both Brynne's hands into his and brushed his lips across her knuckles.

She trembled at the resulting sensations. "Eli?"

He sighed, but his eyes never left her face. "I don't have a ring yet," he began. "I don't have flowers or a horse-drawn carriage, and if I try to get down on one knee right now, I might not get up again." He paused, drew another deep breath, exhaled slowly. "Brynne Bailey, I love you more than I ever thought I could love anybody. I want us to share our lives—the good, the bad and the in-between.

"Will you marry me?"

Brynne was undone. She cried. Threw her arms—very carefully—around Eli Garrett's neck.

"Yes," she said. "Oh, *yes*."

"Hallelujah," Eli replied.

And then he kissed her.

"It's absolutely *beautiful*," Alice Bailey exclaimed, studying the glittering stunner of a diamond on her daughter's left-hand ring finger.

Eli and Brynne had chosen the ring together, within an hour of Eli's proposal, over at Johnson's Jewelry, and then, at Brynne's request, driven straight to Bailey's to tell her mom and dad about the engagement.

"Must have cost you a serious chunk of change, son," Mike said to Eli, looking somewhat concerned.

Eli smiled at his soon-to-be father-in-law. "I can afford it," he assured the older man.

Alice jumped in to scold her husband, though gently. "Mike Bailey," she said, "it's none of your business how much Eli spent on this lovely, *lovely* ring." As if to soften the remark, she moved to Mike's side and slipped her arm through his, gave it a squeeze.

"When is this wedding taking place?" Miranda wanted to know. She and Frank had been hovering on the periphery of the small gathering.

"We haven't set a date," Brynne said, feeling as though her face might fall off if she didn't stop smiling so hard. "Sometime in June, probably, after Mom and I have had time to design and make the dress and make solid plans."

"*This* June?" Alice asked, and Brynne couldn't tell whether she was relieved or disappointed.

"This June," Eli confirmed.

"You and I have a lot of planning to do," Brynne told her mother. "And my schedule is packed—Davey and Maddie will be here for a week in early April, and then there's everything concerning the Anderson farm."

"We'd all better sit down," Eli said, amused by Mike and Alice's surprised expressions.

"The Anderson place?" Mike echoed.

"I want to buy it," Brynne said, dropping into the chair Eli pulled out for her, there at the center table. The restaurant was empty of customers since the lunch rush had just ended. "I'm making an offer first thing tomorrow morning."

"I'll make a fresh pot of coffee," Miranda said. "Since it's too early for champagne."

"I just put one on to brew fifteen minutes ago," Alice told her longtime friend and employee. "Sit down with the rest of us, Miranda, and let me get the coffee."

"Are we *sure* it's too early for champagne?" Mike asked, his tone slightly plaintive.

Eli laughed. "I'll buy you a beer later, Mike," he promised. "Just you and me. Over at Sully's."

"Throw in a game of pool, and I'm in," Mike replied.

Brynne watched the two of them with a soft smile and bright eyes, while Alice and Miranda, apparently unable to agree on which of them should fetch the coffee, both left the table.

"I guess I should have asked you for your daughter's hand in marriage," Eli told Brynne's dad, as Miranda rattled over with a tray of cups and saucers and Alice followed with a full pot of java.

"That's old-fashioned," Mike answered, with a dismissive wave of one hand. "Brynne's a grown woman, fully capable of deciding for herself." He paused, winked at his daughter.

"I *do* reserve the honor of walking my girl down the aisle, though."

Alice filled everyone's mug, including one for Miranda, with the deftness of a woman who has waited tables for nearly three decades. Frank, who might have been invited to join the party, had disappeared into the kitchen and busied himself with the usual chores.

"How many bridesmaids?" Alice asked, taking her order pad from her apron pocket and plucking a pencil from behind her ear to make notes.

"Sara and Shallie for sure," Brynne answered. "Melba, too."

"Flower girls?" Miranda prompted.

"Junior bridesmaids, I think," Brynne said. "Maddie, if she can be here, Melba and Dan's daughters, Jill and Carrie, and, of course, Sara's girl, Hayley."

"Perfect," Alice decreed, scribbling away.

"Is this going to be a hen party?" Mike demanded goodnaturedly. "Because if it is, I think I'll take Eli up on his offer to buy me a beer."

"Go," Alice said, without looking up.

Brynne smiled at Eli and formed a subtle kiss with that remarkable mouth of hers.

"Sounds good to me," Eli said, pushing back his chair. "Get your coat, Mike. It's cold out there."

With that, he stood.

Mike stood up, too.

"Only one beer," Brynne said, addressing Eli. "You're still on medication."

Mike rolled his eyes, but they were twinkling as he laid one hand on Eli's shoulder and said, "And so it begins."

EPILOGUE

Nine months later…

Eli stood gazing through the wide window of the hospital nursery, wonderstruck.

Two babies, side by side in their cots.

His sons, and Brynne's.

Before Brynne had admitted she loved him, overcome her fears about throwing in with a cop and finally accepted his proposal, he hadn't believed in miracles.

Loving Brynne, and being loved by her, had transformed him.

Eli Garrett 2.0.

And now there would be *another* transformation.

"How did this happen?" he murmured, thinking aloud.

His friends J.P. and Cord stood on either side of Eli and somehow, without touching him, kept him upright. They both chuckled.

"I reckon it happened in the usual way," J.P. observed dryly.

Of the three of them, he was the only one without a wife and children. Cord and Shallie had Carly, of course, and now a healthy son named Grant, after Shallie's closest friend, Emma Grant.

Eli let his head rest against the glass. Fogged it up a little with his breath. "What if I screw this up?" he asked, supposing he could be forgiven for losing his grip a little.

Cord rested a hand on Eli's shoulder. "You won't," he said, with the quiet assurance that comes from knowing someone for most of their life. "You're a good man, Garrett. You're a fine husband and you'll be rock-solid as a father."

"What is this, a rerun of *Oprah*?" J.P. interjected. "Let's not go to pieces here."

Both Cord and Eli laughed at that.

Then Cord said, "Relax, bro. We're not going to talk about *feelings* or anything as terrible as that."

"Shut up," J.P. retorted, but he was fighting back a grin.

Just then, Sara and Melba—aka chief Summers—entered the small room and squeezed past the men to get close to the window and admire the new additions.

"Are they identical?" Melba asked, favoring Eli with one of her dazzling smiles. She'd been a lot easier to be around since (1) she and Dan had decided to try again, and (2) she'd been appointed to head up the Creek's municipal police department.

Sara, for her part, was a happy mess, in her crumpled clothes and with her famous braid coming undone. She'd been in the vicinity since Eli had called the night before to tell her Brynne was in labor.

"Yes," answered the proud aunt, before Eli had a chance to speak.

"You might as well tell the people their names, while you're at it," Eli told his sister, without rancor.

Sara gave him a sisterly look, part love, part putting him in his place. She often forgot that she was two years older than he was, not twenty.

"That's for Brynne to do, not me," she said.

"Speaking of my beautiful wife," Eli put in, "I'll be getting back to her now. My turn to sit by a hospital bed and be incredibly vigilant."

"The least you can do," Melba remarked cheerfully.

After that, everyone went their separate ways: Sara home to rest, J.P. back to his work on the ranch, Cord to his wife and family, Melba to the station house.

When Eli reached Brynne's room, Mike and Alice were just leaving. Mike, the new grandfather, was beaming with pride, and Alice was still crying tears of joy, in juxtaposition to her wide grandmotherly smile.

Alice paused to kiss Eli on the cheek, and Mike shook his hand for about the hundredth time that day.

"She's resting," Alice whispered, pressing an index finger to her lips.

"I'll be quiet," Eli promised.

Brynne lay with her eyes closed, breathing slowly and deeply.

Even after twelve hours in labor, she was so beautiful Eli wondered how he would bear it.

This woman. The mother of his children.

Walking quietly, Eli stepped close to the bed and bent to brush his lips across the crown of Brynne's head.

She opened those indigo eyes of hers. Smiled.

"Sorry," Eli whispered. "Didn't mean to wake you."

"I wasn't asleep," his lovely wife confided. "I just wanted

Mom and Dad to go home and get some rest. They're both exhausted."

Eli grinned, though his heart felt as if it would burst with love. "How like you, Bailey, to worry about other people when you just spent half a day delivering our sons."

"I'm *fine*," she insisted. "Now that it's over, anyway, and we have two beautiful baby boys to show for our hard work."

"*Our* hard work?" Eli had never been a "we're pregnant" kind of guy. *Brynne* had been the one to carry twins to term, while being the best wife imaginable, purchasing the Anderson farm, overseeing the ensuing construction projects *and* entertaining Davey and Maddie Nicholls. They'd visited the Creek twice in the past year, first in April during a school vacation and then again in June, to participate in the wedding, and Eli had come to understand his bride's lasting love for them; they were great kids. "Seems to me, Mrs. Garrett, that you're the one who should get all the credit. All I did was have a lot of fun."

Brynne smiled, placed her hands on either side of Eli's head and drew him down for a kiss. "We're in for a wild ride, Sheriff," she told him. "Identical twin boys growing up in rural Montana. They're bound to be a little wild."

"Tricky, too. Telling them apart might be quite a challenge."

Brynne frowned prettily. But, then, she was *always* pretty. "What are we going to do about that?" she asked seriously. "They'll fool us constantly if we don't figure out a way to defend ourselves."

Eli chuckled. "Sweetheart, they're little boys—*very* little boys, at the moment—so I don't think we need to worry about being fooled—*or* defending ourselves. We'll come up with something."

"Like what?"

"Tiny tattoos?" Eli suggested, grinning. "Don't look now, Bailey, but this is definitely a first-world problem." He kissed her forehead. "Suppose you get some sleep now."

"Later," Brynne said. "It's almost time for a feeding." A pause. "You're not serious about the tattoos, right?"

He laughed, low and gruff. "Sure, I am," Eli teased. "*M* for Michael and *J* for Jesse. One tiny initial each, maybe on the inside of their wrists. That way, when they're trying to pull a switcheroo, all we have to do is ask them to show us their palms."

Brynne pretended to punch him. "Did you tell Cord and J.P. about the boys' names?"

Eli shook his head. Michael's middle name was Cord and Jesse Patrick was named for J.P., whose full name was John Patrick. "Sara said that was your job," he replied.

"Dad was so pleased to have his first grandson named after him," Brynne said, grinning at the memory of Mike's reaction, which had been very moving indeed.

"Cord will be happy. J.P. will ask if we remember why he goes by his initials instead of his full name, since he never liked it. Just the same, he'll be flattered, whether he lets on or not."

Brynne looked mildly troubled. "You're sure you don't want to call one of our boys 'Eli'? We haven't signed the birth certificates yet, so there's still time."

"I'm sure," Eli replied. "I like my name just fine, but I think every kid deserves his or her own. Just my humble opinion."

Brynne's worry was replaced by a sweet smile. Again, she pressed her soft palms to the sides of his face.

"I love you *so* much," she said.

Again, he kissed her. "And I love *you* so much," he replied.

Just then, two nurses entered the room in single file, each one pushing a wheeled cot containing a brand-new—and very hungry—baby boy.

Eli stepped away, moved one of the two giant blue teddy bears occupying the only two chairs in the room, and sat down.

And so it begins, he thought.

★ ★ ★ ★ ★

Can't get enough of Linda Lael Miller's
Painted Pony Creek series?
Check out this sneak peek at Country Born.

J.P. McCall's charity work training service dogs is incredibly rewarding and he's grateful for it. But he's secretly envious of his friends, Cord and Eli, because they're both happily married. He's dated many, many women but he can't seem to find the right one. Imagine his surprise when he realizes she's been there the entire time...

Single mom Sara Worth has her hands full. Between her two children and her successful—and secret—writing career, love is the last thing on her mind. But when she realizes that her bestselling hero, Elliott Starr, bears a striking resemblance to J.P., her brother's best friend, she can't deny her growing feelings for J.P. any longer.

But when someone from Sara's past appears in Painted Pony Creek, turning her life upside down, it threatens everything between J.P. and Sara...

Don't miss Country Born
coming soon from HQN Books!

Preorder your copy today!